PLAYBOY

NEW YORK TIMES BESTSELLING AUTHOR
KATY EVANS

Copyright © Katy Evans

First paperback edition: June 2018

Cover design by Sara Hansen at Okay Creations
Interior formatting by JT Formatting

10 9 8 7 6 5 4 2 1

Library of Congress Cataloguing-in-Publication Data is available

ISBN-13: 978-1717420077

To the risk takers and the love makers . . .

TABLE OF CONTENTS

PLAYLIST

"I'm Gonna Getcha Good" by Shania Twain
"Who Knew" by Pink
"The Good Parts" by Andy Grammer
"Always" by Andy Grammer
"Poker Face" by Lady Gaga
"Next to Me" by Emeli Sandé
"Bad Romance" by Lady Gaga
"3 AM" by Matchbox Twenty
"Never Gonna Leave This Bed" by Maroon 5
"Be Here Now" by Robert Shirey Kelly
"Feelings" by Maroon 5
"100 Years" by Five for Fighting
"A Thousand Years" by Christina Perri

THE GIRL

Wynn

"Are you sure this is safe?" I ask as my date parks his car in an empty parking lot next to a dozen others.

All of them too elegant for the surroundings.

My fingers tremble as I open the door and step out into the eerily quiet night, then I watch as my date hops out and takes a selfie standing next to a royal-blue sports car. I frown in confusion. What is he doing?

God. I'm not really out on a date with this guy? Am I?

"Relax, this'll be fun." He motions me to a huge looming warehouse. My heart gives a little kick of dread as I follow him.

After he picked me up, my date let me in on the fact that he was taking me to this clandestine poker game in the underground of Chicago. Now I'm wondering about my judgment and if it's kind of like a girl's virginity. Once it's gone, there's no getting it back.

I mean, we're in the worst part of town. In the distance, the city's skyscrapers hover like concrete bodyguards. It's intimidating and comforting at the same time, but I'm not naïve enough to think I'm safe here. We're in gang territory. Whoever runs this game is paying a steep tax to stay and play.

As I glance around the empty lot to be sure we aren't held up at gunpoint before we reach the building, I smooth a hand nervously down my dress. This night out was supposed to be fun.

This was supposed to be a nice change for me.

A distraction.

An evening out of the apartment.

Except jail was never on the menu. Just stepping past those filthy-looking, crooked doors of that huge warehouse, I'll be breaking the law.

I *never* break the law.

I'm a solid, responsible girl at thirty. Hell, I'm already way past the age I thought I'd be married and having babies. My friends are married. Rachel has a boy and a girl, Gina a girl, and Livvy is getting married this weekend. Me? I have a long string of breakups. Starting with my most recent one, from a relationship that lasted like four or five years and amounted to a big chunk of nothing.

I was dating a commitment-phobe. I didn't know it at the time, and he sure as hell didn't know it either. He could never take that step of proposing—much less the dozen steps it took to walk up to the altar and wait for me there. He asked for time and time and time, and I gave it to him. I gave him *everything*. I used to think he was the One. I used to think the One would come when I was ready.

"No, he wasn't. He's not the One, I tell you. If he were you'd be—"

"Married and popping out babies," Rachel finished for Gina last week when we discussed my breakup.

I sat in sullen silence as I stared at the tissue box in front of me. Unable to believe that he threw me away the way he had. Still struggling, even now, to put the pieces of my life back together again.

"If I win over this guy, I can do fucking anything. Anything. Even win the Texas Hold'em Championship Tournament."

My date's voice has a slight tremor of excitement in it.

If Rachel or Gina could see me now, they'd fall back from the shock. They've always seen me as the sweet one. The innocent one. I've never even gotten a parking ticket.

Now I'm going to illicit poker games with a guy I just met?

Of course, my date is nice and moderately handsome. Medium height, nice brown hair, brown eyes crinkled at the corners. We met at the gallery when he purchased a work from my last exhibit, and I always admire people who love art like me. I'm not even sure why I agreed to the date in the first place, except when he asked me out and I weighed the option of spending the night alone in my apartment versus going out, there was no contest. Although I'm not interested in reliving a broken heart nor interested in anything with *any* man, I also know I need to get over my ex and it can't happen if I don't allow some new things to come into my life. I plan to focus on my gallery and stay off men completely—or at least stay off anything serious with any. But I still need to distract myself if I'm to get over him.

Emmett, a legendary chef in the making, wouldn't take me down the street for a hotdog unless he prepared it in his restaurant kitchen. And even then, I'd need to make an appointment.

Maybe that's why I'm here.

But as soon as my eyes land on the crooked doors of the warehouse we're about to enter, I'm reminded of all the bad choices I've made in my life. Life choices involving the men I've decided to date.

I decide to be less demanding (a problem Emmett claimed I had) and have some good old illegal fun as we head inside.

There's a cloud of smoke and several games underway across a line of round tables.

Dark wood. Low ceilings. The place is straight out of an old movie with its Bokhara rugs dividing floor space and black-and-white photographs scattered across the walls. I recognize a few legendary Chicago criminals.

It's a sign. These games are off the books. A poker room like this can shut down on a dime. I know this because I've been watching movies, not because I've decided to take up with Clyde and would enjoy being Bonnie.

"Shit, he's here."

He exhales, then pinches his nose and tries to draw a breath.

"Who's here?"

"The fucking Tsar of poker. Current worldwide champion. A veritable legend. Ice-cold eyes, you never know what he's thinking. Best poker face around. I'm telling you, if I beat him, I'll be unstoppable. My name will be everywhere." Carson, my date, glances across the room.

I'm not a poker fangirl, but given how my date is acting, maybe I should ask the guy for his autograph.

"Shit, it's really him. I'm sorry, my hand is sweating." He ushers me forward with a motion, and I'm glad he doesn't take my hand because lately I just don't even like it when men grope me anymore. I follow him to a table at the end of the room, and I can feel a guy at the far end of the table watch me.

I gulp.

The man doesn't look polished, not one bit. He has an earthy, raw, compelling presence. Something magnetic makes it seem as if the whole room gravitates around him. He looks to be in his early thirties. Hot as fire.

A shiver runs down my spine as his gaze rests on me.

Silver eyes like diamonds dipped in platinum, cold as ice, gleaming like shards. His jaw square and hard, his lips immobile but wickedly plush-looking. His black sweater stretches over wide, hard shoulders and I can make out the muscles beneath, his biceps straining the fabric as his hands rest on the table. For some reason, I notice the fact that he has long, strong fingers and tanned hands.

I gulp. His gaze is tactile. I can feel it on me and it makes my skin do funny things. He runs it down my black stretchy cotton dress, down to my thighs. Checks out my legs. Down to my ankle boots. *Breathe, Wynn.* Exhaling nervously, I follow my date. And the Hot Gambler with the Silver Eyes continues to watch us approach.

I'm the one walking; but the guy's the one stalking me with his gaze.

My mouth dries up, and I'm suddenly self-conscious about how small and tight my knee-length, long-sleeved black dress is.

"He's looking right at us, *motherfuck me*," Carson says.

Right. Motherfuck *me*.

Carson pulls up a chair across the table from the guy, and I lower my butt to it, aware of the men at the table watching me. Especially *him*.

"You're late." His voice is deep and rich, and terribly, terribly sexy.

"I'm sorry, I'm sorry. My date took a while to come down—"

I hate feeling the flush creep up my cheeks as Carson blames me for not being ready on time. I'm a redhead, so I hate flushing and getting a red face. Isn't it expected that the girl needs to be five minutes late—at least—on the first date? You can't look too needy. But then again, I'm thirty and *single*. Maybe the strategy needs some rethinking.

The guy just looks at him, and I somehow sense he finds his excuse distasteful. I'm beet-red, feeling like I should scrape myself off the side of the moving bus this jerk tried to toss me under.

Silver Eyes gives me a brief look, and something between my legs tingles. I glance away as my date pulls out some bills and gets a tray of chips in exchange.

"I'm Carson, by the way . . ." he belatedly says, standing and leading me forward by the elbow toward the guy.

"I'm Carson," he repeats. "And this is . . . my date." He introduces us awkwardly.

"Hey. I'm, uh . . ." Did Carson just forget my name? I'm about to say it, but as the guy's silver-grey eyes stare at me from this close, I seem to lose all power of speech.

God, do eyes this color really exist?

Yes, they do. Metallic, sharp, and hypnotizing. I extend my hand. He takes it, his grasp warm and firm.

"You were saying?" There's a smile in his voice. In his deep, terribly masculine voice.

I pull my hand back and rub the tingling sensation he left it with against the side of my dress. A thousand eyes are on us as we head back to our seats. So he is the guy my date has been rambling about?

Obviously I *get* the rambling now.

I become nervous about this whole thing. I glance around the room and notice there are plenty of women here—many of them glancing in the direction of who I'm sure is the Greatest Poker Player in Town.

I don't think I've ever reacted to a guy like I'm reacting to this one. My heart is beating so hard I think it's on the speakers, blasting across the neighborhood.

As the table gets organized for the next game, I try to breathe and chill and remind myself this is supposed to be fun.

Silver Eyes is blatantly watching me.

When he starts giving me that slow, lopsided smile, my lower body starts getting much too involved for my liking. *Fuuuuck*, how am I supposed to sit here and fake it?

I close my eyes and breathe.

"First timer?" he asks, as if there's no one else seated at the table but us.

Hell and fuck me. Does he have a crystal ball? Clearly he has two steel balls the kind that some men never will.

"It would help knowing what 'first timer' means," I stall.

He lifts his hand and instantly a waiter is at his side. "A whiskey on the rocks for the lady. One for me."

Well. Smooth, isn't he?

"First game?" he specifies.

"Yes. Poker virgin." I'm saucy on purpose.

"Good. I like going first." His expression remains a blank page. For a second, I think he might drag me off to the nearest dark corner and I'm surprised how much I like that train of thought.

"Let's get started then." His lips curve ever so slightly.

He watches me as if he knows what I'm thinking.

And wow. This guy is more illegal than this gambling establishment.

Cards are shuffled then dealt. Each player gets two cards and after they peer at their hand, the betting begins. There's an order to follow but I have no idea what it is. It probably has something to do with that plastic white button on the table. I'll figure it out, assuming my date stays in the game long enough.

I watch as Silver Eyes checks his cards to see what he has. He slips them down to the felt in one smooth motion and then leans back and crosses his arms, his features unreadable as he studies his opponents, until . . . his eyes lock on mine.

He doesn't smile this time.

And it makes me nervous.

He continues to look at me. I sense that he knows I'm squirming but doesn't care. A hot little frisson starts in the pit of my tummy as I return his stare. I sit very still, trying not to let on that he affects me. But how can he not? He even affects my date, who's palpably nervous beside me.

Silver Eyes finally reaches into his pile of chips and tosses half of his money into the pot.

Some men back out of the hand. One or two say, "Fold." My date reluctantly adds half his chips and says, "Call."

They play out the hand. My date loses and Silver Eyes wins with three-of-a-kind. Queens.

The irony doesn't escape me.

The cards are dealt again.

I try not to look at the guy, but once again, he plays his hand, and then does nothing but watch me. He's intimidating, his stare laser-sharp and direct, and very, very tactile. I can feel it on my face. His masculinity makes my own femininity come to life.

Thank god I'm sitting down, because if I were standing, my knees would be wobbly and I'd be maybe making a fool of myself.

Rachel would know how to handle a hot stud like this one. She was pursued by the most legendary manwhore in town, Malcolm Saint, and was able to withstand his attention without caving in. At least, for a little while. Me? Three minutes and I'm already wet in my panties.

This guy . . . I can tell that he can have any woman he wants. The waitresses walking around the warehouse keep giving him interested looks. But he ignores them. I can also tell that he's very, very interested in playing cards with my date—for now his attention is on Carson, which seems to make my date nervous—and the tension in the room has escalated substantially.

Some of the players fold as if they sense the game is about something more than winning chips. Silver Eyes studies Carson and then thoughtfully strokes his chips before shifting one stack under the other. Carson, jittery as ever, knocks over his short stack.

Embarrassed for him, I quickly focus elsewhere.

"You a gambler?" an older gentleman asks as he twirls three chips close to the felt.

"No." I sound too evasive. "I mean, I could play." Anyone can lose money here, right?

"Wanna place a prop bet?" I don't respond and he adds, "Your boyfriend will lose his bankroll in five hands or less."

"He's not my—"

"I'll raise," Silver Eyes finally says, jumping in at a convenient time. He commands attention and gets it. The other players sit up and take notice.

My date stutters, "I . . . I can't call you . . . I'm out of chips."

Silver Eyes slowly slides his gaze back to me, his expression unreadable. "The girl."

My eyes widen.

My date looks at me wide-eyed too.

My heart stutters.

I scramble to my feet but Carson grabs me by the elbow. "He wants you to stay here," he hisses. "He's forcing me all-in."

"By the looks of things, he's forcing *me* all-in." I lower my voice. "Look, I don't care who—"

"I've got a great hand. Please?" Carson discreetly shows me his cards. He's got a full house. He sounds desperate, and I feel bad. At the same time, I'm mad. This dude is out of his league.

"Please, Wynn."

And the jackass *now* remembers my name.

So I sit.

There's an unspoken exchange between Mysterious Gambler and the old guy. The old guy shakes his head disapprovingly then folds. "If you say so."

I don't hear any other words pass between them.

The guy across the table makes me nervous. He's not looking at me right now and is instead eyeing Carson, but I can't stop looking at him—Silver Eyes. He's got that kind of mouth that is set but makes you wonder how it feels, and a hard jaw, and . . . stop it, Wynn! You're off men, remember? Except for sex, and you're not going anywhere near Casanova over there!

I chew on my lower lip, acting as if the guy across the table doesn't nerve-wrack me as he seems to nerve-wrack my date.

Once everyone folds, except Carson, my date shows his hand, and the guy turns over his cards and crosses his arms. He's got a straight flush. Aces high.

I blink.

What the hell just happened?

My date lost? And sold me to this guy in the process?

The guy's eyes glimmer in victory. "Want to bring that chair over here?" he asks me, nodding slowly at his side.

I really don't know what I got myself into, but I decide getting out of it is my best bet. So I stand and spin around to leave, telling Carson, "I am seriously not . . ."

Silver Eyes stands, comes around the table, and suddenly his chest is a wall I'm about to crash into as I try to leave.

"Stay," he says, his voice low, his hand curling warm and strong on my wrist.

Every part of me feels that touch.

I jerk my hand back, feeling singed and a little concerned about his effect on me.

He's so tall I need to crane my neck back to look up at him.

"Look, my date may have offered me up, but I didn't agree to this."

"Name your price," he says.

And god, he smells really, really good, like soap and cologne and the scent of a winner.

"Price for what?"

"To park your gorgeous ass on that chair, right next to me, and play."

I exhale. "Just that?"

"For now." His lips twitch again, ever so lightly, and stirrings of lust awaken in my body. Damn it.

I watched *Indecent Proposal.* To be honest, I lusted after Robert Redford for a while. I blame Hollywood and my subconscious for making me feel like it might not be a bad idea to just do as he says. After all, I'm only agreeing to sit my "gorgeous" ass on that chair and play. Did he really think I had a gorgeous ass? "All right then," I hear myself say.

The guy motions to the waiter, has them move my chair next to his, then leads me there to sit. He lowers his black-clad, sexy-smelling male body next to mine, and asks them to deal. Once they deal, he pushes the stack of cards in my direction.

"Play it."

"What?"

He meets my gaze with unerringly direct silver eyes. "You heard me."

"You're crazy."

He leans back and links his hand behind his head. "I've heard worse."

"I'm sorry, Wynn," my date says as he stands to leave.

"Wynn," that deep, resonating timbre repeats.

I turn to face him, flushing. "Don't call me that."

"Explain why."

"Because it's my name and I don't know yours. I'm at a complete disadvantage here."

"Playboy."

"Huh?"

"They call him Playboy," my date says before he's escorted to the door.

Playboy smiles.

I'm dumbfounded, shaking my head in disbelief. "Wow, my luck with men has hit a new low."

"Don't stress. I don't pay to get laid. Correct me if I'm wrong, but I just rid you from the lamest date you've ever had."

"It actually wasn't lame. 'Cause you were in it."

"And I'm exciting?"

"No. More like . . . a slasher movie."

"She's playing my hand," he then tells the other guys at the table. "You all okay with me instructing her on how to play it?"

"Play it, Playboy," they simultaneously agree.

He taps a finger to the green felt table and nods toward the cards in my hand. "Let's see our hand."

"My hand," I contradict.

"What's yours is mine," he whispers as I show him the cards, ducking his head close to my ear as he peers at the cards.

He tells me what cards to give back and how many to ask for. I do as he instructs and still end up with only a pair.

"Why am I playing this?" I ask his profile when we lose and get dealt a new set of cards.

"Because I was losing until you arrived."

"We're losing now."

He eyes me thoughtfully, then the new set of cards in my hands. "Obviously you need some coaching." He pries the cards from me and starts playing the game. "Just stay there and don't distract me. Distract the others."

Detecting his brook-no-argument tone, I play with my hair, twirling the loose red strands around my index finger while I stare at each of them hard enough to make them look up.

"On second thought, forget that."

"Huh? Who understands you?" I glare at the guy, and he glares back at me.

"I'm having trouble understanding myself right now. Just stop twiddling your damn hair."

He wins the game, and the subsequent eight games. His pile of chips is so large that the establishment managers keep bringing him larger denomination chips to help him conserve space on the table.

When it's all over, the men at the table start dispersing while we remain at the table. With new drinks, our chairs angled and almost facing each other, he asks me about myself.

I shrug. "You know my name. Wynn. Age thirty. Gallerist. Recently out of a relationship and completely over love."

"Mmm. I believe you left out the best parts. Like what you're doing here."

I take a slow sip of my whiskey. "I have to admit, you have a wicked thing going here. But I'm still trying to figure out why I'm here."

"You expect me to believe you didn't know I would be here?"

"Excuse me?"

"You expect me to believe you don't want me and weren't looking to snag my attention? Inventive, I admit. I'm curious."

"Wow, cocky much. Um, no. You're much too scandalous to bring home to my mom. But I'm determined to have new experiences . . ." I swear I'm making this shit up as I go. "Especially since I just came out of a four-year relationship," I lavish. "I am determined to use guys the way they like to use us."

"Is that so?"

"Of course it's so. Do you ever wonder why you have so many women at your feet?" I motion to the crestfallen waitress who's sending me eye-grenades from afar.

"I don't sleep at night I'm so puzzled." He's amused. I'm amused by his teasing manner too, but I continue.

"Well, it's because you know how to play the game. I want to see how you play it. Then know when I'm being played," I say.

"Is that so?"

He doesn't buy it.

Fuck me, he's laughing inside.

"Yes, that's exactly so. You don't believe me?"

He's smiling, still amused. "Somehow the words are there but I don't believe a single one coming out of that pretty mouth of yours."

The way his eyes land on my mouth makes something hot and achy settle in the pit of me. "Wow, you're jaded. What is it you think I want?" I counter.

He scratches his chin, the rasping sound of his five o'clock shadow sensual in the dark. "Whatever it is, I'm going to provide."

"Okay then," I say, knowing I've got nothing to hide. "Find out what you will and let me find out what I need: how you play women."

"I don't think so, Red."

"Not even after I dressed like a slut to get in here?" I say to tease him.

"Look around you, Red. You're like a monk in a strip club. You're the most conservative slut I've ever met."

"Fine. So I should've hiked up the hem a little more. Just let me watch you woo a woman. Any woman. Call one of them over."

"You want to watch me woo a woman?" he asks incredulously.

"Yes." I scan the crowd and spot a sultry waitress who's been hovering over him like mad, who'd die right now of happiness, I'm sure. "That one."

"I don't want to woo her."

"Okay then, who do you want to woo?"

He stares at me. "I don't woo, Red."

"But you play to get laid. So. Play to get laid tonight."

"Not tonight."

"Why?"

He shrugs.

Then he reaches out and pulls me to my feet and puts his hand on my lower back as he leads me away. I'm careening out of my axis, my senses out of control. I don't understand it.

"And why not tonight?" I semi-whisper, semi-pant.

"You're Wynn Watson, aren't you? Gallerist and serial dater."

"I'm totally not a . . ." How did he know my last name? And then it hits me.

I'm shocked out of my mind, my brain needing a moment to rearrange itself.

"You're Cullen Carmichael. The gambler. Serial fucker, anti-monogamist, and brother of my bestie Livvy's fiancé."

"Life's a little surprising." He eyes me, opens my palm and puts a ten-thousand-dollar chip in my hand. "There you go, sweetheart. Don't spend it in one swing. Save it until our next game."

"Never, thank you. And I'm investing it, maybe. Probably. I'll ask your brother for investing tips."

"You're welcome," he says.

"No, *you're* welcome."

A surprisingly soft chuckle leaves him as he tilts his head and studies me. "Thank you," he says seriously, and just like that, he kisses my lips. "Be a good girl and go home now," he says, patting my ass.

"Was that . . . ? Were you wooing me?"

"I don't woo."

"Were you playing—"

"I'll let you know when the game starts. Go home now."

The guy opens the door of an Uber that seems to appear from out of nowhere. And because it's already three a.m., I get in without argument and head home, reeling a little bit.

Cullen freaking Carmichael. Obviously in town for the wedding, and I stupidly didn't put two and two together. Hell, I couldn't even press my legs together with the guy around.

I can't believe the way he bought me. Like . . . a car. Like he deserved me and like he can get anything he wants. The way he threw chips on the table like they were nothing and there went my whole life's earning, in one play.

I turn the chip in my palm and shine my phone light to inspect it.

Ten. Thousand. Dollars!

I wonder what would happen if he were to teach me to gamble with my money. I'd finally be able to pay my business loan after years and years of renegotiating extensions.

Nah. I'd lose it all and then what? I don't like gambling; it's completely superficial. I believe in work, not luck.

I also don't believe in love anymore . . . or so I tell myself.

Even now, I am tempted to fantasize what being made love to by Cullen Carmichael would feel like, and I can't breathe at the thought. Stop it, Wynn. Stop romanticizing every man you meet. They're not worth it. No man is, especially one they call *Playboy.*

The high of the night, along with my smile, fades the moment I get into my apartment—the apartment I rented after moving out of Emmett's. Sometimes the pain is so crippling, I double over in bed. Nights are bad. The loneliness—the void—is everywhere. In the empty pillow beside mine. In the cold bed sheets, warmed only on my spot. In the dreadful fucking silence of my apartment.

But mornings aren't much better. Somehow I drop my guard at night. Relax. (Sometimes.) Wake up, safe in my bed, staring up at the familiar white fan above my bed. And for a second, I'm fine. Until I remember. He doesn't want me anymore. And the torture begins all over again. Forcing myself out of bed, to live, but barely. Forcing myself to eat; to eat, not taste. Forcing myself to shower, to get wet then dry. Get dressed, to pretend to be normal. Human. Forcing myself to go on when still a part of me is stuck on all that I had that crumpled the day he told me he fell out of love with me. Love. Real love. Happiness. A future, the kind that felt complete. I have none of that now.

Weekends are the worst. My days off from work, no distractions keep me from thinking about it. Turning it around in my head like a shock victim does. Finding some new clue. Some other sign that something bad was about to happen.

I spend the night restless, and the next morning I nurse a coffee cup at noon, skimming the news on my laptop, dreading the wedding tonight. It's not even the event itself. Not really. It's the reminder of what I have here and now. In the present. And what I don't. It's depressing as hell when there's not a future to anticipate, not a romantic one anyway.

I'm not alone. A million other women are undoubtedly in the same boat. They woke up this morning only to realize the rest of their lives won't be the way they'd hoped. This day is different because their happy ending faded to black.

This day is minus one.

I feel exasperated, like I've already been here and done this so much that it's not even about the broken promises and shattered expectations anymore. It's about the time lost as much as the derailed dreams.

At least I still have the gallery, the Fifth Street Gallery.

I like the sound of that. Pepper, also known as the most extraordinary assistant *ever*, came up with the name.

I take a sip of my coffee when I hear the rattling of keys, and I set my cup aside as two of my besties, Gina and Rachel, burst into my apartment.

"Okay. We knew it! We knew you weren't getting ready." Rachel and Gina, one blonde, one brunette, both happily married, slam the door shut behind them and storm forward.

"I told you I'd call if I needed help," I protest as they slam my laptop shut and get me to my feet.

"You'll never call."

"How do you know?" I ask Gina.

"Because you never do. We're going to get our hair done."

Rachel heads to my closet, grabs a sweatshirt and sweatpants, and brings them over. "Come on, you'll feel gorgeous and when you see Emmett tonight, you'll rub it in his face what he's missing out on."

"I got home late and barely slept! Can we do this later? I'm not depressed, I swear!"

"We'll see about that," Rachel says dubiously, pressing clothes to my chest.

"Ugh. I hate you."

"You love us."

I groan and start changing. "Yes, I do," I concede. "But for the record, I'm a gorgeous single girl and in charge of my life. I sold two paintings yesterday, and I had a date last night, too, so really, I'm doing fine," I tell them.

"Really? Oh, Wynn, that's great!" Rachel's eyes widen with excitement and she literally leaps in the air with a little clap at the news. Meanwhile, Gina brings over my sneakers and my bag.

"Is he a keeper?" she asks dubiously.

"No. God, no. He sold me." I carry my empty coffee cup to the sink and wash it before leaving.

"He what?"

"He sold me. It was a game. And I ended up meeting this other guy. He was unexpected but . . . well, he was hot. So at least my hormones got a workout."

"He was what? Wynn!!"

I smile at their excitement and decide not say anything else. One, because they will probably worry, and there's nothing to worry about with me and Cullen. Really! I'm not going to fall for a guy like that—I'm not going to fall for *any* guy, period. And two, because Cullen Carmichael looks like someone's dirty little secret, and it seems like, in some weird way, he's now mine.

FOUR OF A KIND

We meet Livvy outside Accents, one of the most exclusive salons in the city, and its owner, Alessandra, waves us inside. "Come in, I'll be right with you." She motions to a few other stylists. The place is usually packed, and when we notice no other customers, the four of us seem to simultaneously realize that Livvy's fiancé, Callan, intends to spoil his future bride and friends as if we're the only women on the planet.

"Did you know about this?" Gina asks Livvy, turning around in amazement.

The salon is filled with white roses dipped in lavender, the delicate color soft and lovely.

"No!" Laughing in delight, Livvy stops long enough to pluck a rose from one arrangement. She inhales dreamily as I help myself to a decadent truffle.

"Someone's getting laid tonight," Gina teases.

"We'd worry about the state of their union if she didn't," I say, giggling.

"I meant Callan." Gina smirks, and I laugh even more.

But a pang in my stomach comes out of nowhere. Like this black hole opened up inside me and all that's there is a void.

I don't want to be jealous of my friends. I have terrific friends and want to always be there for them. True, I sometimes wish I'd have already found the One too, but that doesn't mean I won't ever . . . right? Malcolm worships the ground Rachel walks on. Gina leads Tahoe around like the smitten man he's become. And Callan dotes on Livvy and tends to always have the best surprises for her, like a romantic honeymoon to an unknown destination.

My friends struck gold with these men and I won the jackpot because I have all three of these girls as my dearest and closest friends.

"What do you say we get this party started?" Gina sits and swirls around in the stylist's chair.

A waiter appears with champagne, and I take the first glass and down it as if I have an alcohol agenda. I do. I'm going to need it.

Rachel lifts her glass. "To love and sexy-as-sin men!"

As our glasses clink together, I shiver at an intrusive thought.

I'm not thinking about the sexy-as-sin men who wooed my friends into lifetime commitments. My thoughts run deeper, hotter, wilder.

Silver Eyes. Die-for jaw. Haunting disposition.

Hot Gambler is complex.

Exciting. Electric. Completely magnetic.

I'm so lost in memories about the previous night, I barely notice I'm seated before the stylist.

She gathers my hair and holds it at my nape. "Are we going for soft and sexy or elegant and risqué?" As I ponder her question, she explains, "Natural contradiction is a subtle way to keep a man guessing."

"And there you have it," I say to Gina with a smirk. "The lone reason I'm going stag to this wedding."

Gina spins around and looks at her stylist. "We'll have what Wynn's having. The bride is the only one who gets to be predictable today."

"She's anything but," I say, laughing as I look at Livvy, whose gorgeous blonde hair is already getting some love from her stylist. She's the most talkative, friendliest girl of all four of us, and today is no exception as she tells the stylist how Callan proposed.

Thinking of the proposal makes me think of Callan, and thinking of Callan makes me think of his brother.

Ugh. Silver Eyes would love that I'm thinking about him.

Last night, that part infuriating, part sexy guy made me forget *everything*. He showed interest in me, included me in his poker game, and made me feel as if I belonged there. When did Emmett ever make me feel as if I belonged anywhere? Hell, he didn't even want me in his kitchen! This is why I shouldn't have agreed to go on the date last night. I really need to forget men altogether and focus on my gallery, the Fifth Street Gallery, my only true love.

"You're thinking too much," Gina whispers discreetly before tucking a lock of dark black hair behind her ear. She says something to her hairdresser then rises from her chair to check out my new do. "We're getting all dolled up for the party of our lives. And it *will be* the party of our lives, Wynn, you little hot ticket, you."

"What do you mean? Of course I'm a hot ticket. I'm the only single one among us now."

"Only that you'll look like a million bucks and we want Emmett to eat his heart out tonight."

"Forget asshole Emmett. His food was horrible, no offense, Wynn. I ate it because of you," Rachel says slyly as she approaches, looking drop-dead gorgeous as usual. "You're better off without him. Trust me. When the right man comes, there will be no doubt about it that it's him."

"Ugh. I almost don't care anymore. After last night's date, I've decided I should focus on work and forget men altogether."

When I start to wonder if Silver Eyes will bring a date, I pull myself out of my thoughts and focus on Livvy as she steps away from her chair, her hair perfectly coiffed and ready for her veil. "You look like an angel," I say, taking Liv's hand as soon as she approaches. "Callan's world will stop as soon as he sees you."

"You're making me blush," she says, fanning her face.

"She's making you cry!" Rachel hugs her.

"Watch the hair!" Alessandra calls out.

"You'll be so happy," I tell her.

While we gush over Liv, I think about Callan and his love for Livvy. Renting out Alessandra's salon didn't come cheap, I'm sure, but he didn't do it to impress others. He wants Livvy to have a memorable wedding day.

"Are you happy?" Gina asks her.

"I'm over the moon!" While she waits for the manicurist, she runs through a list of Callan's plans for their future. "He wants a house in the country that we can hit up often to get

away from the city . . . And he talks about kids. All the time."
She hushes and looks at me in concern.

I blink, suddenly realizing that she's holding back because of me. Because she knows that I've always wanted . . .
well, this. A part of me sometimes hurts to hear about it because it's something that feels so out of reach. But on the other
hand, if I don't hear about it, I'll miss out on the highlights of
my friends' lives and I can't have that. What kind of best
friend would I be if I didn't stick around and watch her ride off
into the sunset? I want to know how the story ends. I need to
witness the excitement because then, maybe, I'll have my faith
restored.

"Go on," I prod with a smile, taking her hand and squeezing to say, *I'm happy for you and I wouldn't miss your big day
for the world.*

And it's true. I'll survive the wedding if it kills me.
There'll be champagne on hand and if Emmett shows, I'll
down plenty of it.

CELEBRATION

Five hours later, we're at the wedding, us and our great hair. I stand in a rose garden with the other bridesmaids, my sisters from other mothers. Due to the full trees, we can only see glimpses of the men.

I go up on my toes in search of Silver Eyes but can't spot him, so I force myself back down. Most of the guys out there are married anyway.

Callan's the dashing groom. Wearing a pointed-collared shirt, bowtie, and black tux, he looks like he's more than ready to take that quantum leap, the fearless jump so many men fail to take.

The one Emmett avoided at all costs.

He's not at all like Emmett.

Callan looks . . . *fired up*. I think Callan wanted to marry Livvy from the moment he first saw her. Now, he's waiting for the love of his life, and I know she can't wait to run straight into his arms.

Liv's more than ready for her big day. And while Callan is gorgeous, Livvy's totally stunning.

The music starts.

For a split second, I panic. I think my knees will buckle before I step up to the ivy-wrapped archway leading to the ceremonial gardens.

Before my knees do just that, Cullen is beside me. As soon as I see him, I *feel* him. He snakes his arm through mine, and the heat of his body suddenly surrounds me.

He wasn't at the wedding rehearsal last week; I didn't know he would walk me in.

I was supposed to walk alone. Suddenly, I'm grateful that I'm not, but I won't let him know it.

I grip his arm tighter when Cullen murmurs, "I thought you and Livvy were best friends."

"We are."

He raises a lone eyebrow, still looking ahead. "Someone should've told the bridesmaid. It's rude to look hotter than the bride."

My skin heats. It's a slow burn from the inside out. I'm uncomfortable but need to hear more. I wonder if *Playboy* has another play in his handbook.

As we pace ourselves and follow Gina and Tahoe, he brushes his fingers across the back of my hand. I shiver at his touch but remain poised, collected.

"Stop the wooing," I whisper.

"Wooing was last night. Tonight, it's game on. You're being seduced."

"Here?" There's a pause in my stride but he helps me find my step again. "Stop."

"Can't help myself."

"It's not working."

"It will."

We reach the end of our walk together. "We'll see." We part ways.

Cullen stands next to Callan. I veer left to wait for the bride, completely breathless by that tiny encounter.

Our gazes touch, part, meet again. If he doesn't stop this now, I'll be one wet bag of nerves by the time Callan and Livvy are pronounced man and wife.

I watch as the rest of our friends make their way down the aisle to stand up for Callan and Livvy.

The gang's all here.

I like that about us. We're devoted to one another.

My eyes find Cullen's, and I don't know why. I guess I'm a glutton for punishment. Maybe he has a lucky charm in his pocket. My gaze dips lower. When I realize what I'm doing, I quickly jerk my eyes upward.

His lips twitch and I curse my existence. I'm eye-fucking at my best friend's wedding. Worse? I'm thinking about getting it on with the groom's brother.

How low can I go?

Whispers ripple across the crowd. I jerk my eyes away from him.

Rachel and Saint are standing under the arch. They're so stunning together and almost steal the show as Rachel holds the hand of their three-year-old little boy, while their little girl, safe in her father's arms, points at Saint and says, "My daddy."

Photographs are snapped. A well-known lifestyle blogger scribbles notes while a reporter from *The Times* takes out her smart phone, takes her shot, and hurriedly shoots off an email. Malcolms and Rachel's daughter just made the news. She's still patting her daddy.

Muted snickers erupt. Cullen watches her with amusement and now?

I'm terribly wooed.

As we wait for Callan's beautiful bride, a full orchestra plays "Never Tear Us Apart" and it's lovely. Absolutely perfect.

Hearing Livvy and Callan say their vows to each other makes me weep. He says he wants to give her the world and that she's the most important thing in his life. And for some reason, I'm still weeping when the wedding march comes on.

I weep because I'm happy for them, and sad for me.

I weep because only months ago, I imagined that one day, one day *soon*, I would be standing up at the altar with the man who loved me—a man with Emmett's eyes and hair and face. And he would be saying his I do's.

I can't believe that this is me, that I'm the only single girl among my friends. That not only do I no longer have Emmett, but that I really don't believe the dream of getting married and loving and being loved "until death do us part" will ever really happen for me.

At the reception, I head to the bathroom to fix my face, and chide myself, *Don't be a crybaby, Wynn. It's Livvy's big day. Be happy for her. Distract yourself. Don't think about Emmett.*

It's easier said than done . . . until *he* arrives.

Cullen.

I spot him and somehow the urge to cry is gone, replaced by some weird urge to look stunning.

I don't know why I want to look stunning but maybe it's just to give him some competition.

Because he looks so damn *good.*

I tell Rachel, under my breath, "If he's a fireman on top of being a poker player, set me on fire, will you?"

She laughs, then eyes him with the eye of a connoisseur. She's married to the most desirable man in Chicago so . . . she knows. "Yep. Very hot." She takes a sip of her wine, eyes twinkling as we watch him. "But stay away."

I want to lick my lips and an image of me licking Cullen's lips hits me.

What am I thinking?

To be honest, I don't know if I want to sell my soul to Cullen Carmichael, but he's hot like the devil tonight. Even the shirt under his tuxedo jacket is black, and the man rocks wearing black like nobody's business.

I keep tabs on him through the wedding reception (which is suddenly moved indoors because of the rain.)

I don't *mean* to keep tabs on him. But a part of my subconscious seems curious enough about him to note that he drinks only water, has smoked a total of half a cigar before he was forced to put it out by Livvy's parents, and laughed a total of once . . . a laugh that was directed at his brother fawning over his wife, so I'm not even sure that can be considered a laugh at all.

After a while of stealing glances, I realize I'm paying too much attention to him, and so I make an effort to ignore Cullen—until my ex arrives.

Emmett.

My lower-than-life ex-boyfriend who is, in fact, not lower than life, but just the guy who broke my heart in so many tiny pieces I can't build it back up again in its complete form because not even a loupe could find some of the shards.

I spot his blond head across the room, greeting Livvy and Callan.

Emmett looks perfect as he hugs Livvy and a roiling tornado starts in my stomach. Trying to get as far away as possible, I shuffle to our tables, and that's when I spot Emmett's name on the place card right next to my own. I blink, looking at the place cards again.

Oh no, no, no, not Emmett next to me!

We've both said all that needed to be said. Talked all we needed to talk.

It's O V E R.

I glance around in a panic only to discover all my friends are either chatting with their husbands or busy mingling. I turn my eyes back to the shocking place card placement, and I know it's not the groom and bride's fault. They've been crazy busy with the wedding and the wedding planner simply didn't get the memo of our awful breakup three weeks ago.

So I do what any girl would do. I search for Cullen's name on the opposite table and exchange it for Emmett's.

Not only will I not have to tolerate sitting right next— right next—to the man I'd loved for four years and who broke my heart spectacularly, I have the opportunity to sit next to a guy who appears single—and it's just a guess, of course, but he seems too quiet and broody for me to imagine any woman actually wanting to commit to all that her whole life. And more importantly, he's a guy I don't care about or need to impress.

So now I'm switching the cards and watching Cullen and all his devilish good looks wind across the room, a drink in hand.

I'm not very sure that I like him at all. It's not that he's hard to look at, it's more that I'm not sure I like Cullen. He makes me too nervous to "like" but he intrigues me enough that I haven't been able to shake him off my mind since last night.

Now he ambles toward me, making my heart thud uncomfortably in my chest.

He pulls his chair back with his feet and sits. He seems a little surly. As if he's irritated with me, and I don't know why because I also feel irritated with him.

I don't even know how a guy can be so hot and not disintegrate the floor beneath him.

The air around him feels flammable.

"Wynn."

"Cullen."

There is nothing from him, just him smiling at me.

"What's so funny?"

"My name wasn't on here."

"How do you know?" I ask.

"Because I checked."

"I . . . oh." I glance at him in surprise, his stoic expression revealing nothing. "And were you disappointed?"

Whoa. Wait. *He checked*? That's kind of badass.

"Terribly," he says in a voice that doesn't necessarily mean he means it.

I roll my eyes. "I don't know why I'm even bothering talking to you."

"Because your ex is looking."

My heart stops beating. I'm not sure if it's because Cullen leaned a little closer or because he's right. Emmett is watching.

"So?" I ask.

"So you still love him." He smirks, those sharply handsome features that mock me and those jeweled eyes of his taunting me. "What did he do? Fail to buy one of your art works on a particularly important exhibit?"

I don't even know this guy and I want to deck him. Instead, I play along and ask, "Are you making fun of my love of art?"

Frustrated, I stand impatiently to get myself a glass of wine. His gaze tracks me across the room.

A vicious knot forms in my stomach as I snatch a glass from a waiter and sit back down next to him.

"What I do is far more valuable than what you do," I add as I shoot him a scowl.

"I have a mind to prove you wrong. But then I'd have to take you with me to Vegas. To watch me win my place at a table of nine for the Texas Hold'em championship."

"Vegas? I've never been."

"Not sure if I want you around for the final. Not sure if I want you around at all." He watches me with that unnerving, unreadable silver gaze and leans forward, a wicked twist in his lips. "I'll tell you what, though. You brought my luck back."

"And you're exactly what I needed to get out of my relationship rut. You make me not want to be in a relationship *ever again*."

"I'm glad I inspire you, Red. You seem to inspire me too."

"You?"

"You inspire my game."

"Ah yes, cards. 'Cause your job is so much important than my job."

"You haven't spent enough time gambling to know for certain."

"Nor do you know anything about art. Art is far superior."

"I'd love to agree with you, but then we'd both be wrong and I'd rather play." He eyes me. "You spend some time at my job. I spend some time helping you with yours. We vote on the best. Winner takes all."

"What does that mean, winner takes all?"

"A hundred grand?" he suggests.

"God no! I'm not betting money. I work for every dime." I shudder at the idea.

"You don't have anything else I want."

Bull. Every man wants *something*. "Really? That money hungry, huh?"

"My hunger knows no bounds."

Now *that* I can believe. This guy will bet on pretty much anything.

At first that excites me, until I consider what he bets on. He probably has a private club and gives odds on marriages and divorces, births and deaths. I gasp at the last thought. How morbid. And yet I know it's true. If there's a game or prediction, Cullen will bet on the outcome.

Now, I wonder. What kind of odds does he have on me?

"Keep gambling for a living and you'll eventually know hunger."

As much as he irritates me, Cullen Carmichael also intrigues. I spent the better part of my day thinking about him. Now, I sit beside him and I'm being crass. Is it because Emmett is watching and I want him to know that a man can be interested while I totally blow him off? Do I look sophisticated or am I going for bitchy?

And why would Emmett care in the first place?

Why do I?

"How can you hate something you don't understand?" Cullen moves his chair closer and rests his arm on the table.

"I understand enough. Maybe it's a great way to make a living." Great for him, I guess, but I won't live that way. "A gambler's life is full of ups and downs. One minute, you're rolling in the money and the next, you can't keep the lights on. What kind of life is that?"

There's a long silence as he debates my answer. Then he says, flat out, "You're coming to Vegas with me."

"What?" I shake my head, certain I've never objected to anything else so quickly. "No. Never going to happen."

"Only way I can prove you wrong." He sits back in his chair as if it's settled. "Gamblers have their own unique set of 'challenges' but I'm not a *gambler*. *I'm* far more disciplined."

"Fine. I'll bite. Explain."

"Poker's different. If you're good at it . . ." He gives me a gaze-fuck that I won't soon forget. "And I am . . . very, *very* good. It can be a lucrative career with perks that'll blow your mind."

"I bet."

"Want to?"

Suddenly I want to do a lot of things to and with this man but gambling isn't one of them.

"You're not satiated with your millions and all your mansions across the world? You want a couple more?"

"I want everything money can buy."

"Well, I may have some things money can't buy. Like really nice cleavage."

"Sweetheart, I get an eyeful of cleavage daily and far more than what you're showing. Truthfully, I'm already zoning out."

He yawns, and my ego pricks. "Butt," I then say. "I have a nice butt."

Really, after a horrible breakup the last thing I need is this guy to give me insecurities, yet I've been baited and can't stop. "If you win, I'll do whatever you tell me to. A dare. And if I win, the same," I add.

"That's too vague. I never play without knowing the prize."

"Let me think."

He runs the tip of his tongue across his lip. "Dazzle me with some creativity."

"I'll blow you," I say.

He chokes on his drink and slams the glass down.

"Creative enough for you?" I smile and rise, deciding to let him ponder it. I want to add something like "I'm all-in" since I learned the term in last night's poker game.

"Hey. Hey." On his feet in a flash, he spins me around by the elbow, looming over me. "Does this mean if you win, I blow you too? I get to eat you up?"

"What?"

"Tell me."

His stillness makes me breathless.

His eyes, still unreadable, gleaming with a new light.

"Um. Yes. I could use some of that," I admit.

There's no shift in movement for a moment, just that dazzling gleam in his eyes, pulsing hypnotically on mine. The power of his grip on my elbow is all that keeps me on my feet, so great is my shock over his interest.

I have doubts about my desirability, but he has eyes riveted on me like he wants to breakfast, lunch, and dine on me.

"Stop," I gasp.

Puzzled, he stares. "Why?"

I blow an exasperated breath. "People are watching."

I realize, all of a sudden, that everybody is watching. That, most especially, Emmett is watching me from his table, with a look of puzzled concern on his face, and a woman sitting beside him. She may not be his date, but still. It's painful to remember that the seat beside him used to be mine.

My eyes fly to the silver ones looking down at me. "Emmett is watching."

"Let him watch."

"No. Okay, yes," I relent. "Dance with me."

"I don't dance. I need a drink." He starts to leave, but then turns back to me as if puzzled. "You want to make him realize what he's missing? Trust me, he knows."

I press my lips together, and nod, not knowing what to do to be sure I look unaffected. Suddenly I don't feel unaffected.

I told myself I wasn't going to hire some date to make him jealous. I told myself I'd act like an adult. But I feel vulnerable and unwanted, like he was right to leave me because he's found something better.

Cullen watches me, eyebrows slanting as he raises his hand and slips it behind my hair. He bends, and sets his lips over mine.

He kisses me drunk. I have no idea of the time, only his name, the moisture, the taste, the heat, the strength of his mouth. The hunger of his mouth.

He jerks free and leaves me with a gasp, his breathing a little faster. His fingers graze my knuckles, prolonging the moment. His attention skimming over me briefly.

The hammering in my heart turns to thunder.

The fire he started impossible to soothe.

I slide a hand over his chest and feel the indentations of his ab muscles and swallow.

"What was I going to say?" I ask dazedly, shaking my head as I try to recover. "Ahh, I remember. *You* were going to apologize," I lie.

"What for?"

"For not dancing."

"I'm not sorry I don't dance. I'm the guy at the bar, not on the dance floor."

"Then for kissing me."

His gaze slits as he looks down at my mouth.

"Not sorry either."

All emotion from the kiss is gone from his face.

How easily he can hide his reactions only magnifies the urge to kiss him again, and see his eyes get all heavy like they had for a few seconds. I must distract myself or else I'll go crazy.

"You're putting a lot of effort into this game," I suddenly say. "Makes me wonder if you really want my lips around you that badly. I might just like to leave you with your pants down and a lick."

"You won't be able to resist the taste."

"Wow, a real playboy, aren't you?"

"Baby, I live up to the name."

"Well, we'll see if you win and I'll get to taste."

"Wouldn't mind *you* winning so I'm the one tasting you."

A flash of surprise hits me, and a flash of warmth follows as I realize his meaning.

He gives me a smile as merry as twilight, his eyes dark with promise.

A tangible awareness of him and how large his body is compared to mine grips me, and a saturating sensation rises in me when his eyes hold mine.

I feel stirrings in all manner of places.

"Gonna pack the dress you were wearing last night?" he asks me.

"Yes."

"And the boots?"

"Yes, they're my fave."

"What about those things you were wearing in your ears, the long gold ones?"

"I . . ." Does he realize he just listed everything I was wearing? Does he always notice things like that?

"Pack those too," he says at my silent surprise.

"Wynn, do you want to dance?" I hear Valentine, one of Rachel's friends, ask.

"She doesn't dance," Cullen growls.

"She loves to dance," Valentine contradicts.

"Not anymore."

Had the atmosphere temp dropped thirty degrees all of a sudden? It feels suddenly chilly, my nipples stiff under my strapless dress.

Cullen drags me back to the table, and I can feel Emmett watching as I mull over the situation. So Cullen and I have a stupid game where we get to rate each other's jobs. More importantly, he gets his luck back and I get out of my rut. And I think about being around a guy I certainly don't want to marry, and the idea is refreshing. And I think about leaving town, and the idea grows on me more and more.

"I'll stop by at eight. You're coming to Vegas with me. Got it?" Cullen says.

"Of course I got it, I'm all for it. But I can only spare Sunday and four weekdays, then you're coming back to help me with my art exhibit." I'm feeling mischievous and don't even regret it. I'm smiling hours later, when Rachel and Saint give me a ride home.

They're discussing the wedding, while I'm staring out the window and tugging my smiling lower lip.

Oh gosh. I just dirty talked a little with the groom's brother. I just agreed to going on a trip with him. Worse, did I demand he help me during my prized exhibit too?

I wonder if my female hormones could have been running through my mind. Emmett had been watching me. Our breakup is still too fresh in my mind, and too painful to think about. I've been working nonstop, trying to stay busy, distracted, trying to not think or feel at all—and Cullen Carmichael is as good a distraction as any.

Not to mention, I may really be looking forward to winning and getting my prize. Emmett, despite being a chef who likes to savor the taste of things, never once went down on me. I should be insulted. Well. Now a man seemed to be savoring the prospect, and it makes me feel wanted again.

I like it.

I need it.

Even if I decide the prize I want is nothing at all.

THE DARE

The following day, he picks me up in a Mercedes Benz sports car, all black. I'm reluctant to meet his gaze as I step out as he takes my luggage and packs it into the trunk of the car. I let him hold the door open for me and I feel him watching as I climb into the passenger seat. His eyes run over my pink shirt dress and sandals.

He climbs behind the wheel, and his cologne blends with the nice-smelling leather of the car. I exhale and try to push his scent out of my system. But it's not like I can live without breathing, so it annoys me that when I take another breath, he's there again.

He's watching me with a frown as he starts the car. I glance into his eyes and wonder what he's thinking before he faces the street and we're on our way.

"Is there something wrong with what I'm wearing?" I ask.

"No."

"Just no?"

He shoots me a sidelong glance and runs his eyes over me again. "Definitely no."

I flush.

"So we're really heading to Vegas," I say to break the ice. "Looks like it."

I press my lips shut and twist them to keep from saying anything else.

"Tell me how you really feel. What do you really think of me?"

His question surprises me. I don't know how I feel about him, or why his looks hold me a little bit captive and his gaze makes me a little breathless.

People don't really know how addictive love is until they fall. Once you're in, you crave the feeling like a drug and you feel lost without it. It's a feeling I have no intention of revisiting.

But this silver-eyed distraction is tempting.

"Nothing is holy or untouchable to you. You'd bet your mom if anyone would take her, I bet."

"How much would you bet on it?"

My brows fly up in surprise. God, he's incorrigible. I swat his arm, nearly bruising my fingers. "Stop trying to make me fall into your addiction." I laugh. "You're crazy. Why do you like it?"

He shrugs. "Pushes all my buttons, I guess . . . Most of them anyway."

"And the ones it doesn't, all those Vegas cocktail waitresses take care of?"

One eyebrow cocks, and Cullen shoots me a dubious glare. "You sure you've never been?"

"I know all about Vegas without ever setting a foot in Sin City."

We head to the airport, and he parks the car in front of a massive white airplane with a black-and-silver stripe down the side. Cullen steps out of the car as a pilot walks swiftly to the passenger side and swings open the door for me.

My jaw is hanging somewhere around the floor as I gape at the gigantic plane. I force myself to snap it shut as Cullen draws me forward, slipping his hand in mine. It feels too surreal, to be this girl, to follow a guy who's a little bit dangerous and a little bit mysterious and all too hot into his plane. The plane, the guy, that are taking me away from it all.

For once I want to have fun. Be free. Stop this ache in my chest. Fill the hole with whatever I can find. I'm not thinking about who will win our bet. I'm just glad to get out of the city. Glad to get out of my head. Glad to give my heart a breather.

"After you." Cullen motions to the stairs as the pilots bring our suitcases to the back of the plane.

I gulp because, let's face it, I've never been in one of these before. I can't believe how comfortable it is to avoid the hassle of airport security.

I board the private jet. There are eight leather seats, all about as wide as first class seats on a commercial airline, each with a small TV and shiny mahogany table before it. I don't know which to pick, so I plop down in a seat facing the front, while Cullen lowers himself on the seat beside mine. I strap my seatbelt and exhale, and when our eyes meet, I feel a little woozy.

He's wearing dark jeans—and the way he sits stretches the material by the muscles of his thighs. His package is a little too large and obvious.

I drag my eyes upward, intending to look away, but my gaze is snagged by the indentations of the muscles of his abs, visible under the black long-sleeved T-shirt he wears. He's still in black, every part of him dark and tempting and very much unlike what I'm used to.

Emmett was blond, and he was a food-loving chef who loved to experiment. This guy, on the other hand? He looks quite the opposite. Dark as the devil, and something about his apparent need for control makes me think he is very disciplined in everything. Even, crazy as it sounds, gambling.

"Nice," I say, motioning to the plane.

"I like nice things." His eyes roam over me.

I look away as I try to recover my breath, something he seems adept in fucking up for me. "How many times have you lost this plane?"

"This particular one?" He cocks his head thoughtfully. "None. A few like this?" His eyes narrow even more. "About six times."

"What do you do when you lose it? Fly commercial?"

"I borrow money and win me another. A better one."

"Is that what you do when you lose a woman too?"

"Of course." He answers in that same mocking tone I'm not sure means he agrees or not. Then he shifts forward, his gaze unreadable as he looks deeply into me. "Isn't that what you're doing?"

Silence. My heart drums a little faster as Cullen lifts his hand and tucks a strand of hair behind my ear, and the skin he grazes with his fingertip burns.

"Maybe," I say.

"We're taking off in two, Mr. Carmichael," the co-pilot says.

"Good," he answers to the co-pilot without taking his eyes off me. I meet his gaze and wonder what's going on. He irritates and excites me at the same time—and this is a first for me.

"So what started gambling?"

Silence.

"Touchy subject?"

"Not really. I'd simply prefer to talk about you." He eases back. "Art?"

"I grew up with it. I am drawn to it. You like nice things? I like beautiful ones."

"You must be full of yourself."

"Huh?" I smile and realize his meaning. Flush. "You're suave."

"You could say I'm honest."

"It's hard to take a compliment after a four-year breakup."

"You better learn to. I don't like my compliments landing on deaf ears."

"I'm not deaf, just have reasons not to believe a guy with the nickname *Playboy*."

"I didn't pick it."

"But you use it."

"I have others."

I shrug as if I'm not insanely curious to know them. "Good for you. Let's talk about that. I'm enjoying talking about you and gambling more than about me."

"You're avoiding telling me about you. That's all right, Red. I'm patient. That's what makes me a good gambler. I always know when to call, and when to up the stakes with a raise."

Whoa and *damnnnnn.*

I smile nervously and glance away.

He's quiet. I wonder what he's thinking. "What are you thinking?" I whisper.

"I'm thinking of our little dare—and how this is the first bet I've ever made I might deliberately lose." He stares at me.

"You're shameless." And yet, I've been thinking the same thing. Having his lips on my . . . mine.

A silence stretches.

He reaches out and strokes my face with his thumb. I'm canting to the touch, liking it, surprised by how much I like it. I don't want to remember him kissing me at the wedding, but I do. My taste buds tingle remembering.

"What are you wearing under that pink dress?" he asks.

My insides go wild. "Guess."

"Why would I guess when I can know for certain?"

My lips part in shock, and suddenly I'm waiting in nervous anticipation as Cullen slips his hand under my dress, stroking the very top of my panties.

His eyes darken as he strokes downward and I feel naked, exposed.

As he inches closer, his fingers dance lower, causing a scandalous fever.

"Lace," he whispers, his silver eyes heating as they hold mine, his touch feathery soft and investigative. "Very flimsy, a G-string. You're definitely aiming to get laid tonight." He shifts his hand lightly, touching the most sensitive place now. "Wet. You're *definitely* getting laid tonight."

"Is that right?" I taunt in my efforts to hide my breathlessness.

"I'd bet on it."

My smile fades because I know how serious this man is about betting. "Really, this isn't part of the game."

"This *is* the game."

"No, Cullen. I . . ." I shake my head, trying to get a grip. "What's the point of betting oral if we're giving it to each other already every night?"

"Sex isn't oral."

He withdraws his hand, licks his finger, and sucks it into his mouth. He releases it with a pop, says, "mmm," and leans back in his seat, and I'm clenching my thighs together in my seat, wondering how many women have made his Mile High Club.

HIGH ROLLER

'm still unsettled by the time we arrive, and really very confused about Cullen Carmichael. Sometimes broody and quiet, sometimes frank and determined, flying so many hours alone in a plane next to a . . . a force like him is kind of exhausting, and yet I'm not one bit tired. I feel, more than tired, a little high. Maybe it's Vegas.

A uniformed chauffeur greets us as we descend the plane at the airport, the Las Vegas Strip standing proudly at close distance.

"Mr. Carmichael," his chauffeur says.

"Oliver, this is Miss Watson. She'll be spending the week with me."

"Pleasure, Miss Watson," the chauffeur greets as he opens the back of a shiny black Audi for us. Once he settles our suitcases in the trunk and Cullen slides into the back seat beside me, we're on our way.

It's close to noon, and I drink in the Strip with growing excitement.

"Wow. The city is . . . really charming. So close to the airport too."

"We're in the desert," Cullen says as he checks some messages on his phone, not bothering to glance up. "It would be unnecessary to make people drive down desert planes to leave it."

"Where are we headed, sir? Home or . . ."

"Hotel." He tucks his phone away. "I'll be playing often. I want her to be able to head upstairs to rest whenever she needs a break."

"Are we feeling lucky, Mr. Carmichael? After last month, didn't think—"

"Very lucky, Oliver," he cuts off his chauffeur.

"So take me to battle," Cullen adds to his chauffeur. He stares at me with his unnerving platinum eyes as he speaks, and though the chauffeur eyes him across the rearview mirror with a smile, Cullen ignores him and keeps looking at me intensely enough to make me flush all over.

We're taken to the hotel, and as Cullen slides out of the car and opens the door for me, I start getting excited at how beautiful and lavish the lobby looks. I glance past my shoulder—and catch his eyes hungrily raking the back of my legs.

"You did not just check me out as I got out of the car."

"Those legs of yours were meant to be seen." He points at his eyes with two open fingers, then we head inside.

A handsome thirty-something guy in a polo and khakis greets us. "Cullen! Good to see you." They shake hands. Slap backs. Seem like old friends.

For a minute, I think they are until Cullen says, "Do I have time to go to the room?"

"You do." He checks me out.

"Mike, meet Wynn." Cullen narrows his eyes suspiciously then adds, "She's with me." As if he needs to make a claim. "See to it that she doesn't want for anything."

Mike pulls out a black-and-silver card. "Had this made up for you, Miss . . ."

"Wynn. Call me Wynn."

Cullen grimaces as if he would've preferred something less casual. "Mike's in player development. If you need something, ask for him."

"Day or night," Mike adds.

Well. Isn't that helpful.

"Whatever she wants." Cullen is firmer this time.

"Understood." Mike is serious and I'm amused.

A bellman approaches. "Mr. Carmichael. I saw your driver outside. I'll take care of your bags."

"Thanks," he says, sliding a rolled bill into his palm.

He and Mike discuss an upcoming tournament then we turn to go. As we're walking, he says, "Whatever you want—food, salon appointments, anything—use the card."

"I have my own money."

"Your money is no good here." He seems offended but then his face softens. "I'm owed a lot of comps. Please use them."

"What are comps?"

"Freebies in exchange for player loyalty."

"Aw, so that's how a gambler keeps his lights on. After he loses all his money, the casino shows mercy and sends the wife at home a check made out to the electric company."

"Ha." He doesn't laugh. "It's more like a percentage of your play and can be used here for rooms, shopping, massages, whatever you want."

"Good to know." I wait a beat. "I'll call the front desk for a room if you piss me off."

"Won't happen, Red."

"If it does," I say, eyeing a shopping window to the right as we walk to the elevators, "I know where to turn." I'm only half attentive now as I eye a skimpy white dress in a boutique window. I wonder how many comps that will set him back.

As if he reads my mind, he says, "Don't worry. You won't even come close to using what's available."

Before the doors close, Mike catches us and hands off a pair of tickets. "Forgot to give you these."

"Thanks, Mike." He waves the tickets as the doors close.

God, this *guy*.

He's cool without trying, utterly sexy.

"Everybody just dotes on you," I comment as Cullen hands them off to me.

"Mike earns a percentage of my play." He shrugs as if it doesn't matter. "He makes my life simple and that's that. Plus I'm a good tipper."

The elevator is empty and we ride up in silence, watching the numbers climb as we do. I don't know why the silence between us starts to feel awkward.

This guy is really hard to read and really magnetic. It feels like an eternity before I feel his hand on the small of my back, the touch causing me to lift my face up to find him looking down at me.

He leans down suddenly and places a kiss on my lips. I didn't see it coming. He's so tall that I have to rise on my tiptoes to meet his mouth, but he doesn't seem to mind that at all.

It's a brief peck, but I pull back because my stomach tangles up with excitement and I want to be sure I'm able to keep my wits about me when I'm around this guy. I drop back down.

"Can we go?" I use the moment to my advantage.

"Where?" He stares at my mouth like he might deliver a bruising kiss then pulls back, holding my gaze in his.

I stick the tickets between our faces. "I know these bands."

"Then we'll go."

"Yes!"

He smiles down at me.

Suddenly I need that kiss again, the one I broke for fear of wanting it too much. I'm standing on my toes when Cullen moves to claim it.

He swoops down and starts slow, moving to a hotter, more searing kiss that keeps intensifying with every nip and taste of his mouth. My hands are suddenly in his hair. His hands are on my waist. The world tilts sideways and I can't help myself from relishing this guy's kiss.

I don't know why I'm responding, except that he tastes nice, and it really does feel as if Vegas is its own bubble. As if I could get away with kissing Cullen right here, right now, and then leave it right here, in this elevator, in this hotel, and in this city, with any regrets I might have too.

"So you just kissed me because you wanted to." I speak on a breath.

"Very good. You're perceptive. Intuitive."

I realize he's teasing me in that low, terribly rumbly voice and I wish he would smile at me.

He takes my hand and fingers my palm with his thumb as he leads me to our suite.

I'm sizzling where he touches me, nervously prying my hand free when he leads me into the biggest, most spectacular two-bedroom penthouse suite I've ever seen. Not that I'd seen one before in person, only movies.

There's a kitchen area, and windows from floor to ceiling. A living room, a pool table, gold brass chandeliers, a brown-and-beige-patterned carpet, dark woods, Italian leathers. Gorgeous! I could move in here.

Now I see the appeal but won't admit as much.

Thinking of our bet, I pay attention to the art on the walls. It's expensive. I can tell by the numbered print and the signature. Painters with indecipherable and artistic signatures are often the artists to watch. It's like they know from the moment they paint their first work that they're on to something big, something that will distinguish their work from all others.

I wish Cullen loved art as much as I do. Maybe I could drag him away from the tables to a local gallery.

"Wow. I could just live he—" I spin around and bump into his big warm body, and he bends his head and kisses my words right out of me.

Kisses me stupid. Kisses my toes curled. Kisses my brain blank. Kisses my heart crazy.

Easing back, leaving my mouth burning from his, his eyes catch mine. He unbuttons my shirt dress slowly, with each button, glancing into my eyes to gauge my reaction.

"Only the top ones," I rasp out.

I don't know why I seem to think that keeping some sort of barrier from him will protect me, at least my emotions, from getting too involved, but there you have it. I feel safe enough with only my tits getting exposed, safe enough to lean up and start kissing his lips as he fondles and touches my breasts.

His hand fits just right over my breast, and I'm surprised by how gently he caresses the swell. How slow and sinuous the pad of his thumb feels as he circles it toward my nipple—and then remains there. Stroking my nipple into the hardest, most painful little peak. All while his tongue and mine swirl. He tastes like bubblegum, and his body heat feels delicious.

"We should probably be friends only," I say, suddenly stopping his hand with mine.

"Is that what you want?"

"I think it's what we both need."

"I'm not sure I agree on that."

"You're thinking with your cock right now."

"Hearing you say the word cock is not helping matters for me one bit."

I feel a blush the color of my hair creep up my face. "Cullen."

He eyes me for a moment, and an unprecedented warmth appears in his gaze as he watches me nervously fiddle with my hair. "Think about it. In the meantime, let's get you in that black dress. Did you pack it?" he asks.

"I have another one that's pretty sweet—"

"Nope. The black dress."

He tosses my suitcase up on the dining table and unzips it. "What are you doing?"

He fishes out the black dress he met me in, then brings it over.

He looks intently into my eyes. "Getting you ready."

I feel dazed and a little hypnotized as he comes close again. I feel his fingers seize the rest of the buttons of my pink dress. Briskly he pops each open until the dress falls at my ankles.

I'm standing there, getting undressed by freaking Cullen Carmichael.

"The black dress is stretchy cotton so I can just pop my head in and—"

"Arms," he says.

I lift them instantly and slip my arms into the sleeves, then pop my head into the neck hole. He tugs it down my body, until it falls to my knees.

He brings my shoes next. Unbuckles my sandals, takes them off.

He takes one of my bare feet in his hands.

I feel him study my toes, caress his thumb along my arch. Gulping, I breathlessly watch him slip my heels on, one at a time. He dresses me methodically, almost ritualistically. He heads back to my suitcase, opens my jewelry roll. "Ah." He finds my earrings among a set of six, brings them.

He eases my hair back and hooks one on. Then the other.

I can't say that watching him work methodically, concentrating as he puts each article on me, doesn't affect me. I really can't say it's something common or normal, because NO man in my entire life has dressed me. Or undressed me like this. With such gentle but businesslike hands. With such expert precision. I've also never really been seen the way his jeweled eyes drink me in. He paces around me. One time. Twice. Thumb scraping his chin, as if he's making sure I am that girl—that girl he met at the clandestine poker game.

"Nothing missing?" One eyebrow cocks thoughtfully.

"Nope. You've been very thorough." I'm almost laughing, he seems so serious.

"Good."

My smile fades when he heads to his own suitcase and withdraws a black button shirt. It fades because he removes one shirt, and he slides into another one.

And . . . I really wish he hadn't removed his shirt in front of me. But okay.

Deep breath, Wynn.

He's gorgeous.

So what? You knew that.

I didn't know his chest was so ripped and muscly but . . . I'll get over it.

He buttons up swiftly, runs a hand through his hair, then heads to the safe in his room. I hear buttons click, instructions on his phone, and when Cullen is back, he looks like he's open for business. Badass business.

"Are we playing?" I feel a shot of adrenaline rush through me at the prospect.

"We're playing."

He doesn't laugh, walks around me, inspecting me again one more time, scraping his thumb along his chin. He stops at my back and eases my hair to one side of my shoulder, inhaling me as he strokes his finger along my nape. "Perfect," he says.

"I've never been dressed by a man before. Just undressed."

"It's a first for me too. Dressing a woman." He sets my hair straight behind my back again, walking around me to face me.

"You do it rather expertly."

"Not too different from undressing one." He eyes me one more time, then takes my hand. "Let's go. I'm feeling very, very lucky tonight."

We take the elevator to the casino.

I don't know what to do.

He just stripped me naked.

Did it affect him? I glance at him in the elevator, and he looks cool and collected. Hand in his pocket, watching the elevator numbers descend. How disappointing.

I wonder if we should discuss it some more. The friends part.

I may be sending strange signals, and I don't want him to think I'm a tease.

I don't know why it matters so much, what he thinks of me. But it does.

"Do you have any questions about—"

"Plenty. But I know when to ask, and when to let you tell me." He doesn't look at me as he speaks, only keeps watching the numbers descending.

The elevator opens on the casino floor, and I exhale a ragged breath. Whew. So we're good then. Friends. I step out, and he grabs me by the wrist. His hold is warm, firm, as he tugs me to face him.

"But you *will* tell me," he says.

His tone is soft but commanding. It might even be a little arrogant, but the truth is, I want to tell him.

He should know, because I'm realizing by the second that I desperately want him.

And it's important that he knows. Because even though he's looking at me with the hottest eyes a man has ever looked at me with, things could change. What I tell him could change things.

The casino is alive with action. It's easy to see the appeal. The air is cool and electric and rapidly pulses with energy and excitement. Multicolored lights, songs and bells, squeals and laughter.

As we pass gaming tables, I hear someone say, "Coming out!" And I scan the casino, half expecting to see the paparazzi and a rock star with his entourage.

"Dice table," Cullen tells me in explanation, apparently reading my mind. "Looks like fun, right?" He leans closer to my ear and gives it a little nibble. "That's because it is."

A handsome dealer wearing a white-sleeved shirt and sharp royal-blue vest twirls a long stick like a baton. "Cullen, my man. Good to see you!"

"You too, Leroy." He shoots a look in my direction. "Take care of my girl when she's at your table."

Leroy looks stunned but rebounds fast enough to say, "Send her my way."

"When hell freezes over," Cullen says to me once we're a few strides away from Leroy's table.

I laugh softly, amused by his uncharacteristic enthusiasm here in the casino as well as his adorable show of possessiveness. It's endearing. And so very sexy. I feel something clutch hard in my stomach. I wonder what else he's passionate about.

I'm about to find out.

We walk through the main poker room to a door with black lettering. He slips his keycard in the reader. Double golden doors with a beveled glass part reveal the VIP suite.

He holds out his arm. "After you."

The room has five tables with players around two. It's a high roller poker game with a tournament set to start. Buy in is steep. A host gives Cullen the particulars but he's distracted. He's watching me as if he expects me to say something but there are no words. I'm impressed with this life and he hasn't even started betting yet.

He's quite the popular guy. Silently, he slips his hand over mine and drags me closer to a table, and a group of young males, one with a cowboy hat, the others in jeans, spot us. Their gazes track Cullen as if he's a man come back from the dead.

One whistles. "Playboy's back."

Cullen releases my hand to greet them all.

"Didn't expect you so soon. Making up your losses in Atlanta or Chicago?"

"Bet's on Albany," someone else says, tossing a black chip at the first man who spoke.

The player nods at the bet, studies Cullen, then looks at the other gambler, "You're on. I've got Chicago."

"You've got the win. Now get ready to lose," Cullen tells him plainly, no smile to indicate he's joking.

The four men laugh, and yet their laughs are as merry as their own funerals could be. In fact, one of them looks damn worried and is clenching his jaw hard enough to warrant a visit to the dentist.

"You haven't introduced us," one guy says, nodding in my direction.

As if wanting them to stop looking at me, Cullen draws me around to a set of chairs to the side of the tables.

"Isn't it rude for you not to introduce me?" I ask him.

"Rude would be for them to jinx my streak."

I realize he's not the kind of man to get drawn into any taunts except the ones he wants, and I smile admiringly.

"Do you really feel lucky?" I ask.

"Do you doubt this?" He lets his eyes slide to the tray of chips they're bringing from the casino cage. He signs a paper and the chips are set in front of him.

"Good luck," the credit manager says.

"Wow. Okay. I need to sit down," I reply when Cullen turns his attention back to me.

He watches me lower myself to the chair with a light of approval in his eye. "Let's do this." He bends and kisses my mouth.

"Cullen, we said maybe we should be—"

"Shh. Be a good girl and watch." He grabs the back of my hair to direct my gaze to his. "And by watch, I mean watch me. Don't twirl your hair."

"Oh, that's right," I tease. "Because it's hot."

"Damn fucking hot." His words are slow and thick as if they catch in his throat.

Releasing me, he heads to the table to take his seat, folding the sleeves of his shirt to his elbows.

I watch silently, trying not to fidget or get kicked out of the room. I wish there were others there to observe and mimic, maybe another player's girlfriend.

Oh, I did not just go there.

Fuck.

I'm in deep and drowning. Cullen is a different kind of danger, a precipice of uncertainty that promises to leave me awakened and alive.

I am so fucking screwed!

His face is in shadows, half in darkness, half in light, and I simply watch, mesmerized, as he plays. He doesn't clench his jaw, doesn't twitch a finger, doesn't do anything to reveal his hand. I've never seen someone so unreadable in my life.

Only when he lifts his eyes does a little gleam of proprietariness show. But it's there so fleetingly that when it's gone I wonder if I made it up.

Whimsically, I roll my eyes at myself. *Really, Wynn. We need to get you off men. If you want anything from him, make it sex.* But . . . I'm starting to like him, which can complicate things. He's more multifaceted than I'm used to, which means if I start peeling back his layers, I'll be surprised by what I find.

My heart is out of order. Which is a good thing.

If it stays that way.

I'm here because I want to be. Cullen was persuasive, sure, but I made the decision to lock up my apartment, slip away from my life, and take a trip on a private plane with a man who knows how to get what he wants.

He wants me.

And I shiver a little. Because I want him too.

Still, it might be better to try to detox from it all. And focus on the bet. Wynn, you have a nice bet going on, and you can blow him as his prize. Or yours. Yep. It's win/win as far as I see. My ego demands I win because gambling is not better than art.

It's a little absurd that he suggested as much.

Yet he makes it look like art as he raises and pushes his chips forward. He slowly stands but I sense I know that move. It's a calculated one, a move meant to intimidate the other players.

It doesn't work.

Another player is all-in, too. He's short a dozen or more black chips but no one points that out. I guess there are rules for this but I don't know what they are.

When my date was short, I was the prize. Guess this player doesn't have a girlfriend to toss in the pot.

As if he reads my mind, Cullen shoots me a sexy, knowing wink.

And for one delicious millisecond, I pretend Cullen Carmichael is all mine.

He plays for three hours, and wins about two hundred and thirty grand. He tosses me two ten-thousand-dollar chips in such a playful manner that my fingers tingle when I catch one in each hand. He then leads me to the elevator. I steal glances at him on our ride to the room, but he's still wearing his poker face. I wonder if he'll want to undress me.

Do I want him to take this dress off me?

Who am I kidding? After our day together, I'd strip down for him. And like it.

Too soon, Wynn. Stay strong.

The internal dialogue bores me when the more reasonable side of my consciousness takes the lead.

As he unlocks the door, I feel his hand on the small of my back, leading me in.

Why does everything he does seem so terribly sexy to me?

I leap away and go straight to the bar, getting a bottle of water from the small fridge.

"I'm hitting the bed," I say, giving merit to my voice of reason. "Goodnight."

His phone buzzes. I hear him say, "Hang on," and curse when I shut the door to my bedroom. Ha! Gotcha. I really didn't want the temptation so it's best that I escaped.

This will make our dare so much more rewarding.

I'm impressed by the suite and take in the huge king bed and the city lights blinking outside.

I shower in the large marble bath, then I lay in bed in my bathrobe with a towel over my head. I check the time and realize it's late in Chicago, so I pull out my laptop and check emails on the gallery exhibit.

Then, I do what all gallerists should swear off—I surf hashtags to see if anyone's talking about the upcoming show.

They are! And I'm stoked I checked.

Once done, I sigh and stare at the closed door. I wander over and open it an inch or two and peer outside. I hear the shower water turn off in his bedroom, and minutes later, I hear him out in the living area, playing pool. I tie the robe tighter around me and step out. He senses me approach, but doesn't stop aiming for the white ball.

Click. He gets three balls into the pockets with a hit. Changes position and aims.

"I have to hand it to you. You're full of surprises. I didn't see you as a runner."

"I'm . . . not." I roll my eyes at his back. "Okay, so maybe I ran for a minute. I'm here now."

He makes another clean shot then props the pool stick under his chin. His eyes are dark, studying me.

This guy has got a winning presence, a brooding confidence.

I know that he's the kind of man who has expectations, but he gives nothing away as to what they are. He's a guy who's highly sexed and works that energy to his advantage.

And I'm eating him up with my eyes.

"What'd you think about it?"

"Vegas?"

"Or me." He takes another shot. Misses.

"I could do both." I take the unspoken dare.

He freezes.

My breath catches when he turns. There's a tumultuous force around him now. It's not just now. He's larger than life wherever he is, wherever we go. He enters a room and makes it his own. And I know from the depths of my soul he takes a woman the same way.

Takes her. *Possesses* her. *Claims* her as his own.

That knowledge should make me run in the other direction. Instead, I'll send him running. I know how to do it, what to confess.

Careful, Wynn. You don't want to push him away entirely. Do you?

I think about consequences before I quietly say, "Emmett and I told each other we loved each other. I dated him for years. I moved in with him. I even had a pregnancy scare, but nothing came of it."

I walk to the couch and sit, trying to decide how much I'll tell him.

"I was . . . disappointed when I received the news." That's an understatement. "He knew how much I wanted to be a mom, so the scare? It wasn't super-terrifying. What was heart-breaking . . ."

"He was relieved when he found out that it was only a scare?"

I nod, the sadness threatening to destroy me all over again. Not because of how Emmett responded to the news. That was minor. What came next was devastating.

"I kept waiting for him to make a move, but he was grow-ing distant. We broke up. I couldn't believe that all that we had between each other was a lie, but it was. We got back together, and for a time he seemed to put in the effort." I shake my head. "It was no use. I tried so hard. I tried to have meals warm, look beautiful, be in a good mood, I didn't even let on when I was tired. Our relationship was hanging by a thread."

He sets the stick down, crosses his arms, looks at me.

"His feelings changed. So I moved out." I need to tell him about Emmett, not because it defines me or where I am in life or because I want to remember the bottom of the barrel that I once scraped. It's more than that. "He says he simply cannot take that next step, but I know it's because of me."

"It's not."

"Sure it was. Is. Things changed after the pregnancy scare. I felt disappointed, oddly, when I realized I wasn't preg-nant." I'm almost there, almost ready to rip open a vein and bleed all over the place.

And why? Why do I want to tell this man, this sexy and present and available man something so personal? So real?

He frowns. "I'm sorry."

"Me too," I whisper, but try to bite back the urge to say enough without telling him everything. To say something like,

"I basically have built-in birth control, which isn't such a bad thing. And I can adopt."

But the words stay trapped inside as I try not to remember the agonizing pain I felt the day I found out that I wouldn't have my own child. I wouldn't have a little girl with my hair or a little boy with Emmett's smile. "He's an idiot." Cullen's eyes are dark, and he seems to be struggling. "That's all I'm going to say about him. As for you. You're . . ." He stops, then says gruffly, "You're perfect. You don't need him."

Deep down inside, I'm screaming, "But I do. I can't adopt a child as a single parent. It's doubly hard!"

He just looks at me, and I wipe my tear. "Anyway. That's why I think I need a friend, more than anything. Just a friend. And I'm sure, judging by your reputation, that you don't lack women who want you in bed. But I doubt you have many people who . . . well, what you said about them liking you because you tip well. I'm not here for that reason."

"No, you're here because you hate my guts—look down on what I do. And I'm about to enlighten you on how thrilling it could be. You game?"

I love that he takes me out of my sorry state and puts the good times back in perspective. "Yes."

"Show me. Come here." He tilts his head back with an easy jerk.

The come-hither call entices me.

He's just too inviting to ignore, so I head over, my heart starting to pound a little faster.

Suddenly my neck is in his hands. He draws me closer. "Kiss me," he husks.

Our lips are a whisper away.

I stretch my arms around his broad shoulders and kiss him like he might get away. I don't want him to go. I don't want to be sent away.

He kisses me breathless then kisses me back to life again.

And I like it. Need it. Because he makes me feel wanted and I need that sense of belonging right now, especially after I poured out my heart.

His kiss doesn't make me feel bought or sold, won or lost. I'm grounded, safe, and feel . . . I can't even think it. It's petrifying to let my mind travel down *that* rabbit hole.

I'm starting to feel too comfortable, *at home*.

"Cullen . . ."

"Shh," he whispers. "Let me have this, you."

"No." But he's already into this, *into me*.

His fingers are in my hair. His lips skim my cheek, ear. Whispering kisses, fluttering tongue, all of it is too much, too soon, and too damn hot.

I'm responding and don't know how to stop. How can I resist the irresistible, sate the insatiable?

This guy is a gambler, a man who wants to win at any cost.

When I finally pull back, I'm breathless. A real wreck.

We take a minute, give each other enough space.

I ask, "Do we have a deal?"

"Hmm?" He drags his thumb across his lip.

"About friends?"

"Deal," he husks out.

The mood is ruined.

I killed it on purpose.

"But Wynn?" The next second Cullen smiles a wolfish smile. "I'm the sort that kisses his friends on the mouth. Fair warning."

"I think we really should—"

"Oh, we will."

"You didn't let me finish."

"You forgot what you wanted to say." He slides his hand around the back of my neck and jerks me against him, teases me with that fierce hot mouth once more. He smirks as if he's playing. I squirm because I'm not.

Before I slip away, he presses his lips harder against mine and delivers a bruising kiss, with that same hint of bubblegum and heat and tongue.

"Goodnight." He smiles, pats my butt, and I turn around and wobble back into my room.

Am I playing the player or has he just played me?

I toss and turn for most of the night. Whenever I close my eyes, Cullen appears with that cool smile and even temperament. My palm burns from the chips he puts in my hand. My fingers ache to touch him. My breathing is labored because I can't get enough.

I'm damp and so fucking turned on. He's not just a fantasy or an image in my head. He's real and he's here.

Right across the hall.

I'm so into the fantasy of him—wanting him, sleeping next to him, fucking him—that I can't stay in my bed. It's four in the morning and if he's asleep, maybe I'll curl up beside him, drag his arm over my waist and settle down.

Just sleep.

Right, Wynn.

I'm padding across the living room with his door in my sights when I hear the clicking of engaged locks. I turn and dart back to my suite in time to shut my door and place my ear against the wall, expecting to hear only footsteps.

Instead, I hear him say, "I left it at the front desk. Ask for Mike in the morning and he'll take care of it."

I frown in concentration. Did Cullen go to a private poker game? Did he lose? Why didn't he ask me to go?

Staring up at the ceiling, I feed into the gambler's superstitions.

He should've taken his lucky charm.

I hear ice clinking in a glass, which speaks of his growing frustration.

"Look, Mom, I'm tired. I don't want to be disrespectful but if you were so concerned about 'family' then you would've shown up for Callan's wedding. At least meet his bride . . . I think you'd like her."

Mom? He was gambling with his mom?

Silence.

"Like I said, the money is downstairs. Mike handles my affairs here and he'll be happy to cash it for you when he arrives. At eleven."

More silence.

"Because it isn't an emergency." He sounds exasperated.

An extended silence follows this time. I don't think Cullen is talking about a poker game.

"I always call you back, Mom." A beat later, his voice is softer when he says, "Because you're my mother. No matter what you do or don't do, I love you. Now get some sleep. Everything will work itself out but nothing good happens after three o'clock in Vegas."

That opinion should be debated, I decide, hoping to have a chance to prove him wrong.

Someday, maybe. But not tonight. Family matters are better left between mother and son. Plus, I've heard the horror stories about Cullen's mom. While I'd love to comfort him, this is one night when he'd probably rather sleep alone.

REDHEAD

Cullen

Several months ago . . .

"Who's the redhead?"

I aim my gaze at the redhead entering the club so my brother knows who I'm referring to.

Callan follows my line of vision. "That's Wynn."

"Wynn what?" I run my eyes all over her, already savoring having my hands all over her.

"Wynn, and she's taken, man."

I stand to leave. I've got a flight to catch. But for some reason, my eyes linger on her even as I slap my brother's back in farewell. "Let me know if she becomes available."

It's not until I'm on the plane that I put together the connection. "Wynn." I toss a few ice cubes in a glass tumbler. A splash of whiskey, a twist of lime, and the first sip burns all the way down.

We're next up for takeoff when it dawns on me.

I should've introduced myself.

A woman who looks like "Wynn" needs to be with a man who loves to do the same. She needs someone who will dote on her and buy her pretty things, someone who enjoys showing her off while introducing her to the world. For some reason, I hope she has these things already. Whoever warms her bed should count himself lucky and spoil her.

I shoot Callan a text:

Is she happy?

Callan: Who?

Redhead.

Callan: Why do you care?

Just answer the question.

Callan: I guess. Why?

She didn't look it.

Callan: I'll bite. What's a girl like Wynn supposed to look like?

WELL sexed. Find out if she's happy.

He doesn't respond until hours later.

Callan: Livvy says she hasn't had sex in several months. Happy?

I slip my arm away from the redhead in my bed.

Me: Very.

"Wynn." It has such a nice ring to it.

"Of course you're gonna win, baby," my date moans, reaching for me. "Want me to give you some luck before I go?"

"I'm good," I say, not meaning to be insensitive, but ready to ditch the broad who was nothing more than a place-holder, a lame substitute for a woman I don't even know.

I'm not the guy who settles but last night, I picked up a generic fix hoping to get name brand satisfaction.

It didn't work.

JOBS

Wynn

I wake up late, surprised that I slept so much. Seeing it's almost noon, I leap out of bed, brush my teeth, comb my hair, and add a little lipstick before I pad outside, my heart sinking when there's no sign of Cullen in the suite. I'm peering into his bedroom to see his bed is unmade, and for some reason I stare at the dent in the pillow for a little while, when there's a knock on the door. I swing open the door, and a man in a uniform stands next to a tall, linen-covered table.

"Breakfast, madam," he says, motioning me for permission to wheel the cart in.

"Please. Come in." I step back and allow him inside, salivating over the scent of bacon. I sign the tab to the room, wish him a good day back, and when he leaves, take a seat and peer around the silver-edged dishes. All of this, just for me? There's everything from French toast, to eggs with hash and bacon, to Belgian waffles with berries on the side.

"Good morning to *me*." I happily pour myself coffee, add maple syrup to the waffles, and dive in.

That's when I see the note resting on one of the silver platters.

Gaming money for you on your nightstand. Look me up at the tables.
CC

Why did I just shiver?

Reading it again, I whisper, "I could get used to this."

And his "friendly" kisses.

Don't go there, Wynn.

You have a bet to win.

I hate to admit it, but if job appeal carries much weight in our wager then he'll win hands-down based on perks alone and I haven't even started shopping yet!

I try *not* to remember the way I opened up to him last night and the way he made me feel accepted—fuck, *more* than accepted, *desired more than anything else*—as I eat breakfast. For some reason, I can't eat fast enough. Once done with my waffles, I guzzle down half a glass of orange juice and run to my room, eager to go downstairs. I don't want to dwell on why.

You don't want him. You just want to win.

I continue to brainwash myself and psych myself into gung-ho, bet-winning mode as I dress in jeans, a comfortable sweater, and my favorite boots. I add a pair of long earrings and pull my hair back into a ponytail. Then I check my nightstand and spot the three ten-thousand-dollar chips he left for me.

Wow. I've never met anyone who parted so easily with his money.

I tuck them into the back pocket of my jeans and wonder if I want to buy something. Buy myself one of the paintings that I'll be exhibiting in my gallery next week. Buy shoes, or a bag, or invest it with his brother, Callan. I make a point of remembering to book an appointment with him when he and Livvy return from their honeymoon as I head down into the casino.

I spot Mike in the lobby as soon as I exit the elevator. He's striding in my direction.

"Miss Watson . . . Wynn." He shoots me a crooked smile. "Is it morning or afternoon for you?"

"Morning. How about you?"

"Evening," he says. "We had an interesting night."

"I already know not to ask. What happens in Vegas . . ."

"Rarely stays here . . ." He walks with me. "Need anything?"

"I just had breakfast." I groan. The man didn't offer to feed me.

"Then you're all set for your salon appointments." He holds up his phone and I can see my email address in his contact list. "Mr. Carmichael asked me to schedule a few appointments for you. Feel free to keep the ones you want. Skip the ones you don't."

I'm surprised. Cullen thinks of everything. A sliver of awe settles in my brain. I'm starting to feel pampered, and very spoiled.

"I appreciate your help, Mike."

"It's my pleasure." He pauses, gives me a quick sweep and says, "Any chance you have a sister?"

I laugh. "Best friends. And they're all married."

"Win some, lose some." He nods in the general vicinity of the poker room. "He's playing a cash game. Have fun, Miss Watson."

"Wy—" But he's already walking away, draping his arm around an older woman who's gushing about her latest slot win.

There's something about the casino ambience that gets my heart pumping. *Thud, thud, thud.* Or maybe it's the fact that I am heading straight for the poker room and feel nervous about seeing him.

There's something about Cullen that unsettles me.

Me and my heartbeat.

Me and my hormones.

I spot him at a table at the far end. *Yep.* Even my pulse seems to skip. He's playing with two others, his dark head bent as he quickly checks his cards. I stifle an unexpected shiver and mentally decree to myself *Thou shall not openly ogle this man!* as I head forward.

He's dressed in a white button shirt and blue jeans. Despite myself, somehow my eyes suck up every detail of the way he's sitting, relaxed, gaze focused. He tosses in a few chips.

He's a conundrum, not only because he's so hard to read, but because he's a little bit surprising and it's hard to peg him. You'd think he only cares about gambling. Winning bets. But he's been nothing but nice to me too. I opened up last night, and he listened. And he seemed . . . affected by what he heard.

I head to the table as he's raking his chips. I feel a prick on the back of my neck, and I chase my breath into my throat when I realize he's looking at me. I'm affected in ways that alternately thrill and frighten me.

"A gambling god left some chips on my nightstand so I thought I'd check and see if he could recommend a good game." I greet him playfully.

He rakes me up and down with his eyes in a way that makes every cell in my body heat up like a boiler room. "So you're ready to play?" His low, deep voice feathers seductively over my skin. "Some require more privacy than we've got at the moment."

He stands and opens a chair for me, motioning for my chips to be changed to smaller denominations.

I take my seat and watch Cullen coil his large, rocklike body back in the chair next to mine.

"If you give way to your nervousness you'll never master the game," he tells me, eyeing me intensely.

I smile and nod, but my mind flutters in anxiety. The cards intimidate me. The other men seated around the table intimidate me. I try to sit still as we place our bets, and the dealer deals. My eyes widen as I look at my cards.

"Treat the cards like you treat the men in your life." He folds his hand. "Do that and I'll back your games for as long as you like."

"Excuse me?" I glance at him, scowling.

"Play it, baby. I'll explain later."

"No explanation needed," I tell him, loving that, this time, he can't read me.

He reaches for my wrist. My stomach churns with anxiety and frustration as his hand engulfs mine. Despite my fears, I feel a heat creep up my cheeks as he holds my hand in his and slowly guides the cards back to the felt. His hand, guiding mine. "Fold."

"Okay."

"Two-seven offsuit is the worst starting hand in Hold'em."

"Got it."

His lips are an inch away from my ear. "The next two should be better."

"Now I see why they call you Playboy," a grumpy fellow says as he rubs the felt with his index finger. "Check."

Cullen ignores him, absorbs me. "Need help?"

"I think I've got it."

"There's something else I wish you had." His silver gaze delivers more promises than an insurance commercial.

"Remember. Luck swings from one second to the next. This could be your turn," he says.

I nod and wait for the next cards. Fucking determined to "master" it, as he says.

The unwelcome sexual tension stretches tighter between us. I feel rebellious but it's hard to part with the money, even if it's money I got specifically to bet.

We play a few hands. He's winning. I'm losing. Until . . .

I check my cards.

Aces. *Yes!*

Cullen doesn't know what I have and furrows his brow as soon as I raise. "You sure you want to do this?"

"Yes."

"Hmmm . . ." He drags his fingers up and down his jaw, studying me. "I'm in."

He doesn't fold?

I jerk to look at him and hope he sees it as a warning. He's amused.

"You should've folded." I sigh. "I'm not above beating you at your own game."

"Do it, darlin'."

"Can you two cut out the narration?" It's the grumpy fellow again.

The flop is full of spades—three-nine-ten—and as far as I can see, I'm still good to go.

Just bet, Wynn! Be reckless!

Grumpy Gambler is all-in.

"Be sure," Cullen whispers to me.

I glance into the stoic dealer's face but she has nothing for me. She'll be as surprised as I am when the next cards fall.

I've watched Cullen play enough now to know I'm still a contender. "Yes, I'm sure."

A lot is on the line but I'm not talking about cards. I'm thinking about Cullen. Because while poker is a very complicated game, our game mystifies me.

Cullen studies me intently and while his tongue snakes across his lips as he stares down at my chest, he's not thinking about sex. Not now.

He's thinking about what I'm holding, what I don't want him to have.

The win.

And suddenly, I'm not interested in the ace on the turn or the one that comes down on the river.

Suddenly, I do want to give him the win. I need to give him everything.

As if he knows an inner war is being fought, he tosses in his cards, allowing one to flip over to show the Jack of hearts.

He smirks. I play.

Three games later, I've won five thousand dollars and I can't bet anymore. It's too nerve-wracking. I've always lived a comfortable life, thanks to my parents. At the gallery, I deal in art, which is always in thousands. But I've always been conservative with money and careful on what I spend. I've always wanted to have savings but somehow I can never manage because the gallery always demands another painting, more money invested in store inventory.

I'm not wired to spend money so carelessly like this. I excuse myself and wish him luck, taking my chips and pocketing them as I start to leave. He's next to me in a second.

"Stay with me."

"Why?"

"I'm convinced you're lucky. Stay by my side," he says as he whips his jacket off his shoulders and covers me with it.

"You weren't even playing well just now. I won more than you did."

"That sweater's see-through. I've taken care of it." He lowers his eyes meaningfully down to my chest.

I tug his designer jacket—huge on my frame—tighter around me. Compared to the waitresses walking by, I could be a nun. Why would a little nipple be distracting?

And why am I *flushing*?

"Any guy would be lucky to have you by his side. I'm feeling lucky today. You game, Wynn?"

I narrow my eyes, mentally devouring that look of pure male ownership in his gaze. I wonder if he truly thinks I'm lucky or just wants me around to torture me. "What is it that makes you want me here?" I ask.

"Insanity."

I laugh, and the smile he gives me makes my whole body shiver.

"I seem to crave your company. Only God knows why."

Gulp.

"Ah, Wynn. Nobody makes me want to lick my teeth like you do."

"What do you mean?"

"Think about it."

I think about it for a moment, and Cullen frowns.

"Be quick about it, will you?" he growls under his breath, finally getting me to nod. He puts his hand on the small of my back as he leads me back to the poker room.

My body responds, though I don't want it to.

"Why are you putting your hands on me, Cullen?"

I'm deeply affected and deeply troubled by those hands.

"You like it when I touch you. Not anyone else. Why?" he asks.

"I don't like it when you touch me, I merely don't dislike it. And I don't want to be touched. I'm turned off men."

"I have this theory . . ."

"Spare me."

"Hear me out."

I look at him.

"You're sexually attracted to me."

I swallow. "So? Aside from our bet, that doesn't mean I'd ever do something about it."

"No, but I would."

"Really? You'd put your life at the risk of my wrath just to add me, another notch, to your bedpost."

"The risk is half the fun."

I part scoff and part laugh. "You're serious?"

He's stroking two fingers over my bare hand, round and round.

I whisper, "I haven't had sex in while. Sometimes I wonder if I can get turned on."

"I'll turn you on."

As he sits me down on the chair, he leans forward and grazes his lips across my nape. The touch triggers a shiver. As does his promise. I suppress it, telling myself this is all for our silly little bet—and I need to win because my pride depends on it.

A few hands later, after he pockets fifty thousand, we head out to walk down the Strip. We're having fun. Stop to have chips at a small snack store. It's easy to like him. He's a mystery, but no doubt a good person too. I don't need to have sex with the guy. If I have sex with him and get attached, it might break my heart. When I'm with him, I have no thoughts of Emmett.

And I can't let go of him, the one person that can take my pain away. Not yet.

That afternoon, after lunch at a café at the Bellagio, we're back at the tables. I watch a few hands until Mike appears behind us.

"Did you forget?" He's looking at me.

Cullen glances up at him and folds his hand.

"She has a hair appointment," Mike explains to him when Cullen only raises an eyebrow in annoyance. "With Gigi."

"Gigi?" I like the name.

Cullen rolls his eyes. I'm guessing he knows "Gigi" even before he says, "Wasn't anyone else available?"

"I can ask," Mike hastily assures as he pulls out his phone, scurrying to accommodate Cullen's every wish.

"Don't," I say, rising. "I'm sure Gigi is fine." I smirk down at Cullen. Now I'm curious. With a name like Gigi, I can guess why Cullen doesn't want me to meet her.

"See you soon." I turn around.

"Later," he promises, patting my butt and watching me until I leave the poker room. I swear I'm blushing and am glad he can't notice how red I get.

He's sweet to say I can have anything and I wonder what he means until I get to the salon and find they have a menu with pretty much everything. From waxing to hair color to manis and pedis and massages and oh my, I've died and gone to heaven. There's even a Brazilian and I think about it. I'm more interested in the one-hour wax and hand massage because I love those.

Alessandra would weep. I overhear one of the stylists motion to Gigi. "That's her."

Gigi is petite, curvy, blonde, and big-breasted. She looks the part of a gambler's girl and I don't know why but I'm not surprised and I'm also not the least bit intimidated. Maybe she had a thing with Cullen. I can see that but I know deep down that, right now, he still wants me.

"Why am I not surprised?" she says rudely.

"I'm Wynn." I stick out my hand.

"Gigi." She shakes. I get the feeling it was an effort. "This way."

I follow her to the back and remind myself that this isn't Alessandra's place and I can't expect great salon services with a side of genuine friendship.

For the next hour, I'm turned one way or another as Gigi works on my dead ends, the ends that were trimmed the week before but now look "hideous and unmanageable." I'm shuffled off to a massage and then led to a large dressing room, which comes as a surprise until a seamstress steps inside with a tape measure.

"Oh, hi. I'm Wynn."

"Delia." She places her tiny hand in mine.

"I know my sizes," I whisper, thinking I can save her the trouble.

"Strict orders. You're with Cullen Carmichael, right?"

"Yes."

"He has a way of spoiling everyone around him. Doesn't he?"

I wonder if I can probe. I don't wonder long. "We're good friends but I've never met his other girlfriends."

"Other girlfriends?" She peers over her shoulder then whispers, "The only person Cullen sends here is his mother. Gigi takes care of her. I assumed she would've mentioned it."

"Well, he probably plays at other casinos. Maybe he sends his girlfriends there."

She spins me around, tosses the tape over my shoulders then pulls it tight. She leans in again. "I'm telling you, Cullen Carmichael spoils his mom and that's it. All the young women here are dying to get at him, if you know what I mean, but he never even follows up on offers for a repeat. Some of them say it's because he won't sleep where he plays but then there's you and now they're rethinking that . . ."

"Then I'm special." I'm obviously joking, but Delia doesn't seem to think of it as a joke.

"I believe it," she says, spinning me around once more. "All finished. Now, let's go shop. Want to?"

An hour later, I'm exhausted. As soon as I entered the casino's boutique, all eyes were on me. The manager ushered me to a large dressing room while snapping out instructions to anyone who would listen.

This boutique is high-end, like a place you'd find on Rodeo Drive. I like that they seem to know me, maybe even realize Cullen's comps are at my disposal, but I would also like to browse the racks, thumb through the shirts, try on the slinky dresses, slip on the ripped tees.

I'd like to play.

They're there to work.

They see me as a commission check, a way to make the rent.

I see the afternoon turning into a chaotic blur of activity.

A waiter brings wine and a decadent cheese tray. Outfits are hung on the right, cocktail dresses on the left. Swimsuits are thrown in a pile on a chair. Handbags and shoes are quickly stacked on two benches. After all that, someone says, "Would you have preferred to do this in your suite? We can take it upstairs if you're more comfortable."

"Are you kidding?" I check out a silvery dress in the mirror, one that is too short for my liking but reminds me of *him*. "I'll take this one."

It's said with such finality that the manager nearly trips over her own feet as she rushes to drape me with a matching necklace. Her assistants scramble, too, pushing rings on my fingers, bracelets up my arm.

"This outfit is perfect!" She clasps her hands together. "You'll knock him off his feet when he sees you." Before I can say anything, she yanks the curtain back and yells, "Lingerie. We need lots and lots of lingerie!"

At that precise moment, a text:

Cullen: What are you doing?

Me: Trying on clothes.

Cullen: Are you having fun?

I smile and shiver a little.

It's so *Pretty Woman*-ish and I wonder if these women see me as that. As a mistress more than a friend.

Me: I am. But I need you to rescue me now. I think I've shopped enough to last me a lifetime.

I lower the phone.

"Um . . . my . . . friend, Cullen . . . he's meeting me here so maybe we could do lingerie later?"

The saleslady looks at me like I've lost my mind. She jabs her finger to indicate Cullen. He's leaning against the wall, tucking his phone in his jacket, and he looks . . . delicious.

I start.

Oh. My. Gosh.

Since when has he been standing there?

"She'll do the lingerie now," he says, his hooded eyes daring me to defy him. "And she looks good in white, black, and translucent, maybe with a hint of soft pink."

"Yes, sir." She darts off.

I can't do anything more than watch . . .

Watch as he strides forward.

Watch as those cut muscles bunch under his shirt.

Watch as he takes my hand.

Watch as he leads me back to the dressing room.

Watch as he looks wordlessly down at me, and I look wordlessly up at him. The whole world fades. How does he do that?

"You were already here when you texted me," I accuse.

"I was," he says, his eyes flickering with amusement. He runs a lone finger over the low-cut silver dress. "Any reason you chose this one?"

"You don't like it?" I step back and twirl around to show him. "I think it makes my . . ."

"Your ass is perfect no matter what you wear."

"My cleavage," I say, holding my shoulders back. "That's what I was going to say."

"Yeah, that cleavage has been a source of many dirty thoughts."

"But you were unimpressed," I remind him saucily. "I believe you said, 'zoning out' if my memory serves me right."

He brackets his arm around my hips and drags me to him. "I lied." And his lips are hungry and possessive on mine. I'm gasping for breath and he's my only air.

I don't want to shop. All I want is this man. This man and his body all over mine. This man and his silver eyes watching only me.

We part as a viewing chair is placed on the other side of the curtain. The sales manager shoos Cullen away from me as her staff piles more garments on another chair.

Behind the curtain, I hear Cullen say, "There's a white dress in the window."

"The one with diamonds?" someone asks.

"That's the one. Send it up to the room. It's her size."

How does he know my size? I gasp. And diamonds? Did he say diamonds?

I wring my hands and look at the lingerie and think *this will be interesting*. Maybe I could slip on another dress first.

And that's what I do.

I pull on a floral mini-dress. It has a lace-filled neckline with whispers of lace around the hem, which cuts high on my thighs. The open back exposes my waist. I glance over my shoulder and decide it's flattering.

The manager returns, quickly zips me up and whispers, "I think Mr. Carmichael was expecting something a little more risqué."

She's right, but he also likes the game. And I'm finding he's a very patient man.

I pull back the drapes with both hands, teasing him as I step out like a showgirl might.

He slowly drags his thumb across his lip, stares at my legs, and motions me closer.

Working my walk, I close the distance between us. He crooks his finger back and forth.

I use the arms on the chair to lean in.

His eyes are dreamy and hazed over and filled with lust.

His hands are on my hips and he rasps, "I was expecting something more . . . telling."

I laugh as his hands slide up and behind me. The zipper drops. His warm palms slide across my skin. "One of the black ones. Now."

"You're so demanding."

"And you like it."

I. *Love*. It.

"Only because you're buying." I push off from his chair and return to the dressing room, unaware that he's behind me.

The curtain shifts and he enters.

"I can do the back," I tell him.

"I could do you," he whispers, his fingers skimming my arms.

His thighs brush mine as he leans over and runs a hand under my dress.

Probing fingers rub against my silk panties.

His expression changes and I gasp as I feel his finger slip underneath.

"Stop. You'll make me . . ."

"Say it."

"Horny." My breathing changes. I can't help myself. I want his fingers inside me. Enough semblance of sanity returns so I can whisper, "I can't try on clothes if you . . . do that."

His features tighten and he eases against me in a slow and tempting grind. "I'd like to finger fuck you right here."

Now my nipples ping. My legs are weak.

He's thinking about it. I can see it in the way his expression darkens, his eyes grow heavy, but before he makes his next move, he narrows his eyes and looks up.

"Damn it." He slowly backs away as if it's a chore.

I glance up too. They have security cameras in these dressing rooms? *Really?*

Considering what I'm now missing? I'm pissed.

He shrugs like he isn't sure then winks, hands me a hanger with his choice, and walks out.

I lean against the wall, trying to catch my breath. Outside, I hear him say, "The dress she just tried on, see if you can get a seamstress to take another half-inch off the length."

It was short enough, but I don't object. He liked the access.

I like that *he noticed* the access.

Gasping at the sexy number he wants modeled, I brave the task of letting go of all inhibitions.

And I slip on the sexiest lingerie *ever*. And I can't help but hope the man who's waiting likes—loves—what he sees.

I'm dressed in the black number when a hand slides between the curtains and dangles a pair of black stilettos with gold straps.

"Really, Cullen?"

"Really, Red."

His voice holds restraint.

And it's a turn-on.

The black bodice is supported by lace and leather straps that cross at the apex and reach behind my neck. Torso is exposed. Sides aren't. Back is out. The garters make me feel . . . sexy . . . but once the stilettos are on?

Oh. My.

I now see why couples shop for lingerie together.

I poke my head between the curtains and meet his curious gaze.

"Don't be shy."

"I can't strut around in this."

"You will," he rasps.

"Okay, so I've tried it on." I clear my throat. "And I think it's a match. I'll go ahead and slip back into my street clothes and we'll be off in a few minutes."

Ducking back behind the curtain, I hear Cullen's quick strides.

He brushes the drapes aside and steps inside the dressing room, taking all the air with him.

"Jesus, woman." He looks down at my breasts and his eyes flicker. He holds me at arm's length and whistles. "You're right. You have great tits."

"Shh!" But I love the compliment. It's raunchy and sexy and not at all what I would expect coming from him.

We stare at each other, the air between us on fire.

My body on fire.

Cullen's gaze the most on fire of all.

He starts to kneel. At my feet. Going lower, and lower, down on one knee, his hand stroking upward, up my thigh, to part the bottom of the black bodice—and stroke my clit with his thumb.

I tense, arch toward him, gasping.

I want him now. At any cost. Without reservations and to hell with privacy.

"Everything all right in there?"

I freeze.

Okay, so maybe I'm a little too caught up in the moment.

Cullen looks up at me and laughs so hard, he falls forward, his face buried in my stomach.

"Um . . . yes . . . we'll be right out." I give Cullen a stern glare.

"Take your time, dear," she says, amusement in her voice.

Cullen slowly rises. "You heard the lady." He drags his hand behind my head and pulls my lips to his in a wicked kiss.

It's brief. Way too brief. It's hypnotic and delicious. Just like Cullen.

"I'll leave you to it."

I take his hand and pull him back for another kiss. As soon as our lips part, I say, "I like it when you can't keep your hands off me."

"Get used to it."

Then he's gone.

And I'm alone with my naughty thoughts . . . and they're all secretly devoted to the hottest man I've ever known.

That afternoon, after I finish shopping and Cullen cashes his chips, we head outside.

"What do you want to do?" he asks.

"I don't know. Surprise me."

Cullen leads me to a black limousine. I'm keenly aware of people in a line outside watching him open the door for me and climb in behind me.

The chauffeur keeps a straight face as he sits behind the wheel and adjusts his mirrors.

"Where to, Mr. Carmichael?"

"Do you know everyone?" I ask, partly shocked and partly no longer shocked anymore.

His eyes glimmer in mischief. "I get around."

"I bet." I smile as he says one word to the driver.

"Summerlin."

"Yes, sir."

"And Tim? It was good seeing you." He hits the automatic button and the privacy glass glides up.

"Same, sir." The chauffeur's smiling eyes are the last thing I see as we're closed off from the rest of the world.

"What are you—"

"This." He strokes his hand down my hair and tips my face up, rubbing his thumb along my lower lip. "I want my hands on you. I want you to myself."

I gulp, look at him. Wondering if I've ever seen a guy look so hungrily at me before.

"Where are we going?"

"You'll see."

He drags his hand down my arm and takes my hand in his, his warmth enveloping me.

"What . . . time do we have to be back at the casino?"

"Work today is done." He surveys me and keeps my hand in his. "The rest of the day, we're having good, *clean*, wholesome fun."

"You? Doing anything that's clean and wholesome?" I laugh and shake my head, tutting at him. "Thank you for the clothes, jewelry, the best shopping experience of my life."

He rubs his tongue over his upper lip. "That was your way of reminding me how hot you look in black."

I grin. "Maybe a little."

"Maybe a lot."

I glance at his lips, unable to help myself before I jerk my eyes up. Cullen fists my hair with his free hands and lowers his head, grazing my lips with his before licking into me. I groan, and he groans in return and pulls back, releasing my hair. His eyes blaze in frustration.

"I'm sorry, I told myself I'd behave."

"Really? You told that to yourself?"

"That's right." His thumb is doing little circles around the back of mine, and my lips crave him. My taste buds like him. "I'm behaving tonight."

"Why?"

"I have a surprise for you." He seems pleased with himself.

"Tell me."

"I'll show you instead."

"What if I don't like the surprise?"

"Then tell me what you *will* like." He leans forward and takes my chin between his thumb and forefinger. "Since you're being such a good girl, I'll give you one wish."

"Kind of like a comp?" I'm teasing him. I can't help it.

"Perks are my specialty." He drags his finger between my breasts. "You choose. But you have fifteen seconds. Then, I'm retracting the offer."

"Just when I think I'm getting anything I want from you, you fold."

"No games, Wynn." He looks at me somberly.

My smile starts to fade.

"And the countdown starts . . ." Cullen glances at his watch and clicks the timer. "Now."

"Cullen, you said no games," I groan.

He looks at me. "What is it you want, Wynn?"

"I don't know!"

"Yes, you do." His eyes glimmer. He leans forward, waiting.

"I want to win this bet, yes, but that's not why I want to win. It's a matter of honor."

"Eight seconds."

"Ugh! I don't know. You're so greedy."

"You have no idea."

"Fine. Maybe I do want to win because of that too," I relent.

"Say it. Three. Two. On—"

"*Because I want your mouth between my thighs!*" I yell.

He's quiet. He's trying to decide whether I mean it, his eyes glimmering. I bite down on my lip, not sure if I really just admitted that out loud.

"You're a player. What's your game?" I ask, suddenly scowling.

"You know what my game is." His voice is almost deathly soft, a whisper in the closed confines of the car.

"Fine. You want the best oral of your life," I whisper, exaggerating my talents. "But the game isn't over yet."

We both stare at each other, the air crackling between us, leaping in arcs from him to me, and from me to him.

His gaze falls to my mouth, and I can taste him there. Still. I want to taste him all over. Lick his skin.

He starts smiling, licking his tongue across his teeth. "Maybe," he says when the car stops.

"We're here, sir."

The voice startles me.

Cullen smiles and jerks open the car door, stepping out and extending his hand. "Come here, Red."

Flushing because Red is starting to sound oddly intimate, I give him my hand and let him pull me out of the car.

"What is this?" I gape up at the two-story mansion. The hissing sound of a sprinkler system draws my attention to a large, well-manicured lawn and the stone path that leads to the front door.

"My home."

"What . . . ?" I'm confused, wondering why he'd bring me here. "You're wooing me now?"

His lips curve slightly as he takes me by the back of the neck and leads me forward. "Maybe . . ."

Cullen leads me into his home. I drink in the black marble floors, elegant stairway, creamy wood-covered walls with exquisite moldings, and arched ceilings, and for the first time, I'm considering changing jobs.

There's a formal study with grand furnishings to the left. Hardback books and hand-painted trinkets line the shelves. Contemporary paintings hang from the walls, which suggests Cullen may have been a collector long before we met. The pieces are showcased in black frames with nickel-plated picture lights mounted above each work of art.

Straight ahead, a white grand piano stands under a chandelier with frosted teardrop crystals. "Do you play?"

"No. It came with the house."

I'm not sure if I believe him until he doesn't smile. He's telling the truth and I love that I'm beginning to read him.

"This is magnificent." I twirl around happily and spot a huge lawn behind the arched living room bay windows. "Is that your backyard?"

"All mine. Every inch of what's here." He's looking at me when he speaks, and my skin prickles under his gaze and words.

"Not everything." I smile, tongue in cheek.

He shakes his head. "Not yet."

Acutely aware that I'm flushing, I shoot him a quick glance to hide the fact that every part of me wonders what it would be like to be his. He's such a force. It would be overpowering, decimating, all-consuming. Incredible.

It's intriguing to watch him, regardless of where he is. It's what first drew me to him at the underground game. His physical presence houses all this power and influence. Even here, in a town known for stripping the average man of his net worth, he's a giant. In a city known for separating a trust fund baby from his millions, Cullen's a whale.

The casinos see him that way.

I see him that way.

But I also see *him*—Cullen Carmichael—the man who has it all but still seems, I don't know, maybe lonely?

He holds all this compelling energy. It's stored in his heart, and methodically released when he sits down to a game.

I shudder to think what he might do in the corporate world, but at the same time I'm already beginning to understand that his way of life is more like an artist's than a businessman's. An artist paints because she can't sleep or eat or enjoy life until the paintbrush is finished stroking the canvas. She can't leave her paints, the tools of her trade, until the art is complete. Once it is, she starts again, because only the art feeds her mind, cures her soul.

She lives for it.

Breathes it.

That's why he plays poker. The game lives in his veins, but is it his life's calling? Can a life-calling be answered by winning a card game?

Can it be found in my gallery? I want to know what he's thinking when he takes his cards, places his bets, calls and raises. Does he cut himself off from the world on purpose and if so, why'd he let me in?

Why me?

I shake the thought aside as Cullen thrusts his hands into his pockets, watching me survey the living room.

There's one silver mirrored picture frame on a side table. It's of a little boy, no more than ten. With gorgeous silver eyes and hair a little lighter than Cullen's. My red hair used to be a little lighter when I was young too.

"Is this you?" I pick it up and stroke my index finger down the photograph and spot another frame with the same boy in it. I set this one down, and go and look at the other. He's playing in some sort of park, his hands on the ropes of a swing. "Where's Callan? Do you have no pictures with your brother?" I laugh. "I'd be glued to my sister, if I had one. I suppose that's why I have my friends."

"That's not me." He takes the photo frame and sets it back down. "You hungry?"

"Actually, now that you mention it . . . playing all day wore me out. All that adrenaline." I smile at him as he leads me to the doors overlooking the backyard. We step outside, and the gardens are fully lit. There's a dining table set for two, with long white linens, and silver plates.

Orange, blue, green, and gold hues stretch across the desert sky, which casts a red tint on the jagged rocks peppering the open canyon.

The view is exquisite and it takes my breath away, but not as much as the man who seems to drink it in, too, as if he's seeing it for the first time.

"Stunning," I breathe.

A sidelong glance. "I know what you mean." Delicious tremors slide down my spine.

"Mr. Carmichael." A man in a black suit and white gloves approaches with a bottle of wine.

"Everything ready, Hollis?"

"Everything is ready, sir."

"Wynn, this is Hollis. My—"

"Butler," I say on automatic, unable to hide my disbelief.

Cullen lifts his brows in amusement when I basically just stare at his gorgeous cocky smile before turning to his butler.

Hollis and I exchange pleasantries. He's originally from New York, but spent some time in Chicago while attending culinary school.

Cullen pulls open one of the chairs for me, and I take a seat, wondering if this is really happening.

I watch as Cullen sits across from me. Only the small rectangular table separates us. He slaps his napkin open. "I'm no chef, yet I may know a good chef around town . . . or two."

"I'm sure. Are you certain you don't know three?" I can't help but tease him, then laugh softly, feeling almost shy. "You shouldn't have gone to this much trouble."

I would've enjoyed cooking for him. It's a strange thought though, so I keep it to myself.

You're being wooed, Wynn. Of course you'll have these silly thoughts. Only . . . I refuse to think of them as silly.

He motions to someone behind me, and a chef appears. "Food is one of the highlights of my days. And I suspect, after dating a chef, it might be the same for you."

A short, stout man in a white chef uniform and hat bows slightly in greeting. "Miss Watson, a pleasure. I'm Henri, your chef for the night. May I tell you my specialties?"

I nod and feel Cullen's gaze on my profile as Henri recites a half dozen dishes. All of them sound mouth-watering.

When I hesitate, thinking that the salmon in rosemary, seared chateaubriand, parmesan-crusted lemon sole, and grapefruit and butter sea scallops all sound divine, Cullen intervenes.

"Why don't you bring us one of each, Henri? That way the lady will know for certain where her tastes run. She'll never know until she tries." A glance in my direction. "Will she?"

"Absolutely, sir. My pleasure." He bows before leaving, and I'm feeling Cullen's stare everywhere in my body.

Thinking, *I'm definitely getting wooed.*

He smiles mysteriously. "I would have loved to dazzle you with my kitchen talents, but I don't have a lot of those. I decided a dinner out of the hotel would be a nice alternative."

"I haven't practiced cooking in a while either. Emmett wanted to cook all the time. He'd almost chase me out of my own kitchen."

He smiles, then his eyebrows lower and he shakes his head. "I don't blame him for wanting to chase you. In my case, I'm doing the opposite. I'm chasing you toward my kitchen, it seems."

I laugh. "No. Not at all." I tip my face up. "But I'd be happy to help the chefs. See how it's all done."

His eyes sparkle, and he sets his napkin aside and pushes his chair back. He extends his hand, and I bite back a giggle as I slide my fingers into his. "Let's go then," he says.

"Really?"

"Of course. Who am I to keep a willing woman out of my kitchen?"

"How gentlemanly. Do you feel the same way about your bed?" I tease.

He laughs and it's pure gold to my ears when he bends closer and whispers, "I want you in my bed, Red. After that comment, I may drag you upstairs and show you how much."

I like that train of thought but know better than to pick him up on it.

When we wander into the kitchen, it's a bustle of activity.

"Mr. Carmichael." A woman in a white apron seems stunned to see him there.

"Miss Watson would like us to help." He grabs an apron from a hook behind the kitchen door and flips me around, putting it on me. His fingers graze along the back of my hair as he knots it behind my neck, and my knees almost buckle from that tiny, searing touch.

The kitchen staff sidesteps to make room for us by the kitchen island.

"Please. My pleasure, Mr. Carmichael. Would you like to cut the grapefruit into slices?" I get the feeling that they're being nice but would've preferred to keep the kitchen as a designated staff area. Still, it's nice to be welcomed into a full service kitchen.

"Of course."

I smile as Henri sets a pair of grapefruits in front of us. I take a cutting board and knife and begin cutting, carefully. Feeling a little awkward, and a lot happy.

I watch Cullen's fingers move beside me as he peels the grapefruit first, and a part of me feels cheated. "Liar," I whisper, part laughing, part groaning.

"What?" He's laughing in silence too.

"You do know how to cook."

"Single for the most part—not always financially secure. Not until recently. Of course I know," he whispers, in my ear. I close my eyes—dating a chef, almost married to him, and not once did I ever stand beside him, chopping our dinner.

I think Cullen planned to woo me with a fancy meal. His gorgeous house. Of course it's all mesmerizing. But what really makes my heart squeeze in my chest is the way he teases me over my awkwardness as I cut, his breath in the back of my ear, and the way his hand brushes mine when he sets down his perfectly peeled grapefruit. He comes to stand behind me and helps me chop mine. And suddenly I'm acutely aware of how easy it would be to fall head over heels for this man, this hot gambler, this Carmichael god. How irresistible this evening is making him out to be.

After we enjoy a feast that would've fed a small community, Cullen leads me to the patio where sparks are flying from a nearby firepit. Wood splinters and crackles.

"I swear I just heard a coyote."

"You're safe here."

Of course I am. It's a gated community. I'm with him.

To feed his ego, I say, "Of course I am. I have you." I tuck my arm under his as we walk.

"Sometime I'll take you to the Grand Canyon."

I stare up at him and think, *Is he planning for a future date? Maybe another Las Vegas visit?*

It's nice to hear him plan. Emmett never wanted to plan, which should've been my first clue.

We reach the cozy outdoor area and I kick off my sandals before climbing onto a comfy sunbrella daybed. It's easy to make myself at home when I'm with Cullen.

Maybe because we're 'just' friends.

He stretches out on his back and it's the most natural thing in the world to lie there facing him. His fingers curl over my hip and he brings me closer.

And *oh my*. His shirt smells woodsy, earthy, and I'm easily reminded of the alpha male who owns the sexy smile, the hands that know where to touch and how to make me feel desired.

"Cullen." I discreetly point to the house staff clearing the table behind us. "We're not alone."

"They're used to it."

"Oh are they?" I laugh. "*That*, I believe."

He watches me curiously before he says, "I don't entertain here but they have their hands full with other private parties."

"Oh. Right. Well . . . I'm—"

"Surprised that your player isn't the wild and crazy guy you'd hoped?"

Surprised, of course, but happy is the better word for it. And suddenly I want to kiss his smile a little wider. "I'm kissing you now, Mr. Carmichael."

"Come and get it," he rasps, pulling back to make me work for it.

I use his shoulder to steady myself and slant my lips over his, easing into an explosive kiss. He tastes like salt and wine, a mix of honey and fruit and spice.

His tongue briefly swirls with mine before he releases me and slips his arm around my shoulders. "Did you have a good time today? Did Mike take care of everything you need?" He brushes my hair out of my face.

His touch . . . spins me, particularly now when he seems unhurried, relaxed.

"He was great," I say.

"Any plans for tomorrow?"

I shoot him a heated glance and enjoy it even more when he returns one of the same.

"Mike said he would set up a tee time."

"He'd like that," Cullen says tightly. "Lucky for me, you don't play golf."

Catching his meaning, I say, "But I've always wanted to learn."

"Have you?" He scoffs. "Then I guess I'll find time away from the tables so I can take you."

"But isn't that why you have Mike?"

"Mike earns a percentage of my play. He doesn't need the added perk of having your company."

"Ah . . . I like it when you're jealous."

"Then I'm so damn jealous."

I laugh but his lips are there to devour the sound. His eyes look like chrome as he ignites several fires in me with one smoldering kiss. His palm rests against my head as his tongue parts my lips and invites me to experience him, to taste him.

When we part, he says, "So you're having a manicure, maybe an updo tomorrow, some more shopping, the concert the day after?"

"If that's what you want to do."

He stills. "Anything you'd rather do?"

"I think you know what that is."

"Are you talking about the bet?" he says.

I wasn't talking about the bet, but probably it's best that I pretend I was. "Yes." I flush and glance away.

He narrows his eyes, as if trying to determine if I'm lying or not. "You've watched me play. Tomorrow I'll take you somewhere you can show me about what you do," Cullen says, his voice low and unreadable.

My heart skips a beat in surprise. "That sounds fun." I look at him cheekily, his expression unreadable while I know that mine is a blank page; I'm too excited at the idea of going around and looking at art. "I'm going to win our bet," I saucily promise.

I smile.

He smiles back at me and chucks my chin, indulging me.

On our way back to the hotel, I'm sleepy from the biggest meal I've ever had in my life. I groan, giggling when I remember the way I tasted every plate we helped make, and every one we didn't. "I won't fit in my lucky black dress tomorrow," I worry in a whisper out loud.

Cullen eyes me and partly smiles, lifting his hand to stroke his thumb along the underside of my cheek. "Not a problem. You're my lucky charm, not that dress of yours."

I smile and want to reach out and kiss him, devour him—I just had the whole contents of his fridge for dinner, but suddenly, the pulsing ache inside me thrums even more mercilessly than any other hunger. This is a hunger I cannot seem to satiate. I'm afraid to even begin to try.

I'm aching, but I don't throw myself at him, and I'm pretty damn proud of that. I used to be so easy before. One nice dinner and a guy would already have gained access to every part of me: body, mind, heart. Life has taught me different. Now I've spent the most memorable day of my life getting wooed and I'm amazed that I have the willpower to withhold my body and heart from him.

I must have learned my lesson. And yet . . . it must be because he's the most dangerous man I've ever dated. He can make Emmett and the way he hurt me look like child's play. And every moment I feel myself slip deeper and deeper into this dark whirlwind called Cullen Carmichael, I'm aware of this. Plus there's something about this man that pricks my pride out to the surface, that challenges me to prove my worth, my value, my best. And I have a bet to win.

Now that I've seen all the things Las Vegas has offered me, I can't even be sure that Cullen will find my job as exciting and adrenaline inducing. I secretly wish he'd learn to love art the way that I do, though.

That night, when we get in, I head to the restroom, and then find him on his laptop in the living room when I come back out. I head to the fridge for a bottle of water. I'm exhausted, physically, and yet a part of me doesn't want to be alone in my room.

I waver, wondering if he's tired too.

Then I decide we still have some days left—and I'll need my energy for tomorrow.

"I'm hitting the bed," I say. "Goodnight."

"Wait." Glancing up at me from whatever it is he was reading, he sets his laptop aside and walks over. "How much fun did you have today?"

"It was actually pretty fun." I grin. "A lovely evening. Thank you."

He squares his jaw thoughtfully as he looks at me. "Goodnight then," he rasps as he reaches out to me. He cups the back of my neck and ducks his head and sets his mouth on mine. I open up instantly, needing this contact more than my next breath. We taste each other, and we taste the same. Like mint chocolate cake and coffee and raspberries. When he eases back, I lick my lips and I take a deep breath and I tell myself it's one of those friendly kisses.

I don't believe it anymore.

Cullen grabs his jacket and swings it past his shoulder as he heads to his bedroom. I watch him leave, sort of wanting him to kiss me goodnight again.

Wanting him to teach me how to bluff and call and raise again.

"Carmichael!" I call. "I bet you can't kiss me goodnight again and walk away a second time."

There. I've said it. He stops midstride. When he turns, I shiver at the sight of his gray eyes, his raw expression, his tense body. His stare, male and *all-knowing*. "Be careful when you call out a player to the new game on the hill," he warns in a low, dominant rasp.

Why is this exciting me even more?

"I'm not scared." But my heart is puttering wildly in my chest, my pulse skipping like crazy . . .

Cullen's lip curls and he tosses aside his jacket before he closes the distance between us and locks his arm around my hips, reeling me toward him. "Baby, you should be."

"With you? Never . . ." I chug in some air. "You can lead a man to temptation, doesn't mean he'll drink."

"Oh, I'll drink . . ." He peppers my neck with kisses. "Sip." Pecks my forehead. My cheek. "Savor every taste."

"Cullen." I breathe out his name, shuddering wantonly.

He isn't finished. His mouth hovers over mine. "You haven't been paying attention, sweetheart." His mouth slides up my jaw to my ear and he's whispering, "Once I get between your legs, nothing's going to stop me."

"Let's hope there's not a big game that night." I flirt, smiling up at him. I want him so much I can almost taste him, the sweetness and the spice. And when he rolls his eyes as if to say the biggest game in the world won't stop him once he starts, I want it more than anything I've ever wanted.

I want the hammering thrusts, the easing forward, the pulling back, the nibbling and teasing.

I want all of it. All. Of. Him.

Damn it, why did I make this bet? Do I want to win or lose?

Here I am, trembling. Standing on my tiptoes, I dare him to show me, beg for that kiss, saying his name. He leans his dark head, teasing my lips apart, then he leaves me, only to come back again, his mouth meeting and parting mine and then his strong, warm, plush lips are meeting mine all over again.

It's exquisite torture, the most painful and wonderful kind. He nibbles on me, and I nibble back at him until, with one fluid move, he jerks me to him and I cop one hell of a feel as he crushes my mouth beneath his own. His kiss is filled with longing and hot as hell. His fingers knot in my hair and he holds me still as Cullen fucks my mouth like only he could.

We're kissing, tasting, inhaling each other over and over again. In one sexy move, he leans over and sweeps me into his arms. He's carrying me to the sofa and I'm already so turned on that I don't know why he wants to start here. I doubt I'd pose any complaint if he carried me to his room. It makes me realize how ready I am to be there.

Instead, we're here and he's kissing me crazy, his body begging mine to act, his lips teaching me to want in ways I've never wanted any guy before.

His lips skim the shell of my ear as his body is flush against mine, his length pulsing against my thigh as he delivers kiss after kiss after kiss.

Oh this man. I could get used to this. Him.

I lift my chin and he trails his lips to my chest. His hands trap mine as he thrusts my arms way above my head, pinning my body under his.

"Cullen." I'm breathless, blown away by the tantalizing promise of how good we'll be together.

He pulls back then dips his head again for another peppering kiss. "Say the word and I stop, but you'd better come up with a way to stop me soon if you don't do it now."

I hesitate, breathless. High on him, on the power his desire gives me.

"I win," I whisper in a lust-thickened voice, grinning, not because I care about a dumb bet. I don't. I care about seducing the gambler. Luring the man. "You can't walk away from me now, can you?" I whisper, praying that this is the case.

Narrowing his eyes at me, he sets his forehead against mine and sucks in a heady breath. "Wynn," he growls in a low, dominant hiss, pressing one last kiss to my earlobe.

He eases back and I notice that he does it with great reluctance. He gradually rolls away from me and, even more gradually, I stand up, letting him help me to my feet while I can still walk away, and before I change my mind and beg him not to stop.

"Never go to the new game on the hill unless you're playing to win," I tease him, leaning up to stroke the tip of my index finger along those lips I just can't get enough of.

"You're a tease." But he likes the play, I know it because his smile gives everything away. "But you're a gorgeous tease, Red."

"I won. You like me beating you at your own game, don't you?" I tease. I should pat myself on the back but suddenly, I don't feel like a real winner, and I hate that I know why that is. I'm staring right at him, and he's looking back at me with amused but hot eyes.

"I'll make a gambler out of you yet."

"You just like my poker face."

He meaningfully sweeps me with his eyes. "I like everything I see, Miss Watson."

I flush beet red.

He turns to go and I head to my room, making a solid effort not to turn around. It doesn't work. I eventually glance back, and my stomach dips as if we're in the middle of a wickedly fierce roller-coaster when I find that Cullen's arms are spread wide. He's gripping the doorframe, maybe debating the same, maybe deciding how far we should take our bets.

"See you tomorrow, Carmichael."

His chin rests at his shoulder. He seems deep in thought. "This one is one I wouldn't mind losing."

"Part of being a good gambler is knowing when to walk away," I remind him.

"This is one time when you should've stayed and played, baby." That rasp and urgency and hunger in his voice makes me a little too melty. And my body is alive with the wicked reminder of his kisses. His touch. I know what I'm missing and I don't know how I'll bear denying myself for much longer.

I smile and watch him disappear with a pang of longing, then force myself to shower and slip into my silk pajama set. I lie down and try not to think of today, but I'm restless beneath the sheets. I toss and turn, consumed by the adrenaline of Vegas and his hotter-than-is-legal kisses. I want more of those kisses, more of Cullen Carmichael, but I don't know how to go about it.

I wanted a distraction. Something to get me out of my head.

Except what I found is more than a distraction. It's a nuclear sex bomb and I don't know if letting it blow up would be a good thing or a bad. I'm betting on both.

FLUSH

The next day, we have a late breakfast at the buffet and once we step into the casino, I tell him of my plans. "I'm heading off to mingle."

"Go on. Have some fun." He hands me a money chip.

"I really don't need to—"

"We're in Vegas."

"And . . ."

"You're my date."

"That's debatable. We're basically in a dare—"

"You're in Vegas, Wynn."

"So?"

"So go win."

He pecks my lips.

I impulsively peck him back, then my eyes widen when I realize what I did. I hear him exhale, his hands, which somehow came up to cup my shoulders, clenching viscerally the moment my lips connect with his.

Startled by the fizzle that runs from the contact-point to my toes, I drop back on my heels and meet his gaze with a smile that isn't as shy as you'd expect. It's actually quite naughty. As is the smile and the smoldering look that Cullen gives me in return.

I spend the next few hours window shopping and ogling window displays, then answering a few emails from my assistant. I even head to the slot machines and play ten dollars, happy when I extract a voucher for eight. Which means I only lost two dollars after playing for over an hour. Yay, Wynn! Maybe I'm not as lucky as Cullen thinks, but I'm not that unlucky either.

I'm standing at the craps table a few hours later, watching it all in curiosity, when I feel his arms slide around my waist. "Hey, beautiful, want to play?"

"Oooh. Well, that sounds like the sexiest proposition I've heard since I arrived here in Vegas." I turn on some exaggerated charm. "See, I've been sleeping alone since I got here and what happens in Vegas? Why, it might as well stay here. I mean, there's no action underneath my sheets." I keep my voice low so only he can hear me. While I speak, he's rocking me side to side and I'm enjoying the feel of him, his rigid cock pressed against my butt.

His body is hard against mine and his arms tighten around my waist. He takes a deep breath and whispers, "I'm supposed to meet this beautiful woman for lunch but if I can help you out . . . maybe help steam up those sheets . . . maybe I can get a raincheck on the meal."

I whirl around and face him. "You're bad." Before I think about it, I peck his lips, kind of like before, and wonder what's up with that.

What's up with us?

The question is still playing out in my mind when we enter the restaurant where Cullen made a reservation this morning. He takes my hand and leads me forward. I let him, though for some reason, I wouldn't have if he were anyone else. Something about this guy simply doesn't broach any argument. And it feels good, sort of protective.

"Callan?" Cullen says.

I lift my head. And spot Cullen's brother, Callan, along with one of my besties, Olivia Roth, now Olivia Carmichael. The couple is seated at a table in the far corner and they seem as surprised as we are as they come to their feet.

"Livvy! I had no idea you were honeymooning in Vegas!" We girls are throwing ourselves into each other's arms in a second.

We're so excited that we're probably jumping up and down and causing a scene, but as quickly as the joy hits, their curiosity follows.

Livvy looks at me then shifts her gaze to Cullen and a dazed, puzzled smile touches her lips. "We're not. Only stopping for two days before we head to L.A. and then Fiji. What are *you* doing here?" she demands.

Cullen.

I'm basically sending Cullen a screaming look, not wanting him to give any explanations.

"It's a long story," I start to answer.

"I can make it short. We da—"

"We dared each other to experience each other's jobs and . . . oh, pooh. It's silly."

"My brother isn't a silly man," Callan says, and he's stoic and not smiling at all. Not one little bit.

"Well, this bet is. You know how he is. He can't stop betting on stuff. Anyway, congratulations!" I hug Livvy again while the men head back to the honeymooners' table.

"Come sit. Join us." She takes my hand and drags me with her.

"Oh, we couldn't." I'm hesitant.

"Cullen? Maybe you should take it from here," Callan says.

"Why? She's doing fine." And he slides me a look that means everything and nothing.

Livvy and Callan notice.

I notice something, too. Cullen and I are thick as thieves, kissing bandits, friends with secrets. Good. Friends.

It's like we're an island unto ourselves.

The thought makes me blush like mad and I'm aware of the heat in my cheeks, the eyes on me, the way Cullen looks at me with new surprise as if he knows what I'm thinking.

And if we're an island . . . and it's just Cullen and me . . . then he knows what's on my mind.

Him. And I'm not embarrassed for him to know it.

There's a new effervescence in the air and it's like a tonic. It's invigorating, sweet, and refreshing.

Cullen pulls out a chair for me, smirking when I hesitate. But then why did I hesitate? Am I so greedy that I want to spend my last two days in Vegas keeping Silver Eyes to myself?

Pursing my lips when I realize the answer, I sit and decide getting some food in my stomach will make the butterflies I'm feeling when Cullen's knee brushes against my own under the table dissipate.

"Shall we order?" Callan asks, looking more amused when Livvy puffs her cheeks and gives him a stern look.

I know what the exchanged couple-looks are all about now because as I swap glances with Cullen . . . I know what he's thinking.

And what he's thinking is all that matters now.

Cullen
Two hours later

"Explain."

"The situation fairly explains itself."

"In words."

"She's available."

"Physically. Emotionally, don't touch her, Cullen. She's a good girl. And she's hurting."

"I know she's hurting. That's why we're here. She deserves to get over him. I mean for her to get over him."

"Let yourself get used so she—"

"No. Not used."

"Then what."

"I get to enjoy her, and she gets all the advantages being with me brings." I wink.

"She's a friend."

"She could be more than that."

My brother looks perplexed. "I meant, she's a good friend to me. I knew her before me and Livvy."

"So what, I can't kiss the family friend?"

"You've kissed her!" He drags his hands through his hair.

"Oh dear God. You did not just ask me that. Hell, I didn't bring her all the way out here just to look at her."

"Well maybe you should've considered that as an option."

"And maybe you should remember that I didn't coach *you* when it came time to watch you and Liv from the sidelines."

"You weren't watching a train wreck."

"Is that what I am?" I'm slightly offended, but then again, Callan's never seen me in my element. He only knows what his rich friends have told him. That gamblers are always chasing their next losing proposition.

"You'll hurt her."

"And what if I don't?" I swallow back the reluctance of telling my brother the facts as I know them. "What if I don't hurt her? What if we have a great time together? More importantly, what if that great time spins out of control and we find that we can't get enough of each other? And if that works, who's to say that we can't fall in love and maybe have a happy ending of our own?"

"Oh my god." He stares at me in disbelief. "Are you listening to yourself?"

"What is it now?"

"You're falling for her. Hard. Fast. But it's still a fall, all the same. You might as well brace for it, Cull."

"I'm not . . ." I stop and think. Wynn's already had someone who told her one thing and did another. I won't be that guy.

"You're not what?" Callan pulls out a pack of Malboros and lights up, twisting his cigarette around to offer me a hit.

I shake my head.

"Thought you quit."

He shrugs. "Stressful shit drives me to smoke. So does Vegas." He grins, eyes twinkling.

And I don't know if I'm turning down the smoke or shaking my head in disbelief because of what I'm about to admit. "I won't deny anything."

Callan watches me, carefully blowing out smoke as he narrows his eyes. He lowers his voice. "Can you be more specific? Because Livvy is going to give me twenty questions about this."

"She could be the one. I could fall for her." Maybe I've already fallen. "Where things go from here, only time will tell." I clench my jaw and lean back in my seat, then steal the cigarette from my brother and take a long inhale.

"Fuck, Cull. This is worse than I thought." He takes his cigarette back and sucks in a full drag.

"Worse?" I shake my head. "Try better." I smirk.

My brother's trying to find the right words but he won't find them on time because I won't give him another opportunity.

I'm not walking away. Why would I?

I want her.

And I always get what I want.

Wynn and I have a great time together and there's chemistry and heat and . . . damn woman should've been finished talking to Livvy by now.

I don't know if Livvy will make Wynn question her decisions but if she does, I'll be there to remind her of what she'll miss if she walks away.

She can't leave. She won't go.

I'm confident because she knows, just as I do. There's something here. Something beyond games and money, beyond art and poker, even beyond the prize waiting for us at the end.

We're not done here yet.

Wynn

"Okay, I'm out. Cullen needs me." I stand up, ready to go. I played ten dollars at blackjack and lost five.

I'm not a loser. I'm a lucky charm.

I smile at the thought but it quickly dims when I look around and can't find Callan or Cullen. What if Callan warns Cullen to stay away from me because I'm a serial dater? What if he listens?

What if he decides to send me back home tonight?

Calm. Down. Wynn.

It's never going to happen. Remember the island! You're not on a ship with a thousand seas before you. You're one woman. He's one man.

You're having a great time. You have a bet going on. Bumping into Callan and Livvy won't change that.

I take a deep breath.

"Hey, Wynn? I bet if you make him a cool mill tonight, he'll make you feel like one in bed too," Livvy taunts, leaving a red chip for the dealer as she stands to leave.

"Nobody's fucking anyone tonight except your husband and you." I narrow my eyes, and Livvy grins cheekily.

"Of course. This is my first time in Vegas too. We're living the life!"

"I can tell, Livvy, I can tell how badly you love that man."

"Wynn, no, but seriously?" She stops me, somber now.

I pause.

"Have some fun, but be careful. Draw some boundaries. Can you do that?" Her sheepish look suggests she thinks it's an impossible request.

"Trust me, they're drawn. Cullen is not a guy who falls in love, and I would never let myself fall for a guy like him. I honestly just want to stop hurting. And I'm having the time of my life. Be happy for me?"

"Okay. Oh, and if you want to piss him off, ask him to dance with you. Callan says he hates that." She exhales, relieved. "He seems to dig you."

"Do you really think so?"

"Of course! Why would he not?" Before I respond, she quietly adds, "And speak of the devil and he comes."

I spin around to find a glowering Cullen before me.

He's not exactly glowering. Just looking at us with drawn eyebrows as if curious about our conversation.

And that look is all-male, all-mine. He seems to take his time as he searches me from head to toe, as if he thinks I somehow changed after we parted.

I feel claimed, owned, and so very much his.

Do I want to be?

Oh stop, Wynn. Just stop!

"I hope I'm interrupting." He takes my hand like it belongs in his.

"You are!"

"Good. Sorry, Livvy. Wynn's going to get busy now."

I groan and shoot him a warning look. "We're heading to the tables now?"

"Not if we don't want to." He leads me away.

I casually peer over his back and wave at Liv. "Wait. So you stole me away from my bestie just because you couldn't share me?"

"I've shared you enough." He laces our fingers together as we walk. "I'm entitled to time alone with you."

Did he . . . just put a claim on me?

I so hope I'm not blushing now.

I nudge him playfully, but the thrilling little frisson of female awareness that runs through me won't go away no matter how much I tease him. "You're obsessive. Superstitious. And a gambler. No wonder you're single. Oh, and you don't even *dance*."

"Right on all counts." He doesn't seem one bit perturbed about it. The more I talk, the more he closes the distance between us.

He stops to get drinks at the bar of a small club restaurant.

"I'll just have iced tea. Thanks," I tell him when he asks. He hands mine over and picks up his whiskey from the counter, leading me to a table.

"Livvy actually *dared* me to make you dance."

"Nobody makes me dance. I'm defective, like a bird with no feathers. Can't fly. No rhythm and no inclination." He shoots me a warning look as we take a small round table. "Don't think for a moment I'll ever try."

"Oh, I know how to get you to dance."

He smiles indulgently, shaking his head.

I twirl my straw in my glass.

"For a bet." There's a silence. I peer up and into his face.

Silver Eyes is looking at me weird.

One eyebrow slowly starts coming up. Followed, very slowly, by the other.

"Damn you." He laughs as if he can't believe I dared to mention it.

"See?" I grin.

"You're a she-devil."

"I know your weakness."

He drops his foot on the footrest of my seat and leans forward, one elbow on his knee. He starts to grin. A grin that would make the very devil run. "How much? What are we betting?"

Red flags start popping up in my brain, but I'm having too much fun to back out. And I really want to make the guy dance. "We're betting . . ." I think about it, unsure of what would tempt him most. "You tell me what will get you up on the dance floor." I nudge him and point at the dance floor.

His hand flies out to curl around my finger and envelop my hand in the warmth of his. The sudden move makes me jerk my gaze up to his. "Fucking. You. All night long," Cullen says meaningfully.

"No. But I'll sleep with you. In bed. Just sleep," I offer. It'd be nice, to be honest. I'm selfish like that.

"What are you wearing?"

I glance down at my clothes.

"To sleep, baby," he says, rolling his eyes.

I flush beet red. "Oh. My peejays."

"Wrong answer."

"Okay, a T-shirt and panties."

"Wrong again."

"Fine. I'll go crazy and shed the clothes. All of them except my underwear. Only if you dance with me."

"You'll wear the lingerie."

"No."

"Yes. It's not even open for debate." He slowly uncurls his body and stands, lifting me up with him. "You didn't ask for it, baby. You begged," he warns.

I'm flushing again. Damn him. I wave that off as if it's due to the lights and brush past him, heading to the dance floor.

He spins me around. He pulls me forward and into his arms, the hard length of his warm body suddenly making me weak in the knees. He wraps a fist in my hair and forces me to look at him. There is fire there, a whole lot of it, and something else. Something questioning, but the question burns out of his eyes when I part my lips in expectation. *Please,* I think. He swears softly under his breath in a low hiss before his lips are on mine, his tongue entering swiftly. Wetly. Hotly.

The music changes and "100 Years" fills the speakers and as he eases back, the way he looks at me sends a little tingle down my spine.

"For a man who doesn't dance, you have all the right moves."

"You think?"

"You dance great."

"I don't enjoy dancing. Don't ask me why, I just don't, never have."

He slows down the dance, slides his arm around my waist and pulls me against him with the kind of grip that makes me shiver and groan.

I squirm helplessly in his arms as he kisses me again, and I kiss him back, wanting to touch him, press him closer.

He pulls free, his nostrils flaring, eyes slitting. "How do you manage to push all my buttons? Huh?"

"I . . . I don't know. I think I'm just uniquely equipped with most of your pet peeves."

"Is that the secret?"

"There's no secret." I feel . . . like the world just disappeared around us . . . like we're on the verge of a zombie apocalypse but we're not scared because we have each other. Even if we *turned*, we'd find our way together.

"What are you thinking?"

"You so don't want to know," I say, laughing.

"If it's that funny, I definitely do."

I hesitate and debate on whether or not to tell him, whether or not he'll think I'm too much of a girl or maybe not girly enough if I'm thinking about zombies and monsters and end-time scenarios.

"It's like we're the only two people in the world right now." I leave out the zombie part. If the confession doesn't scare him off, the monsters might.

He rocks his hips.

Once.

Twice.

Pleasure starts bubbling inside me. I rock back to him, clutching him to me, grabbing the back of his head and kissing him hard.

I don't know what happens as he rocks his hips to mine, as he dry-fucks me on the dance floor, but suddenly my world crumbles and burns, nothing exists but earth-shattering, convulsing, soul-blinding pleasure. I don't even know if he comes with me and for how long or for how long I've lost reality, but when I'm back in my body his kiss is deep and slow, absorbing my cries.

What a liar.

"You're not too bad," I say, breathless.

"Really? I'm not noticing." His voice is husky, his gaze half-mast and heavy.

"You're not?"

He gives a slow shake of his head. "I'm noticing you're breathless and flushing." He ducks his head to my ear. "You just fucking came in my arms."

I cut my gaze up at him, boldly admitting in a breathless whisper, "And I didn't hold back."

Wow. I don't know how I can say these things to him. I instinctively seem to know they're the kind of things he wants—needs—to hear.

His whole body radiates strength as he clutches me tighter, gaze direct and unflinching as he looks down at me with hooded eyes.

I swallow thickly, and he sets his hand tighter around my waist, gripping me as he drops a kiss on my temple and heads back to my ear. "Do you want more? What are you thinking about? What's got you so turned on, hmm?"

I swallow, breathless, limp in his arms after my O.

"Winning." I tip my chin up at a proud angle, unable to hide the sound of my haggard breaths.

His gaze glimmers in heat. "No. Not winning."

"Yes, winning our bet."

"You really want my mouth between your thighs, don't you, Red?" He's looking down at me with twinkling eyes and almost purring low and thickly.

"I . . . uh, no! It's an ego thing!" I counter.

"Or a mouth-between-your-thighs thing."

He seizes my hand and starts leading me out, to an empty playing table.

"Come here. Sit. I've got something better to do."

He sits at the table.

I smile back and sit beside him.

After what just happened and the way I came undone, I'm embarrassed. I stare around the casino nervously. "Focus," he says.

"On what?"

"On me, Red."

I swallow, my eyes jerking to his unreadable features. His eyes gleam. He relaxes.

"I'll play for more. More than you sleeping in my arms tonight," he tells me.

"For what?"

"Three minutes, my tongue in your mouth."

"Ugh."

"It's just a game, Red."

"More like war."

"Why?"

"Well every time you bet you're either losing money or clothes or self-respect."

"That's the principle of everything in life. Everything has a price. The price of winning is betting—sometimes more than what you're comfortable with. You win some, you lose some." He gathers me up from the table. "Let's take this upstairs." He dials his phone. "Oliver, meet me at the elevator bank."

"What's the most devastating loss you've ever had?" I ask him as we board and Oliver slips in with us.

Oliver clears his throat. "I can say it wasn't on card games, miss."

"Thank you, Oliver," Cullen says with a stony growl and a bleak glare.

"Yes, sir."

Oliver closes his mouth, and I'm left wondering what he means. We step out of the elevator and straight into our suite, Oliver following. "Every time I lose I'm wearing this." Cullen jerks his white button shirt off. "Burn that." He tosses it at Oliver, who catches it midair.

"Yes, sir."

"Get me a few of my black ones. Three or four. I always do well in black."

"Done, sir."

"That will be all, Oliver. Goodnight. Get yourself a good dinner, sign it to the room and head back to the house. I'll call if I need anything." He shuts the door behind Oliver and eyes me in interest. "Now where were we?"

"We were saying you need institutionalization." I shrug somberly as if I'm not teasing him.

"No. We were saying you're overdressed for the occasion." His gaze rakes me up and down.

He sits on the living room couch, leaning forward as he speaks.

"Strip poker. We play to the end, then I'll go all in for three minutes with your mouth."

I gape at him. I can't stop swallowing the moisture in my mouth. "So . . . if I win, you take your clothes off?" I ask, hedging.

"That's right, we play for clothes. Then I play for your mouth."

I laugh sardonically. "You'd need to go very far to get to that point and I'm not letting you get that far. You see, I'm feeling lucky tonight too."

I'm not about to mention the few bucks I lost at black-jack.

That unlucky streak at the tables wasn't exactly unlucky; I only lost because I couldn't stop thinking about Cullen. And his mouth. His eyes. His touch.

God, I don't know what's wrong with me.

Cullen smiles, a smile all too clear and adrenaline-inducing. A smile that says,

It's on.

Once we say it, there's no turning back though. Cullen pulls out two decks of cards, and I sit at the edge of the huge living room couch, fidgeting as I watch him shuffle them. It feels like I locked myself in a hotel room suite with a wild cat. My heart stutters with all the testosterone in the air.

The word handsome is far too tame for this guy. He's so much more. Darker, harder, more man. More . . . magnetic.

All sex, and I agreed to play strip poker with him. Something I've never done in my whole life.

"Are you comfortable there?" he asks.

"Not really," I admit.

He slides his eyes to the floor, and I settle on the carpet.

He pulls out a tray of chips and each is worth a hundred thousand dollars.

"I don't have a hundred thousand dollars."

"We won't be betting money. We're betting what you're wearing, like we said."

"And you?"

"That too." He settles down across from me.

The game begins, and after the first three rounds, I've on-ly had to remove my shoes and necklace. Cullen still hasn't removed anything.

The next two hands, I have to tug off my dress, and Cullen has to remove his belt.

I'm in my underwear. He's still in slacks and his undershirt. Blast him.

I'm getting more and more into the game, and more and more naked by the second.

I might be seeing things, but I swear his pupils go blacker every time I cast an article of clothing aside.

My physical reactions to this guy astound me. My insides seize every time we show our cards and our eyes meet, and when my insides finally relax, everything resumes at a frantic pace. My breaths, my pulse, my thoughts.

He's big, at least six feet two, and dark as twilight. Everything about him is dark except those diamond-platinum-jeweled eyes, eyes he tracks me with as I stand to undress.

He drags his open hand around his jaw while studying me with a gripping focus, the kind that he uses when he's at the tables with a real player, someone he views as his equal, someone with the potential to ante up and stay in the game.

Win or lose.

A fight to the death.

The lamplight casts shadows over his face. Las Vegas buzzes outside the window, but suddenly, inside the suite, things have gone very, very still.

We deal again. I show him a straight flush, while he just has a pair.

He grabs his undershirt and pulls it over his head. He looks frustrated and I love it. It's my turn to eat him up.

Oh my.

"Let the angels sing," I purr, whistling.

He growls, that little tell of his when he doesn't want to smile or laugh.

"I like what I see."

"Oh you wanna play that way?" He drags his eyes over the swell of my breast and I know I'm at a disadvantage.

Still.

I look.

My breath catches at the sight of his bare chest. His arms are ripped and muscular, defined and so strong my stomach's got a fire inside it. I admire how smooth and tan his skin is and try not to notice how thick his neck is, his Adam's apple bobbing as he speaks.

"Good girl, Wynn."

I try not to notice his mouth moving, talking, but it's hard not to want to shut him up with my own and let the hot bastard have his three minutes times a thousand.

We deal again, and soon I lower my cards, afraid that I don't have much to win.

Shit. My bra is gone now.

Cullen rests back on his elbows and watches me take it off. I feel restless now, unable to play. Trying to cup my breasts in each hand and hold the cards is impossible. So I cross my arm over my breasts, frowning. "Last one or I'll have nothing to bet."

"Your mouth, Wynn."

He's watching me for a moment, his breathing even, but the shade of his eyes is swirling, darkening by degrees to a molten metal.

His words reach me, scrape me. I feel like a raw nerve, a live wire.

"Okay," I breathe.

He smiles then, a smile so honest that I want to kiss his mouth and suddenly, desperately, want him to win the next one.

A rush of sensation slides under my skin as I absorb his smoldering gaze. I've never seen eyes in that exact shade before. They look almost transparent now. But it's the unreadable, mysterious look in those hooded eyes that draws me in even more.

Imagining those eyes seeing me as we have sex takes over my mind, and my girl parts tickle so hard I want to squirm.

We deal.

I win. To my shock and disbelief.

"I've got nothing," Cullen growls.

With a slow, uncharacteristic smile, he stands and unbuckles his jeans, lowering the zipper. My jaw hangs open as I notice his huge cock straining against his boxers. I can see the tip of that cock pushing out of his boxers—fully erect. Very pink. Very swollen.

When he discards his jeans, I'm raw with desire.

I long to touch and kiss him, but he's dealing. Again. And it's sinful torture, the kind of torture that makes my eyes grow heavy while my mouth turns dry.

My hands shake as we play another game—and now I'm desperate, desperate, for him to remove his boxers somehow.

I lick my lips and study my cards, noticing how Cullen is studying me.

"Nothing again." He tosses his cards to show me he had nothing, and my heart starts to pound as he stands to jerk off his boxers.

Oh my god.

My eyes hurt from the beauty of it.

"You didn't even play," I accuse.

"Oh. I played. We're still playing for those three minutes with my tongue in your mouth."

I can't concentrate with the sight of his beautiful cock on display and naturally I lose the next game.

"Come here, Wynn."

"You—you want your prize."

He nods very slowly, almost warningly, watching me approach, still with one arm covering my tits. The way his eyes drink me in and travel from the top of my head to the tips of my feet makes it hard to breathe.

When I reach him, he grabs me by the hips and drops me down to his lap, and then his hands are engulfing my face and he bends. His lips part my own, his breath on mine as his tongue flicks into my mouth. I can't remember my name.

Flutters of heat bubble in my veins.

A shot of heat races through my bloodstream as his tongue flicks my mouth again. His hands fist in my hair as he tilts my head sideways for better access, and then his tongue is all over mine, rubbing and stroking, wetly caressing.

He scrapes his fully-hard cock against my sex, the only thing separating me and him is the flimsy fabric of my panties.

He makes a low, savoring sound, a long, drawn-out *mmm*. I'm breathless when I ease back. I wonder who else he makes those sounds for.

He comes back for the full three minutes and lays me down, all the while kissing me, and I don't want to stop, my lips moving with his. I feel so hungry, so hungry I can't stop my hands from wandering up his arms, around his shoulders, into his thick, dark hair. I grab him and hold on, my mouth parting wider beneath his, his tongue devouring me, flick by flick, plunge by plunge. I part my legs, needing something, some sort of pressure, between them. And when the weight of his body comes down on top of me, his erection feels so good that I arch up to get closer.

He groans softly, fisting handfuls of hair as he tears free and looks down at me with heavy-lidded silver eyes. "Tease," he says. "You're sleeping beside me tonight."

Cullen helps me up, gathers our clothes, then guides me with a hand on the back of my neck as he walks me into his room. He watches me obediently climb into his bed as he sets our clothes aside. He reaches beneath my body to pull the comforter back, and then joins me from the other side, his hard arm sliding beneath me.

I watch the muscular curves of his arms flex with the move. I look into his eyes as we face each other.

My fingers want to do things to him, and so does my mouth and every part of me that can move or taste or hear or see. But I don't let myself move. It takes every inch of my willpower not to.

"I said you'd wear the lingerie."

"This reveals more. I'm basically only wearing panties," I contest.

He's already naked, and I can't get enough of looking at his ripped abs, his chiseled chest and arms, every part of him defined, hard, athletic, proportionate, perfect.

"We'll save the lingerie for next time."

His eyes darken as he drinks me in semi-naked in his bed, and he leans down to set a kiss on my lower abs, between my pussy and my belly button, right above the edge of my panties. Then he sets one on each of my nipples, which are peaked and hard, begging for his attention, whispering, "I like you just like this," and I groan and say, "Don't cheat," before he lies down next to me and slips his strong arms around me again.

"We said you could kiss my mouth, nothing else," I breathlessly remind him.

"You can't blame me for trying." He pulls me closer. So close that I can feel his cock deliciously, soul-searingly hard against my abdomen. He looks into my face, and I shift my hips a little closer to his.

"I want to know how you feel," he says. "Before we head back to Chicago, you'll be dying for it."

"Ha. No doubt you think I'll be dying for *you* like all your—"

He reaches up with one hand to tip my face up, and then he slowly parts my lips and gives me his tongue. I shudder uncontrollably as that hot, wet, familiar tongue flicks over mine.

We kiss for a little while, until I'm panting and his cock is so hard that I feel moisture against the skin of my abdomen. My whole being is undone with the way this guy kisses me.

When he strokes his hand down my cleavage, spreading his fingers out to touch my ribs, my waist, I could swear he's touching the most sensitive places of my whole body.

He groans as I stroke my fingers along his chest.

"You feel good," I quietly admit. "You work out, don't you?"

"Inside you, I'll feel better." His expression is dark and savage as he hisses out that promise. "And yeah, I do."

I relax in his arms and press my cheek to his chest, listening to his strong, steady heartbeat, and before I know it I'm asleep.

I wake up to the sunlight, relaxed and snuggled into a delicious warmth. When I realize it's Cullen and his smooth, muscled chest and hard arms around me, I take a brief moment to help my ovaries settle down from the happy shock. My eyelids flutter, and I find him staring at me.

We survey one another.

Silently, I reach out to touch my fingers to his jaw and the light stubble there. "I slept divine," I admit, voice sleepy. "Thank you. Did you sleep at all?"

He studies my features as he brushes my hair back, a gorgeous smile on his face.

"What? You didn't film me while sleeping, did you?"

"No. But not for lack of wanting." He studies me. "We should probably get dressed."

I shut my eyes and relish the feel of his hand on my back. The nearness of his dick to my pussy. The sound of his low, deep breathing, which is slow and even compared to my choppy little breaths.

"Yeah, we should get going." I ease out of bed and get dressed, aware of him sitting up in bed, propped with his arms behind his head and the sexiest, most kissable smirk on his lips.

"Do I sense hesitation in your voice?"

I halt in the middle of zipping up my dress. "What?" I'm breathless. "No. I'm . . . if you think I'm going to tell you your life sucks . . ."

He nods somberly.

"It doesn't."

He frowns at that, and I shake my head and continue dressing. "I just really like it here with you. But gambling is still wrong, and art is magic. I need to head back in two days . . . let's make the most of today. I'm hopping into the shower. I'll see you in a bit," I say from the door.

He gives me a gut-wrenchingly sexy smile, and my toes curl against the carpet as I lift my heels and walk barefoot to my room. What is going on here?

The butterflies the mere thought of repeating last night give me are the craziest little things I've ever felt.

The thought of curling up in bed to him at night. Nothing but him and me. I'm scared by how much I want that. I'm scared that it's been . . . days and all I can think about is Cullen. Breathe Cullen Carmichael. Live Cullen Carmichael.

Because this life? It's not real. Las Vegas is a fantasy. Thinking of anything long term with Cullen is a fantasy. It will only leave me feeling even emptier once it's done.

TONIGHT

Cullen
Last night

I didn't sleep. I kept watching Wynn sleeping soundly beside me, my chest heavy, my dick hard. I'm not big on sleeping with the women I fuck. But something about this girl has always struck a different chord, something has always made me feel protective of her. Interested, and also possessive of her. I haven't felt like that in a long time. And I don't remember being this interested in a woman ever.

She looks down her nose at what I do, but I see the look in her eyes when she looks at me. Interest. Curiosity. Desire.

Makes me want to take her and brand her and make her scream Cullen until her voice is raw.

I think back to fourteen years ago, to the only other woman I was once obsessed with. It didn't turn out well but it began on fragile soil anyway.

"I'm pregnant. God, how am I going to take care of this baby, Cullen?"

I was shocked. Part elated, part confused. I assured her, "I'll find a way."

"Your dad." Her tears vanished as if they were never there in the first place. "You'll go talk to him. He'll set us up and everything will be fine."

"It's not my dad's responsibility, it's mine."

"What? You're seventeen. You're getting a nine-to-five job, and earn what? Twelve bucks a day? How will that help me and the baby?"

"You're crazy, you know that?" As I said the words, I believed them. She wasn't crazy as in fun-crazy but more of an insanity-plea kind of crazy.

I never even considered asking my dad but if I had, he would've shouted alternatives while asking his secretary to type up a bullet-point list of why I should've been running in the other direction.

Still, I couldn't resent her. While I'll always think she wanted to get pregnant and saw me as some sort of meal ticket, I don't hate her. How could I?

She gave me the best gift in life. She gave me my son.

In some ways, she gave me my career, too.

I didn't have a lot of options so that very night, I got a fake ID and drove to the Indian Reservation. I went straight to the poker room. Back then the casinos used the virtual tables, which were more like video games, but they paid out like any other machine.

I took one thousand dollars out of my savings account and played all night. Looking back, I don't know how I did it. I was green or young or dumb. Maybe all of the above.

And so into her that I couldn't imagine life without her. A week later, I called her up and asked her to meet me. I handed over every last dollar from my winnings.

"Here." I forked over six thousand dollars, wadded up in an elastic band.

"What is this? Wow. It's . . ."

"Don't abort," I told her. "Marry me."

"I don't want to marry you. I'm dating Cody Baxter. You know, from Baxter Group. They're really rich. Like your family, except he doesn't mind asking his dad for money."

"My dad lives across the country in Chicago, Sondra. It's not his responsibility. It's mine. You're carrying my kid. Marry me."

"You cannot give me what he can. You don't even talk to your dad, and your mom spends money, not earns it."

"I'll have an empire one day and Cody Baxter will have nothing but his dad's money—or what's left of it."

I was devastated when I heard she was seeing Cody and Cody wanted to make an 'honest woman' out of her. She was just a girl, a stupid girl who focused on money and things rather than having a real family with a man who would've given her everything.

A few months after my son was born, she called me up and said, "We're married. He wants to adopt him. You have to agree."

Looking back now, I don't know if she was caught up in this ideal world filled with big houses and luxurious cars or if she wanted to hurt me. Sometimes I think she regretted getting pregnant even though I still think it was planned. It was like she thought that the pregnancy would speed things up, throw her into adulthood before her time.

She used my son against me and even now, when I think of that call, I still feel my heart clench and can almost hear her whispering in my ear, "He wants to adopt him. You have to agree . . ."

"I won't."

"I'll sue you. You cannot be close to him. You're a bad influence."

"I did it for you, for him."

"Nobody asked you to gamble."

"You're a bitch."

"You're a fucking loser. You know why you gamble? Because you know you're a loser and the only way to counteract that feeling is by winning as much as you can."

"Fuck you."

The joke was always on her. I didn't care what she thought about me and I didn't care that she didn't understand. It was the greatest career, the best job I could've ever hoped to have.

She didn't have that with Cody. She didn't even have Cody.

The money I won at the tables could've taken her away from a real job, any real forty-hour commitment because the money and the perks . . . every last one of them . . . were exactly what she wanted from the start. It was why she married Cody Baxter and that was the saddest part of all. He married her for sex. He wouldn't have found anyone else so willing to sleep with him, but I have to give him credit, after he tired of her pathetic little games, he grew into a man who wouldn't be controlled.

He didn't give her anything more than the bare essentials, the necessities. In that regard, he was much smarter than most.

I push the memories aside and shift in bed, my eyes falling on her. Her hair liquid lava on the white hotel pillow. I skim my knuckles across her cheek. I smile.

She's available now.

I want to tell her everything now. She should know.

Maybe. Maybe not.

I blow out a hard breath and drag my hand through my hair thinking that maybe the time isn't quite right yet. Maybe I should wait until she asks. Will she ask? Doesn't she wonder why I've been so intrigued by her? Why I'd give her everything just to keep her in Vegas a little longer?

She's beautiful, so damn beautiful, but it's more than her looks that drive me to want and need her. She's smart and talented and has the kind of personality that will keep a man guessing.

She keeps me guessing.

Even when we played strip poker. I wanted her to drop her hands and sit there confidently, defiantly, and she could've. She almost did, but it's like the devil sitting on her shoulder, sitting there and whispering, "Don't do it. Make him suffer. Make him wait."

And suffer I did, but not through the game.

The long wait for her breakup from that chef was pure torture. I couldn't ask Callan to keep an eye on her but I knew when she and Emmett were over.

From the moment I boarded the plane in Vegas, I knew my luck was changing. Before the underground game, there was something different in the air. It was like my life had been on full tilt waiting for the slow play of a lifetime.

I brush her hair away from her face and know that this woman changes my game.

She. Changes. Everything.

She never saw me that night months ago. She pressed closer to the guy she was with. It bothered me, but I watched like it was me her hands were on.

Sometimes I wonder what might have happened if I'd thrown caution to the wind and bought her a drink. Her ex wouldn't have minded one bit.

I bet he cares now.

Callan and Liv's wedding reception and that kiss? I wanted her right then and there. I did little to hide it. My interest. Real interest. I didn't do it for show. I did it for me.

I think her ex saw her then just as I see her now . . . strong and beautiful, untouchable by those who want to hurt her and unattainable by those who actually believe she's sitting on the sidelines waiting.

She's not a girl who waits patiently for anything.

I scoff as I think of how she gravitates toward me in the poker room. How her body curves closer to mine as she sleeps.

She's in my bed now and I'm determined to have her here again tomorrow night. She's scared I'll hurt her. And that's all right and valid. But I'm going crazy here.

We have a bet going on. Either I give her oral, or she does. I have a mind to lose if only to get my mouth between those thighs tonight.

SHOW

Wynn

Cullen is looking at me almost with that same intensity that I feel when I look at paintings, and I feel so seen and bare. "The art is over here," I point with a smirk, sashaying to the next work. A part of me tingles in excitement over his male appreciation. This guy is so blatant it's . . . *hot*.

He reaches out. "Not all art is on these walls."

"Ha. You're smooth."

He runs the back of one finger down my hair. "You're gorgeous."

"Cullen," I groan, flushing all over. I raise my eyes to his—and suddenly I believe him. I feel perfect, and gorgeous, and hotter than I've ever felt in the last few months.

Smiling cheekily, I turn away and keep walking. We view another painting, one which is full of vibrant colors but with two shadowy figures, young boys facing different directions. It immediately reminds me of Callan and Cullen, of the different lives they've chosen and how their paths have inevitably led them down different roads.

"Why did you and your brother end up living separately?"

"Our parents split when we were both teens. Callan stayed with Dad, I went with my mother."

I eye him quietly. "It must have been hard."

"It was harder for me knowing that she would be all alone. I couldn't let her go without one of us."

"So you chose to be the one?"

"I'm the oldest."

"How often do you see Callan and your dad now?"

"I travel quite a bit, but I try to make it a point to stop by when I can. Dad's getting older, but he's healthy as a horse."

"Lucky you, you get good genetics," I tease.

"On my dad's side. My mom is a whole other thing. Shopaholic to the core."

I laugh.

"My mom's not easy to live with but she's alone. I'm all she has, really."

"Does Callan see her?"

"Once or twice a year. Took him a while to get over the fact that our mother chose to leave Dad when he wanted her still; hell, he still does. She just fell out of love, I guess."

"I'm sorry."

We fall silent for a while.

"And your parents?" he asks me.

"They're the best. Happily married. They own a couple of candle stores. I used to help out until I went on my way to open a gallery. They're not rich, by any means, but we got by and I've never lacked for anything." I smile. "I've always wanted to find what they have. I sometimes feel wanting it to this degree has only decreed it impossible for me to find."

"Why?" His interest brings us both to a halt.

Him, because he wants an answer.

Me, because his interest seduces me.

"I don't know." I laugh nervously, his unwavering attention making my cheeks feel warmer than normal. "Because maybe nothing lives up. Maybe all these failed relationships are my fault."

He stares with drawn eyebrows. "You believe that?"

"I . . . no," I admit, a soft laugh escaping me. "It wasn't my fault. It was just . . . not meant to be. I guess. I was willing to give them a shot far longer than most of my exes were willing to work for it. Bastards."

"Bastards," he agrees, more effusively than me.

I smile, my stomach knotting painfully in yearning when his hand encloses mine again.

Suddenly what happened with Emmett seems like it happened to another girl, in another lifetime. But I remember what happened that drove him away . . . remember that I won't be able to have a family in the way I always envisioned, and my smile fades. I'm about to pull my hand free, but Cullen watches me, as if reading my mind.

"I have a son."

My eyes jerk up to his. "What?"

"I have a son."

Shock doesn't even come close to what I'm suddenly experiencing. I blink as my world spins, confusion making me reel. I search Cullen's implacable features and realize . . . he's not lying. Realize, from the set of his jaw, the fierceness in his metallic eyes, that this is a subject he may not usually talk about. That this is a subject that gets to him—deeply. He's watching me back, his gaze as intense as a loaded weapon trained on me.

"What happened?" I ask softly.

I remember the little boy photographs I saw in his home—and suddenly I *know* that's his son. My heart melts remembering that he looks just like Cullen. That I even thought it was Cullen in those photographs.

"Is he the boy from the pictures in your home?"

"Yes." We continue walking, but I'm not interested in the art anymore.

"He's beautiful."

"He's a great kid. I just don't see him as much as I'd like."

"Why?"

"His mother wouldn't allow it. I'm a bad influence." He shoves his hands into his pockets and scrunches his forehead thoughtfully.

I feel livid. Like punching whoever keeps a man, any decent man, from seeing their own flesh and blood.

"Where does he live?"

"Santa Fe. Close but not close enough." His eyes twinkle, but the frustration is still there. "I fly in to see him once a month . . ." He shakes his head, chuckling. "He loves it when I fly in."

"Of course he does. You're his dad!"

He smiles at me in silence.

"What's his name?"

"Adam."

"It's a beautiful name. And he's not bad to look at, either. Like his father."

He crosses his arms as we stand before another painting, both of us staring at it. "Never really pictured naming my son Adam, but he's a good kid."

"Do you want more children?" I ask, my heart stopping all of a sudden over my question.

Cullen looks at me, frowning, as if I'm asking a trick question. Maybe I am.

He glances past his shoulder, spotting something behind us. "The artist should be here somewhere," he murmurs. Cullen points at a flock of people around the corner. "There she is," he says.

I spin around and spot her at the very end. Excitement rushes through me at the prospect of meeting the artist. I tell Cullen to give me a moment and head over to greet her and inquire as to her other exhibits. Once I'm able to push past the fans surrounding her, I also hand her the card to my gallery, in case she's interested in representation in Chicago. It's not New York, but we have amazing art in Chicago.

She seems impressed over my determination to get her to come, and we've begun talking about my gallery when, out of the corner of my eye, I spot Cullen as he motions to his phone and to the doors, indicating he'll meet me outside when I'm done.

"I wasn't interested, but now I am," the artist assures me once we're done.

"I'm so pleased to hear that." God! This is so fabulous.

"Give me a call next week. Let's set aside some time next week, look at a few options, and see what we can do."

"Fantastic!" I'm over the moon but hold it together enough to casually say farewell.

I need to go find Cullen and tell him the good news. I've just won a jackpot. I think.

KING OF HEARTS

After my chat with the artist, I feel high on my own luck and head out to where Cullen indicated he'd meet me. I spot him standing beside Oliver as I stride toward the car, and they're discussing something, Cullen looking at me.

He pushes himself off the hood of the car and walks forward with something terribly deep and dark in his eyes.

"She's super interested. She's calling me. I can't believe it."

As he opens the car door for me, there's pride gleaming in his silver eyes as he leans to whisper in my ear, "I lose."

"Excuse me?" I glance over my shoulder as I slide into the backseat, and then watch him settle in next to me.

He shakes his head, those silver orbs dark and hot enough to make me cinder. "There's no way I'm going to win this, Red. I lose."

"What?"

He circles an arm around my hips and leans toward me, and again, whispers in my ear, his voice getting thicker and hotter with each word, "I'm going to taste you now, Wynn."

I clench my thighs together, the idea of having his mouth between my legs too hot to stand.

"You really believe I win?" I ask, disbelieving as I push him back.

"I believe in this," he whispers, and then his hand bunches my hair. He lowers his head, and his lips feast on mine.

Am I in a movie, living a fantasy, creating a dream? *Living* the life?

Cullen is kissing me like he's never going to stop. The illusion is real. The life is mine.

My whole body catches fire. Whatever this is, I want . . . need . . . must have . . . much more. My fingers are suddenly in his hair, gripping him.

"Closer," he rasps, dragging me across the seat until my chest is flush with his.

I kiss him back because he's the most delicious thing I've ever tasted. He tastes of bubblegum, his rich cologne intoxicating. He smells like confidence. And the urgency of his kiss? OH MY . . . I need to savor, enjoy, but it's impossible when I want to eat him right up.

And he's eating me up and up and *upppp*!

His mouth is at my ear. His hand rests on my knee.

He drags me closer still, pulling me onto his lap.

I straddle him. My hands are on his face and I'm pampering his lips like they're mine to savor, mine to keep.

He lets me guide the motions before I'm cradled in his arms. His fingers tease me as he pulls strands of my hair, tucks them behind my ears.

I'm flush against his chest. Catching my breath as we look at each other.

His ragged breathing makes my head stir with salacious thoughts, lecherous desires.

His lips come back and are all over mine, claiming and giving, *owning*. He retreats. And I feel the void as if he's left me alone on a busy street.

I reach for him and he returns, this time with promise, an impassioned attitude that suggests whatever I want, I'll have.

This isn't blind lust. I can plainly see. He wants to lead, but I'm too eager to follow.

I. Need. His. Kiss. Need to be ravaged and cherished . . . I desperately need this void filled and yet I sense that there's something more to these emotions, something dangerous right under the surface.

It's unfair to Cullen . . . because I don't know why. Maybe because I'm looking at him and expecting him to save me. And he's watching me as if to say, "Ask."

And I might.

Ask, that is.

We're alone in a city built on sinners. And while it might be wrong and it might be immoral . . . I want to drink in the most primitive moments and bask in all transgressions because if I let myself experience the power of passion, I can be raw and naked.

And then I'll be free.

This is what it'll take to get over Emmett, I think, shaming myself for letting the memory of my ex almost spoil the moment.

Why should I give him that? Why should I let him intrude here? I don't want to think about the past. I don't want to plan for anything more than this hour, minute, second.

This. Man.

I come up for air. "What's the equivalent to the Mile High Club if you're in a limo?" I breathe, my crazy ego letting me revel in the way he's watching me.

His hard cock is rocking his blue jeans and I can't help but look. I'm dying to touch.

"You're beautiful," he says, studying my lips. "*And* funny."

"Because the Mile High Club is a laughing matter?"

"Because you want me to win the bet." His hand guides mine lower, but he then lifts my arm and walks his mouth from my wrist to my elbow. "And I lose."

I laugh when it tickles and also melt from the top of my head to the tips of my toes. My nipples perk. The tips ping. What kind of kiss was that?

I'm shuddering. He's leaving me in ruins and I don't know how this is possible.

I try to keep my distance but he keeps pulling me closer.

I'm salivating.

I'm excited.

Horny out of my mind.

"We said you'd help me with gambling, I'd help with your job. We'd see whose job was better. And I lose completely. I want to taste you now," Cullen says.

I swallow. He leans forward. I do the same. I kiss him. He kisses me back.

We tease, play.

The give and take is competitive. It's the gambler in him, the seductress in me.

I pull back, gasping for breath. "Okay. I mean, I can't be a sore winner." I look deep into his eyes, absorbing the fires blazing in his gaze. "But are you sure you don't need more proof? I thought—"

"I have all the proof I need."

I'm flushed. He keeps my hand in his for the rest of our ride back, lifting it to torment me with delicious kisses on the inside of my arm that make my nipples ache, and I'm hot all over by the way he runs his lips all over me. "I was surprised you'd bet against me. I thought you were smarter than that," I whisper, trying to keep a level head until we reach the room. Where I plan to jump him.

"My slowest moment to date." He covers my hand in his again and lowers them to his thigh and inclines his head playfully in agreement.

I narrow my eyes, laughing and too nervous to name. I'm having my suspicions by the time we reach the hotel and head to the room. "Did you plan this, Cullen?"

"Planning's over," he rasps, kicking the door shut behind us as he shrugs off his jacket, pulls his tie free.

He grabs me by the hips and lifts me up in the air.

"Up on the pool table."

He sets me down on the edge of the table.

"Cullen—" I protest with a squeak. "I thought we would head back to Chicago so you can really see me in action."

"I already did. I know when I've lost a game."

"Really?" I say. Wow. I just can't believe I won so easily.

He nods somberly, those unreadable silver eyes drinking me in before he slowly bends.

He nuzzles my stomach over my skirt, using his nose to tease my top upward. I pull it over my head and my lungs work overtime as he groans softly, his tongue flashing out to lick across my belly button. I tense as my whole body constricts in desire. Keeping his mouth on me, he unzips my skirt and grabs the sides of the waistband, tugging it down my hips as he licks a path around, and down, my belly button.

Desire pools between my thighs.

He runs his fingers up the back of my legs, caressing my skin as he bites the bow at the front of my panties and tugs it downward.

Oh god. I clench my hands against the table beneath me as he drags my panties down, down my legs, using his *teeth*. I whimper when he removes them, grabs them in his hand, inhales them, and tosses them aside.

"Cullen."

He comes back. His tongue flicks out to lick my skin as his hands wander the insides of my thighs.

I'm so wet I'm embarrassed. He moves his thumb along my sex, and I arch my hips.

He licks into me. I swivel my hips up, violently, unexpectedly. He thrusts his tongue more deeply into my sheath, moving it as I move my hips in need—passion, sexual frustration, everything he makes me feel.

He slants his head, his hands sliding up to grip my waist, press me down so that he can fuck my sex with his mouth. And what started out as slow and easy is becoming wild and crazy, undoing me.

I moan.

He groans approvingly, the sound muffled by my folds.

He grazes his teeth over my clit. I'm grabbing at his hair, both of us sort of out of control as he tastes me.

He. Devours. Me.

And I can't think of anything except how much I want this—him—how much I ache all over. How good he smells, how much I love not thinking, how great his tongue is.

Oh my, that sexy tongue.

He spreads my legs wider. "No closing them, Red," he says, caressing my pussy with his eyes before he settles between my legs, and continues to take his slow, sweet time devouring me.

I groan because I want him. I want to pull him up to me. To feel him inside me. I want him to fuck me, I sort of crave him to be rough—but instead he pulls my hands away as I tug on his hair, and pins them at my sides, continuing to lick and eat from my pussy, his eyes opening and locking with mine.

I can't stand it, but I can't stand *not* to have it. I want to watch. I need to see. Can't believe what he's doing to and for me.

I'm just breathless. Hot. Dying.

And yet right here, right now, I realize—I've never really lived. Not like this. Not with anyone else.

Eyes locked, his are gleaming hot and silver as his mouth works between my thighs. I clench my thighs around his shoulders, and he pushes my legs apart again. My hips start swinging upward without rhythm. It has never felt this amazing. It does. It startles me, and my eyes widen, and Cullen shuts his eyes and pushes his tongue back into me.

"Cullen," I groan, tugging him by the hair again. Aching for his mouth on mine. Him inside me.

I'm breathless, my voice raw with desire, my fingers cramped from tugging so hard on his hair.

"I know I said no sex but I am *dying* to have you inside me."

It takes him a while to come up and ease his hand between my legs, then he rubs my clit with the pad of his thumb. Little circles. I'm shaking between the pool table and him, my legs skewing apart wider as he inserts his middle finger inside me.

He groans at my moan, devouring it with his mouth.

I kiss him back without restraint, our tongues going wild on each other.

The tremors in my body won't stop. Cullen's breathing is fast as he fingers me, tearing his mouth free to watch me. His jaw clenches hard, a muscle working in the back, when he scoops me up and carries me to the bed.

He tosses me in the center, then jerks open his pants.

I sit up. And whoa. Suddenly my windpipe is swollen with desire, my eyes wide as he strips off his shirt, slacks and boxers, and I drink in every ripped inch of his body.

He crawls toward me—eyes predatory and determined. Excitement bubbles in my veins.

I don't expect his groan, the hungry way his tongue drives into my mouth as he bends his head, repeating the same rhythm of his finger, which is back between my legs. Easing deep into my sheath. I thrust my hips up, mewing softly at his touch.

His voice, thick and guttural, as he inserts a second wicked finger inside me, gives me goose bumps. "Lie down, Wynn."

He bends, placing his mouth over mine, tasting the finger with me, then dropping his hand as his tongue and mine connect again. Twirl and lick again.

My throat constricts with need.

"Good girl." He flicks open my bra and discards it, then grabs his cock. "Look what you get." He's fisting the base of his dick, and I watch as he drags the head of his cock up and down my folds, teasing my entry.

My wet, aching, hurting, pulsing entrance.

"Say you want it."

"I want it," I beg.

I'm waiting, panting, watching him grab me by the side of the thighs and drag me down to him, where he kneels at the center of the bed.

I watch him position me. He splays my legs wider apart until his long, thick cock is right there, right *there*, then he grabs my arms and lifts them above my head. He secures both in one of his hands, and he uses the other to trace down my body, as if memorizing me. He keeps me pinned down, grabs the base of that glorious cock, gleaming with pre-cum, and in those five seconds, Cullen feeds it to me.

One breath, I'm waiting and anxious. The next, I'm moaning and near exploding. I gasp from how good it feels—how amazing HE feels—and he drives out and then back in, a little deeper and harder. His cock so big my walls are stretched way beyond what I thought possible.

I whimper a silent plea so he does it again. My pussy squeezes anxiously around his length, clutching him hard every time he drives out and stretching to welcome him when he rams back in.

He looks gorgeous, a look of concentration on his face as he moves, his eyes more brilliant than ever. They look nearly white, the silver so shiny and bright. Expression taut and raw, his muscles flexing as he thrusts. He holds my wrists imprisoned in one hand, the other torturing me. Pinching my nipples. Caressing my clit as he drives in and out.

"How good is it for you?" he asks me in a thick, raspy whisper.

"It's beyond good . . . don't stop." And I don't want to talk. Not yet. Not now. I just want to watch and see and feel.

He drives harder and my muscles tighten, nerves shatter.

Each breath I take is one more than I thought I had.

That low, guttural sound of his voice is toxic, so very, very toxic. He bends and suckles a breast into his mouth, suckling my nipple, teasing it with his wet, hungry tongue. His hand cupping the other. My sex grips as my orgasm builds and builds. "Cullen!" I cry as I tighten my arms around his neck, my head thrashing back as he gives me what I need. Fucks me like I need.

"Cullen," I groan, my muscles tightening more and more, the movements of my hips getting faster and more reckless as I roll them up to his.

He groans deep in his chest in response, our bodies moving in unison. Faster. Faster. Harder. I'm too aroused, too out of my mind, he feels too good.

We're both losing it. Cullen grabbing the back of my head and kissing me like he's out of breath and I'm oxygen. I cry out pleadingly, wanting, needing, my nails sinking into my palms as he restrains my wrists.

His hands tighten as the tremors take over me, his muscles straining in his release as I twist beneath him, a thousand stars bursting before me.

My body twists beneath his and I cry out, and I hold on to him as he drives me harder. His body tightens, his every muscle straining until he snaps, and then Cullen comes, his big body trashing against me, hips pumping, never taking his mouth off mine.

We continue moving, our pelvises rocking as our orgasms start to recede. Cullen's mouth gentles over mine, his body still taut with desire, warm with sweat, and more addictive than any addiction on this earth.

I'm quaking even after my orgasm stops.

He grabs my butt and rolls to his back, bringing me with him, before he rolls over yet again and sets *me* on my back. He grabs my hips and rolls me onto my stomach and props me up on all fours.

I gasp in surprise, but when I realize what he's doing, a new pool of moisture gathers between my thighs.

I feel his cock bob against my ass as he reaches around me to caress and fondle my breasts.

A low groan leaves me, and suddenly he folds the front of his body over the back of mine.

And I don't know how I ever survived the week without this.

What the hell were you thinking, Wynn? Look what you missed!

His muscles surrounding me, his breath on the back of my ear. "I'm not done with you," he whispers, fingering my earlobe, bringing a strand of hair—wet with my sweat—behind it. "What do you say, Wynn?" he wants to know, his warm lips brushing my earlobe.

"Please," I breathe, so weak with desire I'm nearly incapable of remaining on my knees, on all fours. I start sliding down, and Cullen seizes my hips in both hands. He props me back up, eyeing my butt, caressing his warm, large palm over it.

My breath comes in quick, fast bursts, and I hear his own coming in fast and haggard as he bends and starts dragging his tongue down my spine. I shudder, aware of my sex leaking wetness.

A wetness he gets to taste over and over again because he lost our bet.

Cullen grabs my hips and suddenly plunges back inside me, hard, deep, holding me still for every thrust. I mew, pushing back to meet him.

"Cullen."

Low, guttural fucking sounds tear out of him, out of us both, as he takes me.

I've never been taken like this. It feels animal, a little wild, and I can't get enough of Cullen driving into me with his big, long, thick, ramming cock.

I clench my fingers around the bedsheets beneath me, hanging on to my life.

"Kiss me, Cullen," I plead, out of my mind with pleasure.

He tangles his fingers in my hair and twists my face halfway around, kissing me senseless as he clenches one of my hips in his hand and fucks me to orgasm.

When we come yet again, this second orgasm lasting even longer than the first, we fall back in bed, struggling to recover our breaths.

I feel like the hottest, most relaxed individual in the planet. Forget yoga, Zen, Mozart, and art, sex with Cullen Carmichael is the ticket.

Hoolly . . . fuck . . . I can't breathe. Sex . . . it just can't get any better than this.

I drape one leg around his and exhale, relaxed, fingering the muscles of his abs and dragging my fingers up his chest, to his sexy man nipples, his throat. Fingering his lips and their perfect, sensual shape. I watch his lips open and his teeth bite my fingertip, nibble on it.

I smile, then watch him raise his head and lean over me, his lips coming closer and closer, down to take mine, and the lazy, satisfied moves of his tongue make me clench my thighs together again as I try to suppress the beginnings of another ache.

God, he's delicious.

Addictive.

What am I to do?

Have him again . . . ?

I can't believe all this time I've believed that sex while in a relationship was better than flings and one-night stands. I can't believe what I've been missing. And yet, I have to admit that I'm not sure it's the relationship aspect that's making sex good with this guy. It's simply this guy. He knows what he's doing. He's also clearly very sexual and hungry, something which seems to drive me wild.

Hell, this guy drives me wild without any effort at all. Even when he's being annoying he makes me rather hot. Go figure. And no fair!

But right now he's nibbling on me, my throat. "Did you know they call me Great White sometimes?"

"Why?"

"Card shark."

I roll my eyes. "Okay, Great White."

"Jaws," he husks out teasingly.

I'm distracted by what he's doing, and it takes me a second to reply. "God, you're totally Jaws." I laugh and let him bite me.

In the middle of the night, we still haven't slept one bit. I stare around in the darkness, too happy to sleep. He's dragging his fingers lazily up and down my arm while I spoon his side. And instead of shifting away from me to attempt to go to sleep, he sort of pulls me closer. It makes me giddy, giddy enough that I don't want to ever stop feeling giddy.

"Cullen?" My voice sounds almost loud in the darkness.

"Hmm." His voice rumbles against the top of my head.

"Did you enjoy today? Or . . . um, last night? I have no idea what time it is." I laugh.

He pulls me back closer to him because the moment I laughed, I sort of almost sat up.

"Immensely," he answers slyly.

"I mean the art and paintings."

"That too." He chuckles, and I laugh softly, shifting up as I try to make out his features in the dark.

"So you enjoyed it as much as I do gambling?"

"You don't like gambling," he rumbles, pulling me back to his side. "You like watching *me* gamble."

"I like it," I contradict, roaming the tip of my index finger along his hard abs. "It's growing on me."

I feel something else growing against my abdomen and smile in the shadows.

"So you enjoyed it?" I insist.

"Yeah." He moves me closer and shifts to face me, his hands wandering up and down my back. "I enjoyed watching you too." His admission melts me as much as his wandering fingers do.

"Do you still plan to come to my show in Chicago? Even if you already lost?"

"Yeah. I plan to go. I should be finished tomorrow with the qualifier."

I smile. "I'd love to have you there and show you the art. It's my biggest exhibit to date."

He shifts up on his elbow, and I can feel his gaze in the shadows. "Tell me about this big exhibit."

Something else that's pretty big keeps nudging my hip-bone.

His interest mesmerizes me.

"Well, it's a collective," I explain, sitting up as I search his gaze in the dark, finding it only because of the silver gleam in his eyes, shiny even in shadows. "All of the artists I represent are exhibiting their newest works, plus a few other artists who've got international exposure that I was able to snatch up. One of them, Yamika Tanato, she's so incredible. They all are. But Yamika . . ." I tell him about her installations and large-scale works, how she uses several layers of paint, how each work takes about six months to dry.

He inhales my hair as I settle back down in bed, runs his lips along my ear.

"Sounds fascinating."

I frown. His voice is so low it's almost indecipherable. "You don't sound fascinated."

"I am," he promises, with a low laugh, as he drives his fingers into my hair. "Not my fault it's such a turn-on to hear you speak about art. Come here."

I giggle, already aching again as he turns my head, and suddenly our lips are inches apart. My breath and his breath mingling. "Have you worked me out of your system yet?" I ask, stroking his nipples. I love how velvety and hard his chest is. I could touch this guy all day and look at him all day, like a living work of art, and never tire of it.

"We're not nearly there yet."

I push him back a bit, and I open my mouth to tell him I'm craving more when he ducks his head, "No more talking, Wynn," he says, huskily. He sticks his tongue into my mouth. He folds my leg over his shoulder, and before I know it, he's inside me again.

"No more talking, Redhead," he says, huskily, "just fucking. If I'm going to *work* you out of my system, it'll take a while . . ."

He sounds lightly amused as he tosses my words back at me, but he shoves his thumb into my mouth, watching me lick it as he starts moving in me, and he's not amused anymore. Both of us quiet, our breaths quickening, our bodies straining. I arch back, closing my eyes, letting Cullen do whatever he wants with me. Letting him tease me, play with me—and fucking loving every second of it.

CRAPS

We spend the morning having breakfast in bed.

"Don't think I've forgotten about the concert." I glance at him across the breakfast (more like lunch) table. "Are you still taking me?"

"It's your last day. Your wish is my pleasure." He chucks my chin, teasing me. I laugh and walk my fingers up his arm, then tease his lips apart with a strawberry. He bites it, enough that his teeth catch my fingertips.

"Ouch. Caveman." I glare playfully but actually it didn't hurt one bit, and I raise those same two fingertips he bit and suck them.

His eyes darken. He shifts back, eyeing me with a smirk on his face as his gaze caresses me. "Why are you so covered up now, huh?" He leans forward and strokes his hand across my shoulders, lowering my loose pajama top to reveal the curves of my bare shoulders.

"Because I'm hungry. I don't want you to get any ideas until my tummy's satisfied."

"Your satisfaction is my aim. Let's get you fed then." He snatches the last strawberry from the plate and raises it to my lips.

I'm blushing the same shade as the fruit he tantalizingly offers me. "You're ridiculous."

"Last strawberry, Red. Do you want it or not?" He teases it away.

"I want it," I groan, opening my mouth. He teases it into my lips, and I part and take a bite, the juice flowing down my throat. "Mmm. It's my favorite fruit. Did you know? It just tastes so . . ." I start to lick my lips when he grabs the back of my head and kisses me, tasting the strawberry on my lips.

"Fresh. Fresh and perfect," he concedes, leaning back to watch me flush with a look of amusement on his face.

"Why so shy with me today? You'd think you'd be less coy this morning after the things I did to you last night."

"It's *because* of them that I feel . . . ugh. You're enjoying this, aren't you? Stop it!" I cover my face, laughing. "Stop looking at me like that, I hate blushing. My hair is red, Cullen. When I blush, I blend straight into my hair and I hate it."

"I personally love it."

"Ugh, you." I toss my napkin at him, and he chuckles and peels it off the top of his head.

His phone starts buzzing on the table, and he frowns when he sees the name on the screen. He answers. "Yeah?"

I take advantage and hurry to the restroom, freshen up, and hear him as I come back out to the living room. He's standing, staring out the window. "That's not possible. I'm busy." He pauses. "I'll send Oliver with some money later."

He hangs up and rings for Oliver, who knocks moments later. I watch Cullen pull out several stacks of bills from the room safe and stash it in an envelope, handing it to Oliver.

"To my mother's," he tells Oliver.

"Yes, sir."

Cullen shuts the door behind him, his eyes finding me across the room. He's wearing slacks only, a hint of stubble on his square jaw.

My heart is doing something funny because . . . he's kind to his mother. He left the comfortable life that his dad provided him to be with his mom, who seems to be less . . . well, dependable. It does something to me.

There's a slim distance between love and lust, and I'm straddling the very middle, unsure of what I feel, unsure of how to stop it, helpless to swing from one side to the other, touched and affected by both.

I realize Cullen is still looking at me too. "Look at you. I can't even take my eyes off you when you're in a room."

"Don't tease me."

"I'm not teasing you. I've wanted you from the first moment I saw you."

I lick my lips, his words buzzing in my head. "When you bought me. Robert-Redford style."

He doesn't move for a moment.

His eyes darken as he remains silent, a suspicious line at the corner of his mouth tempting me to believe he's about to smile.

"Had a good time last night. Let's get ready. What do you want to do on your last day?" He pats my butt on his way to the bedroom.

I follow him and watch him flip on the shower. "Aside from going to that concert tonight and the obvious . . ." I smirk. "Working *you* out of my system," I tease. "I'd love to learn how to play craps."

He rounds back to look at me, surprised. "You're kidding."

"Nope. Are you game?" I throw myself on his bed, curling my legs beneath me as I watch him get undressed, my whole body responding by what I'm seeing.

His grin is absolutely devilish. "I'm game."

He eyes me on the bed, the twinkling lights in his eyes intensifying.

"*If* you come wash me," he adds.

I gape and drool a little in my mouth as I watch his gorgeous ass flex as he walks toward the shower.

Exhaling, I quickly strip and join him, pulling the door open, steam covering my face and body as I step in. Cullen was dragging his hand down his face, but his entire body tenses when I press up behind him and wrap my arms around his waist, leaning my cheek to his back. I close my eyes, exhaling, loving when he reaches behind to hold me still before he turns around and pulls me right into his arms.

He rocks me under the water for a moment—and I know it's not true, but it *feels* like the first time he's ever held me like this before. He smiles down at me, and I smile up at him, before we get into the sexiest fucking of my life. And I just can't remember anything exists outside of Vegas and this man.

"You've never shot dice before?" he asks when we arrive at the craps table.

I shake my head, and Cullen smiles down at me and places himself behind me as he instructs me.

"On your come-out roll, seven and eleven pay. Two, three or twelve are craps, and they lose on the come-out roll. If you hit any other number, you'll establish the point you need to hit again before seven rolls out," Cullen says as the stickman shoves the dice our way.

"Okay." I smile.

"Pick up two," he says, nodding at the dice. I miss his heat when he steps to my side, but adrenaline already pumps in my veins.

Forty-five minutes later and we're on a roll.

I'm throwing the dice, confused by the rules, asking Cullen, "What do we need now?"

"Seven or eleven. You're coming out again."

I nod and blow on the dice, throwing them down the table, squealing when a seven appears.

The table gets hot. Other players are coming in to place their bets.

I do it again, and again, establishing the point, hitting that same point with no seven in sight—which apparently is a good thing. It's a good thing to throw sevens on your come-out throw, but not when you've already established a point.

I blow on the dice again, throwing the dice, squealing again when I hit my number. I'm giggling, having the time of my life, the adrenaline rushing through my veins as Cullen places bets for us and manages our winnings like a pro.

When I throw a seven, and my winning streak seems to be coming to an end, we collect our winnings. I grab Cullen's jaw and kiss him, saying, "Nobody told me gambling would turn me on this much. That it could be so sexy." I squeeze his jaw and kiss him again, ecstatic. "It's because *you're* sexy."

I'm all horny, wanting to lead him upstairs, or to a nearby restroom. I want him all the time, every second. I want to go down on him, devour him.

I want him to devour me.

"I love this game!" I throw my arms around him and whisper in his ear. "Can we go now?"

He looks down at me, our lips a hairsbreadth away. He pecks them, squeezing my waist and letting me feel how hard he is. I squirm needily, pecking him back and tightening my hold on him.

He nods and says we're cashing out our winnings.

"Good roll," a lady says, tossing a black chip my way. "Shooter tip."

"Aw! Thanks!" And I sound like such a girly girl.

Cullen growls when I lean over to pick up the chip and my tits almost spill out of my dress.

And I'm no longer a girl. I'm *his* girl.

While the dealer counts our chips, I push myself into Cullen's hard chest and breathe, "I am lucky, aren't I?"

"You're fucking Lady Luck on legs," my Silver Eyes husks down to me, smiling teasingly.

He looks at me like he wants to take me up to the room and do me. He tucks our chips into my palm, and as he hands me the large denomination coins to store in my purse, I know he might have done just that if Mike didn't appear.

"Cullen. There you are. I'm sorry to say . . . I've got some bad news." Looking worried, Mike scrapes a hand along the back of his neck. "Qualifier has been postponed."

Cullen looks at him with a mild arch of one brow. "When's the new date?"

"I'm awaiting confirmation, but three days after tomorrow at the latest."

His jaw squares, and his voice drops a decibel. "Fuck that, Mike," he growls.

I feel my own smile fade as Cullen shoves his hands into his pockets and looks at me. "He'll be here," I quickly tell Mike, and Cullen turns to me with laser-like intensity in his gaze.

"Cullen?" Mike waits for his confirmation.

Cullen nods tightly, still looking at me with curiosity.

Mike excuses himself, and we stare at each other for a beat. Two. Three beats.

Aware that I'm flushing and my expression could give me away, I begin walking, looking down at my feet, trying to hide my disappointment. "You can't skip your qualifier. This is what you do. Besides . . . you've already lost our bet so it's not like you need to come help with my exhibit after all. I only said you should because—" I trail off.

"Because you wanted to strut your stuff for me," Cullen says. "I know that, Wynn."

My eyes widen, and I laugh and shoot him a glare. "See? And I didn't have to, to win. So . . ." I sigh. "It's tight, but you could still make it to my show if you finish on time. It won't be as fun without you to impress—your presence alone would dare me to do my best."

I hate the disappointment in my voice, but I can't help it. I raise my eyes to his hard profile.

He's staring straight ahead, a slight frown on his features, then he eyes me, giving me a wan smile. "Tell me you'll kick ass with this exhibit, though."

"Of course I will. I won our bet, didn't I? That artist I told you about last night? She's bringing her best work, a massive painting, the crown jewel of the exhibit. It's almost a mural, only someone with huge spaces and bankroll can afford it . . ." I shake my head, unable to describe how jaw-droppingly stunning her work on such a grand scale is. "I adore it. It's called 'future that will never be' and is the most incredible abstract landscape you'll ever see. It's magical, you see? So beautiful it can't be real, but when you stare at it you're hit with the fact that it *is* real. It could be real, because reality is subject to perspective, and perspective can change reality. I'm proud of this particular artist. She went through tough stuff in her life to be where she is now. I'm proud of all my artists, but this one—that piece . . ." I shake my head, sighing when I realize I must be boring him. "Anyway. Invites have been sent, and there's already some buzz on the internet so I'm thrilled . . ." I glance up at him, grinning sheepishly.

He stops me from walking, a hand on my wrist, looking even more intent than before. "Stay for a few more days. We can leave together."

I hesitate for a second, Cullen's gaze searching me intently, almost as if he's prying my secrets away from me. Especially the one I'm clutching closest to my heart, which is that I don't want to leave.

But I have to.

Stomach clutching at the thought of never again seeing Cullen like I did this weekend, I groan. "I can't. I need to unpack some of the paintings, get everything ready—I fear I've already asked too much of Pepper this week."

"Damn," he growls.

"I know. But you need to be in that qualifier. I mean, this is what you *do*." I roll my eyes in fake mockery. "It's still not art, but . . . it's your thing, *Playboy*." I shoot him a grin as I tease the sound of his nickname, hating the butterflies that awaken in me at a hint of a smile. "It's my last day—our last day here together. So let's make it count. I'm ready for that concert. And I know you're dying to dance with me!"

"Right," he says flatly, and I laugh when I see the amusement in his eyes.

CONCERT

"Drop us here, Oliver," Cullen says. Next he smothers my lips with the hottest kiss I've had since . . . oh, maybe five or six minutes ago. We've been kissing all the way to the concert. I already sort of wish we'd stayed in the room so I could truly make the best out of my last day here.

"Do you have your tickets, sir?" Oliver asks.

"Got 'em," Cullen answers. He checks his interior coat pocket before taking my hand. "In case I haven't told you tonight, you're beautiful."

"You don't look too bad yourself, Mr. Carmichael." I eye him in those dark slacks, black button shirt, and black coat jacket. I could lick my teeth. To be honest, I can easily accept and dish compliments with Cullen because it's like we fit, like no one else is breathing our air except me and Cullen and we can say and do whatever we choose.

Oliver pulls to the curb. Cullen exits then helps me out as well, taking my hand and pulling my arm through his.

A reporter closes the distance as if she wants an exclusive, but Cullen puts up his hand. "Privacy tonight, please."

"Cullen," I whisper, letting him lead me. "Was that reporter . . . waiting for you?"

He laughs. "Me and any other familiar face she sees."

"Do you want to go back? Do you need the publicity?"

"No. Sorry. You're all mine. They're not taking you away from me."

I like that he's already noticed that I get nervous in the spotlight. Besides, I don't want to share him tonight. This is our last night together.

Don't go there, Wynn. You're out on the town tonight with the hottest man in the city.

Enjoy it. Enjoy him.

I turn to drag my fingers up the front of his shirt and before I realize what I'm doing, my head is up. I reach for a kiss.

He pops my lips and smiles down at me. "Let's go have some fun."

Behind us, the crowd erupts in cheers as a sleek SUV limo arrives with the headliner. The New Vegas Pack is known for their outstanding renditions. Tonight they'll bring Mendes, Puth, Sia, and Adele to the stage, working with a full orchestra.

Cullen laces our fingers together and flashes his tickets at the VIP entrance. We enter a fancy event tent with a lot of bells and whistles. Gaming tables are set up with high limit tables and complimentary champagne.

I can hardly believe it.

It's like the games follow you everywhere you go when you're here.

"Does everything revolve around gambling here?"

He slides his arm up and around my neck. After a succulent kiss, he reminds me, "Every good time starts with a bet. Don't you think?"

I shiver a little. "You won't hear me argue that point."

"It's your night . . . we don't have to spend it at the tables."

I smile, admitting, "I've found I've quite enjoyed the tables. If you're in one."

He smiles at me, then leads me to secure a fabulous place close to the stage.

By the time the concert starts, I'm already sweating and ready to dance.

Throughout the first ten songs, I'm screaming my lungs off. I haven't been to a concert in a while, and it's like this is the last concert I'll ever go to. With him, maybe. I love knowing he can't take his eyes off me as I dance.

I'm jiggling my shoulders and hips as Charlie Puth's song "How Long" fills the outdoor arena. We're all the way up front so I have room to shake and move. I especially love that Cullen's hands land on my hips, where he keeps me still against him whenever a song stops. The roped-off section accommodates tables, chairs, and standing room only for about seventy-five people, but the concert is sold out and I feel like a real VIP.

The band's lead singer works his final number like he has something to prove. "This one goes out to those of you who love to win!"

He's standing in front of me as he starts singing The Calling's "Wherever You Will Go." He walks down to the other side of the stage as the song begins, then he returns for the chorus and stays right there . . . in front of me . . . singing to me!

And I'm loving it.

I'm loving it because Cullen's hating it.

I'm grinning.

He's frowning.

I'm singing aloud and barely hear my guy until he pulls me hard against his solid cock, dragging me as he sways gently one way and the other.

My whole body electrifies as I lean back against him. I let him sway me.

I already know my guy can dance when he's inspired.

His arms tighten and he breathes at my ear, "I'll go wherever you go."

"Will you?" I play, glancing over my shoulder.

His lips take mine and his kiss makes a statement. It's one that shows ownership and makes me forget everything else, even the concert.

When he releases me, the band's lead is nowhere in sight.

I shoot him a playful glare for scaring him off.

Then it's over.

"That was incredible!" We're walking back the same way we entered, and he's holding my hand. I'm so happy I'm swinging our arms. The desert air is nice and warm, but not humid and thick. "Thank you."

"It was my pleasure."

"I'll bet," I say, when suddenly a drunken woman stumbles up to him, feeling up his dick as she tries to straighten up. "Hey." She blinks up at him. "I remember you. You're the one they say can win it all this year at the final table." She practically purrs when she adds, "You feel like a winner to me, *Playboy*."

"I think you've had enough to drink for one night, sweetheart."

"Cullen?" I whisper, suddenly bristling. She knows his nickname? What the hell?

He called her sweetheart?

Unfortunately, he helps her to her feet and smilingly tells her something that makes the girl—a drunk girl—*blush*, and I grit my teeth.

"Really?" I search his eyes and take off at a faster walk.

I can walk.

Independent women—sober women—can do things for themselves like, oh, I don't know . . . keep their hands to themselves?

Actually, I have a tough time with that myself when it comes to Cullen but *still*.

He *wants* my hands on him.

Does he want drunk chick's too?

Apparently so . . .

Cullen catches up to me within a couple of minutes. "Really, Red?"

He sounds amused. It pisses me off even more.

I stop. "Really. That's what I asked you. *Really, Cullen?* How could you?"

"She grabbed me. Believe me, it wasn't invited."

"You didn't look too distraught."

"And you didn't stick around to help."

"Help? Are you kidding me?"

"Why not? Faith Hill made a public claim on Tim McGraw one time at their concert. You could've done the same."

"They're married. She should've!"

I keep walking. I'm so damn pissed and even madder that I don't have claims to him. If I had claims to him . . .

Shit, Wynn, what are you thinking?

I stew on our ride back to the hotel and the smile Cullen is wearing makes me even madder. He holds my hand and I try to take it away, but he only tightens his hold and won't let me retrieve it.

I let him have my hand. That's the only thing he'll get tonight. And I look out the window, avoiding his penetrating stare.

"What did you say to her that made her blush?"

"Only to watch her step next time before she fell onto someone that would be more difficult to pry away from."

I huff angrily. "You're incorrigible, Cullen!"

"I meant some other loser. I'm not interested in her."

I shoot him a glare. I hate this feeling and I hate that he made me feel this. Him and his playboy ways.

By the time the car halts, I admit to myself that I'm more mad at myself than at him. I'm mad by how jealous I feel. How . . . fragile this thing with him is. I feel things for him. Crazy, deep things. And yet I'm leaving tomorrow, and it's starting to make me panic.

When the car halts, I open my own door and step out. I cross the lobby and hear his footsteps close behind me. "Wynn." He grabs my elbow and spins me around when a little boy bumps into him.

"Sorry!" he calls off to Cullen off-handedly as the mother hurries over. "Sorry," she tells him, then hurries after the boy and catches up with him. "Carson, what did I say about running off?" she asks.

I realize the little boy's name is the same as my date when I first met Cullen. I'm about to smile, but Cullen has fallen still, and I can't help but notice the yearning in his eyes as he watches the boy and mother walk away. He shoves his hands into his pockets, watching intently, a soft smile on his lips.

It's the first time Cullen isn't wearing any poker face at all.

And what I see there kills me. Makes my heart burn and crumble. My stomach sky-dive. Because I could never, ever be able to fulfill the yearning in this man's eyes. It's physically impossible for me.

And suddenly I'm done with men—with everything.

"At least Emmett wouldn't have flirted with some drunk at a concert," I whisper, needing an outlet for my frustration and anger, unable to admit to him my failings. The reason Emmett couldn't take the next step with me and I'm sure, the reason no other man will want me.

His attention whirls toward me, his smile vanishing from his features.

I hate how catty I'm being but I'm desperate to push him away and remember what we have between us is nothing. Can go *nowhere*.

Striding quickly away, I enter the elevator a few minutes later and punch the button, trying to get to our suite ahead of him. Cullen slides between the doors as they're closing and he looks at me.

"Emmett," he says, his voice like ice.

"That's right. My ex! The last man I will ever lo—" Before I can say anything else, his mouth is on mine, and he's giving me a punishing kiss that makes me gasp. His tongue is sliding across mine.

His hands are in my hair. On my shoulders. On my ass.

He frames my face, sucking my tongue just a little at a time, the anger and frustration in his kiss matching mine.

"Stop," I groan, trying to remember why I'm mad in the first place. "I can't think when you—"

The door opens on our floor and I dart out. My key is in my hand and I enter our suite ahead of him.

When I turn to say something, he's already ripping his tie away from his neck, kicking off his shoes, undressing right there in front of me.

"Now *you're* mad? Why would you be? We're talking about this," I say.

"No," he says, his belt following his tie. "We're fucking through our differences first. We can talk later."

"The hell we are."

"Glad you agree," he says, catching me before I have a chance to get away.

His lips crash down on mine and he's feeling me up, working one hand under my skirt while the other strips the material away.

I remember again the look of raw yearning in his eyes when he saw that little boy and I want to comfort him. I wish I could give him the thing he most wants in this life. Instead I clutch him to me and can't fucking let go. Wanting him like I've never wanted anything.

I'm on fire and this isn't one of those delicious slow burns. This is one of those, fuck the foreplay. I need you inside me, somewhere and everywhere . . . now.

"Cullen."

He turns me to the wall, and he rips my thong away and growls in my ear, tells me that he wants me, only me, and that he's been doing me all night long in his thoughts.

Holding onto my anger in self-preservation mode, I groan, "If that's even true then you should've told her you were—"

"Fucking crazy for you?" He leans over my back, palms my ass as if it's the most fragile thing in the world, and in contrast, he thrusts inside me like I'm elastic, then growls, "Dying to be inside you?" His voice thickens in my ear, his tongue licking me. I groan, parting my legs wider, bracing my hands on the wall. His hips roll forward and mine rock back. "Can't get enough of you . . . this?"

He's breathless now and the hammering begins. He nips at my ear, runs his tongue down my neck, turns my head to my shoulder where he meets me with a soul-stealing kiss.

"Oh Cullen," I whimper, clutching his hand as he drives inside me.

Our fucking is uncontrollable now. He drives inside me with no control and I want him to be like this with me. Want him to take me as if he's never had me, claim me as if he plans to keep me.

He pulls out right before I come, and I'm so wracked with sexual frustration I wheel around to face him and jump into his arms, locking my legs around him.

He enters me again, grabbing hold of my ass as he drives inside my pussy with rapid strikes.

"Cullen." I hang on for dear life, dragging my fingers up and down his arms, back and forth as I ride him.

"What do you want, Red?" He rips the top of my dress down and buries his face in my tits. "Because all I want is this . . . you."

He pulls out, backs me up a step or two. My back slams against the bedroom door. "Only. You." He boosts me up again.

"Fuck me." I squeeze him as he impales me on him, grind and ride him.

"How much do you want me?" he says. His lips skim the peaks of my breasts again.

"You have no idea," I moan, unable to think when he buries his face in my hair.

Then we're kissing. I drive my fingers into his hair, fisting him as we come together. He clutches me as I shudder, and shudder, and shudder. Cullen growls softly as he follows me. We pant together minutes later, our lips mashing for one last kiss before he pulls out.

He runs his fingers gently through my hair as he watches me straighten. I look at him, his hair mussed, his lips reddened by me as he watches me rearrange myself.

I'm scared of what I feel. Of how out of control this man makes me.

"Don't pull away," he husks. His hands fly out to halt me when I try to move back.

I exhale, prying free to finish righting my clothes. "I had a moment of weakness, but I think this isn't going anywhere." *I saw the way you looked at the child and mother and I could never give you that*, I think helplessly. "And I don't want . . . this is getting out of hand."

"Meaning . . . ?" He starts to frown, bringing his slacks over from the living room. He pulls them on with a frustrated yank and zips up quickly. Almost angrily.

I groan. "Meaning, I saw the way you looked at that mother and her child in the lobby and it made my heart hurt. I just wanted to comfort you."

"And I wanted you coming," he growls back at me.

We face off, narrowing our eyes at each other.

"Fuck you!" I explode. "You won't even take anything tender from anyone, you try to act as if you don't really need anything—everyone needs something! You want it, Cullen, you want it all, don't pretend you don't!" *And I hate that I can't give you that!*

"I want it! So fucking *what*? I don't want your pity," he growls. "Save your pity, I don't want it. Do you hear me? All I want from you I got right now."

I punch his chest with my fist.

He doesn't even move.

"If that's not just damn epic," he hisses.

"Want epic? I'm using your comps to get myself another room!"

I stare at him, spin around, grab my purse, and storm away. I hurry to the elevators, wondering what the hell I'm doing. I've never dated such a conflicting, infuriating guy. I have no idea what I'm doing with him! I have no idea what to do with *myself* around him. I march across the casino and grab the first cashier I see. Cash one of my chips, get a hundred dollar bill and push it into a slot.

I'm pushing the button with tears in the back of my eyes. I don't know why. It's because I'm leaving. It's because I'm mad at him for being so . . . so goddamned wonderful. More than I ever expected. I'm angry at myself for coming here and exposing myself to this man and his charms in the first place. I'm mad because his last words hurt me. Because I want—deep to the very deepest part of me—to be more than just another of his flings. Ugh.

I sense a shadow behind me. I stiffen, cash out my ticket, and turn around in my chair.

"Come with me," he murmurs, his gaze dark and forlorn. He looks bad.

I hate that I can't breathe when he's near and I can't breathe when he's gone. I especially can't breathe when we're out of sorts with each other.

I hate that I can't think when he looks at me. And I can't think of anything else but *him* when he doesn't.

I press my lips angrily and stay silent.

He reaches out to tuck a strand of red hair behind my ear. "Come with me."

A swarm of butterflies flutter in my stomach.

"I came down to be alone."

"Want to designate areas?"

He smiles a little as he teases me. But his eyes are tortured and heated. My breath catches as he takes a step forward. I can almost hear my personal bubble pop. My lungs strain for air as he trails his fingers up my cheek and cups the side of my face.

"Don't," I warn. He leans down and kisses my cheek.

His arms envelop me—locking around me as though he never plans to let go.

He pulls me up on my feet and brings his lips down on mine.

My breath leaves me. My toes curl. My lips open for his. The warm, wet flick of his tongue teases me open.

"I apologize."

"Stop it, Cullen, just stop," I beg.

"I will when you forgive me." He nibbles me more. "Please forgive me. I'm unhinged and I don't know why but I know it's because of you."

"I'm unhinged too and I blame *you*. Let's just forget about it. We came here to have fun—"

"We came here so you could get over that bastard. Don't mention him to me again," he warns, angry, as he holds my face in one his large hands.

I swallow, nod.

He takes my hand in his. "Ready to go back up?"

I let him lead me to the elevators. "I lost eighty bucks. I feel so bad."

He smiles in amusement, and when we board the elevators, I lean on him on our way up to our room. He stands behind me, embraces me, pulls me closer as he leans his chin on the top of my head for a moment. He drags it down so he can kiss my temple. I'm clutching in anticipation all over. In aching, in yearning.

"Let's get you to bed," he murmurs.

He gets me to bed—where we kiss like maniacs. Where he kisses me raw. The way this guy makes my body sing mesmerizes me. A body I have hated because it can't give me one of the things that I most want—a family. He makes me love this body like I used to . . . before I knew.

We fuck so hard and fast, we never really get our clothes off, and I can barely remember my name after. Much less why we fought.

Oh yes, I was jealous because of the drunkie.

He got fucking pissed that I mentioned Emmett.

Both Emmett and the drunkie can go fuck themselves. I've got Cullen, and right now, I'd rather have him more than anything else, even food or sleep.

"I want to do it again," I quietly whisper up at him.

"That's the plan."

"I love having sex with you."

"I aim to please."

"That you do." I feather my fingers up his chest. "You have very fine hands, and a very fine . . . umm, you're so fine." I bite him a little, slide my hand down the sheets.

He bites me back.

"You put your hands on my dick and I'm not going to last."

"Mmm, I like that you lose control a little."

"I'd say more than a little." He eyes me. "Strip."

I strip my clothes nervously. Watching him do the same before he crawls over me.

He cups my sex and parts my thighs. "Give me this."

I do.

"You're gorgeous. Look at me."

I do.

"Don't close your eyes."

I can't. I won't.

I keep them on his as we start doing it slowly this time. Every scent, every sound, every sight, every taste, every touch, intensified. I watch as his eyes haze up and my own blur and still, those silver orbs are all I see.

WHAT HAPPENS IN VEGAS . . .

This morning, right after a round of shower sex that left my legs weak and the rest of me on a cloud way above nine, we got dressed. We've sent my luggage downstairs with Oliver. I don't know what it is about Cullen. The more sex we have, the more I want him. Last night we bickered like a married couple and then made up like one. The feel of him, smell of him, his touch, his looks—I'm addicted to all of it. Isn't it supposed to be the opposite with a fling?

Now we're walking across the lobby, heading out to my waiting car, when Cullen checks me out rather blatantly. "Now you decide to wear the white dress?" His breath is hot against my ear.

"Makes me look innocent."

"On what planet?"

"Yours," I mouth.

He smiles, and that smile kills me. "Want me to phone the pilot and tell him you'll go home tomorrow?"

"We discussed this already. I have to get back." *And I thought you would come with me.*

That was the first plan anyway.

He drapes his arms over my shoulder and presses his forehead to mine.

"I'm sorry." He looks sincere. "If I don't play this out, I won't have a seat at the final table."

I nod. "I know." I sigh, disappointed as I drink in his gorgeous features and those hypnotizing Silver Eyes one last time.

He's drinking me in too. Intently. And when he speaks, his voice is deep and solid.

"Wynn. The bet . . . there's more to the story. You bring me luck, sure, but luck had nothing to do with why you ended up on my plane. I'm not playing games with you, Wynn. I wanted you. I still do." He holds me by the waist against him, cupping my cheek. "I'll be at your show, Red. I promise."

I catch my breath, absorbing what he has said. Does he mean . . . does he want to continue? Does he want *me* like I want him? "What if they move the qualifier again?" I whisper, dreading to hope.

"They won't move the qualifier again," he assures.

"And if they do?"

"I'll still be there."

I feel lightheaded and weak, giddy and revived. He's staying in Vegas only to qualify and coming back . . . for me. And maybe it's because he also feels . . . come on! Am I really considering . . . what? Playing happily-ever-after with Cullen?

My heart hurts at the thought, and I hate that he's making it hurt.

I mean this guy, he kisses his friends.

He *is* a friend.

Or he was . . . At the moment, he feels like everything. In the space of a few days, he's become everything.

"Red . . ." he warns, smiling down at me.

I exhale. "Good luck. Keep me posted. Okay?" I laugh, a little in encouragement, a little to cover the fact that I miss him already. Before I turn to leave, I whisper, "Cullen?"

I want to tell him that I want him, want this. To tell him I want it beyond reason.

But all my past heartbreaks, and a feeling of impending doom, weigh down on me. I hate that I can't be sure if he'll look at me like this if he knew everything about me. I try to shake it off, because I don't want to leave on a bad note.

I go up on tiptoes and drop a kiss on his lips. "Thank you for the most fabulous trip of my life. Go get it, champ."

Before my emotions get the best of me, and the knot in my chest expands to my throat and does shit to my eyes, I turn and walk away, feeling the unmistakable weight of Cullen's gaze as he watches me leave.

I don't want to leave.

I want him to *stop* me.

I want him to *come* with me.

But he doesn't because he has another game to play. And I have my own job to do.

But as Oliver drives me to the airport and the distance between us stretches, my smile begins to falter, and my chest begins to ache harder and harder, and my eyes don't feel as dry as they should in the Las Vegas heat anymore.

I can't believe I was able to hold it together in front of him. Maybe I did learn quite a few things in Vegas, after all. I learned to bluff like a pro.

I feel off when I board his plane. All the excitement of Cullen's lifestyle isn't exciting without him.

The week before I was flying out to Vegas with Cullen and wondering what it must be like to fly on this jet alone.

Now. I. Know.

And I wish I didn't.

More than anything, I wish the little boy and his mother hadn't chosen our very last night together to bump into us. I wish I hadn't seen Cullen's face as he wished for things he didn't have.

There's nothing I can do.

I refuse to think about the family I can't give Cullen. I think, instead, about the week we spent together. I slow it down. Play it in reverse. Shopping, strip poker, and romantic dinners. And how we partied all night, feasting on one another as if sex were our drug and the only fix we needed was another round of fucking.

"Ah jeez," I whisper, exhaling.

If I keep reminiscing, I'll never make it back to Chicago.

But it's lonely to be on a great big fancy plane, all alone and headed home. I replay the scene when I was leaving in that white dress he bought for me. The way he looked at me. He didn't pull me back. And I couldn't run back to him. The gallery will be a chaotic bubble of activity as we get ready for the upcoming show.

I need to be in Chicago.

Still, I feel like we should've said or done something more.

Maybe.

Then again, maybe not.

It was a bet.

I won. Maybe if I hadn't, he'd have come back with me as I'd hoped to help with my exhibit. Instead he's staying for qualifier, and I'm left with the best oral of my life and then some. And now it's over . . .

I knew it would have to end.

Didn't I?

"Miss Watson, are you ready?" The pilot looks at me, and I nod quickly and inhale.

"I can't . . . breathe. Is there enough oxygen in here?" I wave at myself.

Suddenly, I feel like I'm dying.

"Yes, miss." He smiles. "Everything is all right. Get ready for takeoff then."

I nod, but I still feel like I can't fucking breathe.

"Thanks," I say, strapping on my seatbelt. Trying to look calm when I am anything but.

He disappears into the cockpit.

I exhale and shut my eyes, telling myself to settle down and leave everything in Vegas. Isn't that how the saying goes?

What happens in Vegas, stays in Vegas. Whoever you do in Vegas, stays in Vegas.

My Cullen.

Ugh.

We had a silly wager.

That's all it was.

But I'm hooked on him, not because of what he is or how much he can spoil me.

It's because of who he is. Who I am when I'm with him. Who we are together.

Are we together?

An island unto ourselves.

It was the first thing I thought of when I saw Callan and Livvy. And it was nice to think of us that way. It was nice to have 'my person' and 'our island' and everything that went along with that. As the orange-and-brown hues of the horizon fade with distance, I feel my chest grow heavier and heavier.

The Nevada sand has now disappeared right along with Cullen.

I don't want it to be over. Maybe we're taking a break, a little breather.

Like Emmett and I used to take?

I swipe at my cheeks. "Don't be so theatrical, Wynn."

No. I shake my head.

Cullen and I aren't Emmett and me.

We're different.

We're better.

I've never been better with anyone. I stare out at the white-blue clouds. I'm all by myself again. I can't do anything more. I didn't tell him how I felt because I was afraid. I still am.

The odds were always stacked against us. We were the underdogs, the longshots, with odds at 35 to 1.

I would've still ended up on this flight bound for Chicago, returning to the life I know.

Is this why Malcolm and Rachel warned me? Is it why Callan had a 'talk' with Cullen?

Is the gambler's life a lonely road, an uncertain path into the luck-filled trenches of the next wager, the next game?

If so, there's no place for a significant other. Maybe there isn't room for anyone. Is that the real reason why he doesn't see his son?

Cullen's wrong. He's wrong if he thinks there's a difference between gamblers and poker players.

The game always comes first.

It will *always* come first.

There's a reason he's single, and yet I want him more than I can stand. Passion isn't our problem, though. Commitment is. And I don't want to go back into this relationship place . . . it has never ended up being a happy place for me. And Cullen . . . I don't think he's ever been capable of going there at all.

HEADS-UP

Cullen

My game is off. Wynn's gone and my luck went right out the door with her.

I want to call her, hear her voice, tell her . . .

Tell her what, man? Get it together.

I peer at my cards again.

"Humph. That's a first." James "The Original Shark" Johnson grins. "Playboy took a second look at his cards, guys. What's that tell ya?"

"Couldn't say for sure," Lucas Ingram says, swirling his glass and staring into his apple juice like it's straight-up whiskey. He frowns. "Come to think of it, you never check twice. What's up with that? You feeling okay?"

I've known the Ingram brothers for over a decade. Isaac is a horse's ass and Lucas never met a stranger.

Normally, I'd be thrilled to find Isaac's younger brother at my table. He's readable and not that great at cards. He's a 'luck' player and well, I don't believe in pure luck. You need skills to keep winning.

There's an exception, of course, and I'm staring at him.

When Lucas Ingram is on the other side of a deal, then everyone wants the same question answered—is he on or off?

When he's hot, the guys in player development stay away from him because he can break a casino in a matter of days, which is why big brother bankrolls him in the first place. It's good for business.

But when Lucas is off, man is he cold. And that's when everybody wants a piece of him.

Right now? I'm afraid he's about to take a bite out of me.

I look around to see if I can find Mike in the crowd, watching us, and when I come up empty, I find my answer.

Lucas is definitely on the take.

With my lucky charm somewhere between Las Vegas and Chicago, I can't be sure of how this all will play out.

Lucas travels with an annoying bunch of poker groupies. He uses them as a distraction. As soon as I spot a redhead in his bunch, I can't help but think of my sweet Red. The woman who twiddled her hair. The woman who was my greatest distraction.

God I miss her.

Without Wynn here, I feel like a shell of a man, an ordinary player who isn't even interested in playing. "Anyone seen Jack? Haven't seen him around for a while."

So I start talking. Lucas can't multi-task.

"Cavanaugh? Nope. Heard he's down big time," James says, whistling low.

I can't help but think I'd be in the same circumstances if I hadn't found my lucky charm. I wish Jack had a good woman in his life.

From what I've heard, he doesn't.

"Cavanaugh will be up soon enough. That guy's got more moves than a hooker," another player says.

Glancing up, I talk directly to Lucas now. "I heard you put together an underground team."

"Yep." He folds and leans forward in a conspiratorial manner. "Card counters. Why? You lookin' for a career change, Carmichael?"

"Nope. But I heard you're on a hot streak." I've also got an inside line on his casino deliveries and rumor has it that Isaac sent his kid brother a care package before his lucky streak began again. "Maybe it's time to come back to the dark side."

"Ah. I'm touched." He places his hand over his heart. "Hear that, boys? Carmichael misses me."

Frank, a player with several titles under his belt, says, "Ask yourself why that is, kid."

"He likes my company," Lucas says, always under the impression that everyone loves him. He turns to the girls. One or two blow him a kiss.

He's feeling the love.

I smile at myself. So what, timing is lousy for me, terrific for him. It doesn't matter much. Not today.

"That flop looks made to order," a tourist says, tossing in a few black chips in a lame effort to represent the straight flush.

There's an eight, nine, and ten of spades on the flop. I've got the nuts with the jack and queen of the same suit. Tourist just lost credibility.

I think about Wynn, and maybe my luck won't tank altogether.

"So tell me about the girl," Lucas says. "I hear you've spared no expense for her. Rumors around here say she may earn the title of Mrs. Any truth to it?"

The two of hearts is on the turn.

"Why? Are you taking notes?" I raise.

"Not even." Lucas rolls his eyes and folds. "So she's from Chicago."

"Is that a question?"

"Is it serious?" he continues.

I know why he's asking.

"Tell Isaac that Wynn's having a show next Saturday." I can't help myself. I'm the devil he knows so I say, "Wynn and I hope to see him there."

It happens just like that and it's that easy.

I'm all-in, staking a claim and making it count.

When I push away from the table and stare down at Fifth Street, it hits me. I'm laying everything on the line now and it's not for a bet that left me well positioned. It's for a beautiful woman who had me wrapped around her little finger long before first introductions.

What the hell was I thinking?

I never should've let her leave Vegas without me.

TELLS

Wynn

I feel better reaching Chicago.

"Look at you!" Gina greets me as soon as I step off the plane.

Rachel is there, too.

My girls circle me and I almost cry. I'd forgotten how much I need my friends nearby, not because I look at them as a support system. It's not that at all. I need them because life is sort of empty without them.

"So tell us," Rachel says, popping the trunk so the pilot can store my luggage. "How was Vegas?"

"You've talked to Livvy?"

"Of course she's talked to Livvy," Gina says. "*I've* talked to Livvy."

"She's your sister-in-law," I say. I turn and smile at the pilot. "Thank you for a lovely flight."

I start to tip him but Rachel shakes her head. Once he's gone, she says, "Cullen's already taken care of it. Saint would flip if I tipped his pilots. I'm sure Cullen is no different."

"Cullen?" I gasp. "How do you know about Cullen?"

"That's not the right question." Rachel scowls, then looks at Gina. "Questions are overrated anyway. An apology is in order. Don't you think? Wynn! You flew in on Cullen Carmichael's Citation X!"

"Oh absolutely," Gina teases, lowering her voice. "Are you insane? You go to Vegas with Cullen *Fucking* Carmichael? What were you thinking?"

"I wasn't."

Rachel sighs as if she detects the sorrow in my voice. "He's the hot guy from the underground casino. Isn't he?"

"Yes."

"Well then, that's understandable," Gina admits with a waggle of her brows.

"Don't tell Tahoe she said that," Rachel says, starting the car as soon as we're all buckled up and ready to go.

"Oh, Tahoe knows he's way hotter." Her eyes flicker dreamily. "Trust me. He isn't worried."

"Why would he be?" Rachel laughs. "I mean, do you guys ever get out of bed?"

"Shh. This isn't about my sex life." She shoves her thumb past her shoulder, indicating me. "It's all Wynn. And *Cullen*."

Hearing his name makes me long for my Silver Eyes. I debate if I should keep some of our more explicit moments to myself. It seems wrong to talk about them when there are so many unresolved feelings, emotions boiling right under the surface and threatening to make me implode.

"So . . . tell us everything!" Gina turns sideways to look at me in the backseat.

"He's . . ." I sigh. "Perfect."

"Oh no," Rachel groans. "Please tell us you didn't go to Vegas to get over Emmett and came back in love!"

Outside, the sky flickers with the occasional star and I feel nostalgic. I wonder what Cullen's doing. Hoping he'll win his poker game. So it will all be worth it.

"Anyone in there?" Gina waves her hand in front of my face. "Hello?"

"I'm a mess." I state the obvious.

Rachel adjusts her mirror. "Wynn. Tell us you're not totally in love."

My eyes feel suddenly stingy and I'm sure it's some sort of allergy I picked up during the flight. I blink a little, and huff, and I'm almost ready to tell them everything, tell them how I had it all and threw it away because of my fears and Cullen not really being into this like I am but then my phone rings.

"Hang on," I say to the girls. "It's probably Mom. I haven't talked to her since I left for Vegas."

"Hello?"

"Wynn?"

My heart drops. "Emmett?"

"Yeah, can you talk?"

I blink and glance frantically around the car at my friends, holding my breath when Rachel pulls over. She parks the car and she and Gina turn around to read my face.

"Actually, Emmett, I think we've both said what we needed to say," I state, deliberately slowly, into the phone.

And I do something I've never done in my life. I pull my cheek away and press the "end call" button.

"That was Emmett?" Gina cries, clearly glad I hung up and equally shocked about it.

I feel a strange twinge in my heart. Because it wasn't the male voice I wanted to hear on the other end of the line.

Ugh.

I glance down at my phone as it buzzes.

And it's a text. From Emmett again.

We need to talk.

I reread the text, my stomach tied up in knots of anger. I mean, really? Does he have nerve or what?

"What does he want?" the girls ask.

I stretch out my phone and show them the text.

"Wow, the nerve of him," Gina says.

My stomach hurts when I remember. "I'm physically repulsed by the idea of being romantically involved with him again."

"What's done is done, what you grew from the experience is grown. What he showed is shown. It's over. Don't answer," Rachel says.

I pause. "Should I answer something short and nasty?" I consider it. I really do.

"Why open a window for discussion? The end will be the same. You're over him. He threw you away, and you're finally back on your feet," Gina says.

"You're right. Delete."

I delete the text. And I feel good. I feel empowered.

I always wondered if he'd ever reach out but always worried that when he did, I'd feel weak. I'd be tempted to go back—to go back searching for a sign that he'd actually cared, that none of it was a lie. But I'm not in love with him, not anymore. Maybe I never was. Certainly not in the way I have feelings for another guy now.

Gina and Rachel look at each other, perplexed, before Gina gives me a stern glare as if to say, "What is going on, though?"

"It's complicated."

How to explain to them?

I miss Cullen like my morning coffee, a ritual I can't do without. If I skip my morning cup, the rest of the day is screwed. Is that how I see Cullen? As the man who came into my life and fucked up the rest of my days?

Is this—whatever this is—as serious to Cullen as it is for me?

If so, then his big game is so screwed.

I look at my besties, hoping they have words of encouragement because I can use some advice.

Gina sighs. "Okay. Start over. Let's go back to where we were before Emmett called and that look of near-retching appeared on your face. Let's go back to the swoony face you were wearing when you landed because Cullen stole your heart."

"He didn't," I lie. "We're friends. We had a moment in Vegas and it was fun and sexy and hot as . . ." My voice trails.

Whatever it was . . . it ended.

Whatever it could've been . . . it's over.

For both our sakes.

Gina reaches over the seat and takes my hand. "Start at the beginning and tell us everything."

"I don't know where to start." I want to tell them that I've fallen for my own playboy and that I need to break it off. That I need to go off him, like a drug.

"Oh that's easy," Rachel says, deliberately trying to keep things light. "Just start with the sex."

WIN AND WYNN

Cullen

With my damn seat at the championship now secured, I tell Mike that I'm checking out tomorrow. I hang up and start packing, wondering what Wynn's doing. I reach for my phone to call her the second my ex's name lights up the screen.

Perfect.

"Hi, Sondra."

"Cullen."

"Glad you returned my call," I greet. "I wanted to see Adam next weekend. I've got a big tournament and I'd like to spend some time with him after my big win."

"I don't think so, he'll be busy doing homework. I wasn't really returning your call, I'm calling because we need to discuss an allowance for Adam. He's playing sports now, Cullen. And Mr. Baxter thinks he has a real gift for the cello."

"The cello?"

"Yes, Cullen. You do know what a d minor—"

"Stop," I grate out. "How much?"

"Six thousand a month should do it."

"What?"

"You have the money, don't you? I mean, seems a shame that a big player like yourself wouldn't have the money. See? That's the reason there was no way I'd ever consider being with—"

"Stop. Right this minute or you will not get another damn dime from me."

Something just snapped. I didn't want to be the long-distance father anymore or the ex-boyfriend that Sondra calls whenever she wants to replenish her wardrobe.

I won't yield to her demands anymore. And I won't spend the rest of my life talking to her several times a week. Adam is old enough to pick up the phone and ask me for what he needs. He's old enough to answer my goddamned calls.

Call it stubbornness or too many years of playing Sondra Says.

I'm sick of living like this.

I think of Wynn. Hell, that look in her eyes when she saw a picture of Adam. That same look flashed on her face when the kid bumped into us the morning she left. I noticed the wistful expression on numerous occasions.

Wynn wants kids. I want her to be a part of Adam's life, nearly as much as I want her to play a part in mine.

"How DARE you speak like that to me!"

"You know what, Sondra? I was a kid when I fell in your honey trap, a real kid. Not even eighteen. And for the first time in over a decade, I'm going to say what you should've heard all those years ago."

"Oh? And what are you 'going to say' now, Cullen?" She coughs. "I can't hardly wait to hear this."

I'm reveling in this because it's a turning point. So for the first time in eleven years, I cross Sondra, and I do it for myself, for Wynn, for my son, for the family I've never had.

"I'll see you in court, Sondra."

"You'll what?"

"I'll see you in court. You're not keeping me away from Adam now. He's older and he needs his father. And I need him." And I want Wynn to know Adam. I think they'll like each other very much.

I disconnect the call and settle in my chair. And as I close my eyes, my last thought is how much I need *both* of them.

I'm on the plane at sunrise. I like leaving the city at dawn. It's the only time when the place looks serene, at least to me. The sun is orange with a captivating ring of light blue clinging to its circumference and it looks like its cradling our plane as we fly east.

I swivel my chair to face Wynn's empty seat.

I lean my head back and groan at the tangled wire of emotions. When did my thoughts become a scrambled mix of Wynn and winning?

When did it get so damn hard to leave a woman's bed?

Or let her leave mine?

When did I begin to think in terms of 'us' instead of me?

I should've seen this coming from a mile away. From the dirty little dreams to our late night conversations, I've been treading thin air since the day I first saw her.

And that day . . . was absolute torture. I spot the wet bar and go there to stand, bending down to peer out the small window as we find our cruising altitude. That's when it hits me. I was standing right about here when I realized she was the ONE.

What the hell is happening to me?

I return to my seat and drag both hands through my hair. I'm staring at *Wynn's* chair and inhaling the rich fragrant leather, angst-ridden because I can't catch her scent, that quiet smell of lust and sex and expensive perfume.

I wish we were at the start of our trip all over again.

She was excited that day . . . and maybe a little scared. And I wanted to fuel that excitement and replace that fear with utter joy.

Fuck, Cullen, get with the program. She's not here and you'll soon have a game to play.

What can I do to get her out of my blasted head? Forget the way her sexy little body tensed the first time I touched her, the way her wide eyes followed mine as I pressed my finger against her damp panties.

That look was damn priceless.

I dream about her. Hell, I dreamt of her before I ever held her in my arms.

The thing is, I never saw Wynn's face in those dreams but yeah . . . I intuitively knew she was the one there arching, moaning, singing that beautiful O song.

I can't help but grin now. No one sings *that tune* in a better pitch. When Wynn opens her mouth and lets the pleasure have her, those sounds are better than the act itself.

Well maybe not better . . .

FUCK. I'm hard thinking about it. Hard because I want her there with me. HARD because if she were there now?

She wouldn't have to ask about the Mile High Club.

She'd earn her damn wings.

SHUFFLING

Wynn

I've been busy with Pepper getting everything ready this past week, busy unpacking crates full of paintings and having them stretched and hung. I'm exhausted, and still can't seem to get a good night's sleep. There's been no word from him. Is he over me already? Did he get some other lucky charm? One who sits on his lap and claps when he wins or goes down on him or something?

Ugh. I'm so jealous I can't stand it.

I flip over in bed and grab my cell phone. No messages.

When Cullen and I first met, he was determined to help me get over Emmett, like it was his duty and mission. Now I wonder if there's anyone out there who can help me get over Cullen?

Why did I fall for this guy? Why didn't I listen to Livvy when she tried to tell me to stay away?

Why'd I listen to my heart?

Why didn't I listen to my head?

I groan and stretch. If I don't get some sleep now, I'll never make it tomorrow.

It's my biggest gallery exhibit and I can't blow it because I'm mourning a guy who tempted me with a love that never was.

I can't do this, not now.

Cullen seems like a lonely creature by nature. Pining over our times in Vegas won't do, especially when it won't happen again.

Later, after the exhibit . . . then I can toss and turn and dream about my sexy and lovely Silver Eyes.

Yawning, I just need . . . sleep.

He leans down, his breath skimming my ear as his fingers trace the line of my back. "Wynn? Are you awake?"

Cullen: I groan his name out softly and I snuggle closer to his warmth, dragging his arm around my waist and tracing the thick veins in his hand.

His cock mashes against my butt and I want him to drag me up to all fours, want him to sear me with his kisses. Those sweet kisses he places along my spine and shoulders, nape and cheek.

What is he waiting for?

My body is alive and sensitized. I flip over and stare up at him, seeing the hunger and desire and unmistakable need. God, I love how he looks at me, how he watches me.

No one has ever looked at me like HE looks at me.

I'm dying for him.

And he knows it.

He drags me to his lap and teases me with the lightest touches against my hip. I groan at the feel of his cock, starting to kiss him all over. From his throat, dropping a line of kisses down the center of his chest, and lower. Lower . . .

He groans. "God, yes, baby," he says when I curl my hands around his thick length.

And I think . . . oh yes, please, now! He shouldn't have had to wait this long.

I eye that gorgeous, straining piece of male flesh. My mouth is watering. I'm dying to taste, dying to lick that speckle of translucent moisture straight from the pulsing head.

I dip my head and my tongue snakes across the crest, pulling him to my lips.

My smoldering-hot Cullen. He tastes like . . .

"Wynn! Damn it, wake up!"

Gina shakes me so hard I swear some bones might snap.

"What is it?" I'm startled awake, looking around in panic until I spot her. "What are you doing here?" I yank the blankets over my head. "Whatever happened to a little privacy?"

"Hurry!" She yanks me straight up and throws clothes and towels at me as she rushes me to the bathroom and slams the door. "And I don't know who you were doing in that dream, but hurry and finish him in the shower!" She laughs. "Pepper has been trying to call you all day!"

"What?" I stare at my surroundings, blinking wildly at the vanity and towels and shampoo and soap. "What time is it?" I stick my head out to see if I can see the clock on my nightstand.

"Four o'clock." She shoves me to the bathroom once again and slams the door. "And don't worry. Pepper's in charge. Saint and Rachel are there now helping her. Take a minute to pull yourself together. You have time."

I open the door again and tilt my head in the air. "Do I smell coffee?"

"From about five hours ago. Full pot. Untouched. Guess your timer didn't shake you. No wonder. Whoa. What a dream you must've been having." She gives me a gentle look of understanding. "He's not worth this, Wynn. You've waited for this day. It's your *big day*. Don't let him ruin it."

I slam the door in her face. Behind closed door, I call out, "He didn't ruin it. You did that all by yourself when you woke me up!"

"Ha! I had to shake you out of it before I got an eyeful of something I wouldn't soon forget!"

I open the door and glower again. "Don't you have a husband to do?"

She shrugs. "Checked him off this morning."

"Such a chore," I tease. "But seriously? I can take it from here, thank you very much. Give me forty minutes?"

"Wow. Must've been some dream."

"What can I say, he brings out the best in me."

"See you at the gallery," she calls out.

It doesn't take long to pick up where my dreams left off, but the hot water rolling across my back and hips does nothing to soothe the ache or still the burn.

I need my hot gambler and those wicked silver eyes.

I need Cullen . . . every thick and delectable inch of him.

And my heart needs him just as much.

ANTE UP

My beautiful gallery is my dream come true. I can't believe I nearly slept through my alarm because of Cullen, plus I was up so late last night going over all the details and final touches for the show.

We're showcasing ten of New York's top up-and-coming contemporary artists and everyone who's anyone will be here. Lifestyle bloggers and pretty much every new journalist in the city lines up for their press badges. While I want to keep the elusiveness about our show, I also don't want to turn away those who can make me or break me.

My artists deserve exposure.

We're giving them as much as they can stand.

When I arrive, I'm glad to find that all of the volunteers, including my friends, are performing their delegated duties smoothly according to the schedule I painstakingly made for tonight's exhibit.

"Hey, guys." I greet Rachel and Saint, joining them at the champagne fountain. "Thank you so much for helping tonight."

"That's what friends are for," Rachel says, giving me a sideways hug.

"Don't mention it," Saint says, nodding at the door as a few of his rich friends enter. "I brought a couple of friends. Let me say hello first, then I'll introduce you."

"Act like you know them," Rachel says. "We sent the invitation on your behalf, remember."

"Of course." I roll my eyes. "I've been in Vegas. I didn't lose my sense of business while I was away."

"Just checking."

I lean to her, tongue in cheek. "I was well fucked. It gave me inspiration and a lot of motivation."

"I'm sure," Rachel replies drolly.

I drag in a breath and whisper, "If you only knew . . ."

"I have some idea. You've spent most of your time in bed recovering since you returned," Rachel says, laughing. "Now come on. Tonight isn't about your Playboy. You're going to pose with your guests, give these bloggers something to report, and make Mr. Carmichael eat his heart out when he turns on his computer tonight."

"It's a nice thought." Even as I say it, I know better. My *Playboy* is probably pulling up a chair to another poker game by now.

I hope you kill it, but I'm killing it even more tonight. Art is art, after all. I breathe out roughly and in a barely audible voice, whisper, "Wow, now I'm talking to him in my imagination?"

"To who?" A rough voice behind me makes me turn around. A part of me is hoping desperately to find Cullen and yet greatly disappointed when I find Isaac instead.

To make matters worse, Pepper is looking at him like he just brought in takeout from Wings on the Corner. I could wring her little neck, but decide there will be time to steer her away from this guy later.

"Good evening, Mr. Ingram. Thank you for coming."

"Thank you for the invitation." He's cool, distant. And for some reason, I don't remember inviting him.

"I ummm . . ." Can't find the right words.

He holds out his arm and leads me to the side. "I'm interested in several charcoals. I'd like to discuss them privately?"

Great. Just what I need at the start of my show. Someone who wants to drag me out of the spotlight.

"Smile!" A petite blonde runs up, flashes her camera, takes a few shots, and while I'm trying to regroup, I realize that I looked like a deer in headlights.

Gina and Tahoe are coming in behind her. I wave them over and Gina holds up a finger then points at the champagne fountain.

Who ordered a champagne fountain anyway? Won't that be expensive? And doesn't it look cheap?

Too many things are going on but I grab Isaac and the little blonde at the same time. "Can you take another shot, please?" I grit my teeth and instruct Isaac. "Lean in and act like you're having a good time."

"I am."

"Then don't frown," I hiss.

"I don't know how to smile."

"Then think about my assistant over there. She's looking at you like you're sex and candy all wrapped up in one."

The look on his face is priceless but I'm not sure it's a smile. It doesn't suit him, but I think I looked like the gallerist, professional and polite.

Plus, the picture will drive Cullen wild.

He continues to frown before he says, "You're probably wondering who invited me."

"I am," I admit, waving at Mr. and Mrs. Benson, an older couple responsible for buying my first painting. I'm relieved they're here. They'll buy.

"Cullen."

My heart leaps at the mention of his name, and my stomach coils up like a pretzel. "Yes, Cullen is . . ." I pause, shake my head, and say, "Why are we discussing Cullen?"

"He invited me . . . by way of Lucas."

"I'm sorry. I don't know who Lucas is?"

"My brother. He's quite fond of Cullen. He's the big brother he probably wishes he had."

"I see."

As if cued, the music playing in the background is from Lady Gaga and "Poker Face" is piped into the gallery.

"Anyway . . . I assume he'll be here." He hesitates, taking in the way my face suddenly goes pale, before he says, "Listen. I don't know if I can help because there's a big difference in waiting for a brother and waiting on a lover. If you need to use me some other time, you know where to find me."

My stomach caves in, and I don't want my disappointment to ruin my evening. I inhale deeply, trying to feel calm and happy. Proud of myself, which I am. Never mind that I wanted him to be proud of me too, for some reason. I wanted him to watch me work this room and admire me the same way I watched him work those cards and admired his savvy.

"Thanks, Isaac," I whisper, thinking he probably didn't hear me. I should've pushed him off on Saint. Malcolm is great at making his friends throw down the plastic.

My back is against the wall and I notice a shadowy figure at the end of the hallway, talking to Rachel and Saint. He moves away from them and starts across the room, and my eyes widen. Disbelief and excitement streaks through me as I register the height of him, the breadth, the shade of his hair, the features of that figure.

All free eyes land on him.

But his eyes are on no one else but me. He runs them over my figure in blatant appraisal as he strides forward. My knees start wobbling.

Sensations tangle together as I try to continue on as if nothing monumental has happened. Is happening. I'm not sure I can do this right now—melt for Cullen right here, in my real world, in my gallery.

I don't move. I can't move.

Cullen.

My heart is near exploding.

Cullen-fucking-Carmichael.

Our eyes hold.

The hammering in my heart turns to thunder. Impossible to soothe.

He frowns at a point in the darkness, and I know Cullen is frowning at Isaac behind me.

Damn him.

I want to yell and scream for making me lose control of myself but my body is already too defiant. I'm not in control here.

He is.

It makes me angry, it makes me rebellious, it makes me feel fierce and like challenging him for making me feel like this.

I don't speak. I shouldn't have to. Cullen stops before me, his scent making me dizzy, his gaze roving over my face as he tips my face back to study me.

"So is this how it's going to be?" he finally asks, quiet but harsh, towering over me, his hands on my shoulders. He's looking down on me. His poker face on.

I clench my fists, dig my nails into my palms. He tilts my chin up. "Red?"

I look into his eyes, those hot silver eyes, the eyes that I love watching as he's thrusting inside me, eating me up, kissing me madly.

This man is my ruin. He's my ruin because no other man will ever compare enough to even make the sliding scale.

"Answer me."

"What do you want me to say exactly?" I'm tempted to tell him about the shower sex he didn't enjoy, about the fantasy sex, the *my mouth on his cock* dream that he didn't get to experience.

"Is this the way it will be if I don't do what you want me to do, you'll what—find the next big Vegas whale and do your damnedest to make me jealous?"

"Are you?"

His lips twitch.

"What I thought." I duck under his arm, but he stops me . . .

"Come here, Watson, we're not done here . . ." His hand lands on my hip. He pulls me closer, his warmth surrounding me.

"I'm jealous. All right. I don't want anyone to share your days with you . . . only me . . . What you do to me, Wynn . . . Don't you see what's going on here? My game is off. I can't focus . . ."

"That's what I am to you," I remind him. "We're playing a game."

"You're playing a game." He shakes his head somberly, his poker face gone, his eyes livid with heat. "I'm playing for keeps."

"What?"

He nods, ever so slowly, as his hand lands on my hip. He pins me to the wall, gently kicking my ankles aside so he can stand between my legs.

I'm dying now. Dying when he rests his arm casually against the wall then places a kiss on my forehead and says, "Think the press will mind if I give you a little kiss?"

"Go for it," I whisper.

"Game. On."

Before our mouths meet, I already know I'm in trouble. I'm in trouble when his lips crash against mine and my body arches to his. I'm struggling to catch my breath as our tongues duel. We're both looking for the lead and if it's the lead we want, it's one we'll easily have.

Flashes of light explode around us as reporters move closer. The room falls still and quiet before the timeless energy is absorbed by a round of clapping and laughter.

I press my lips together and sort of fall forward, my hands balling in his shirt, more of an effort to hang on to him rather than push him away.

Malcolm Saint is a LIFESAVER when he stands in front of us and steers the onlookers back to the heart of the gallery.

Tahoe hangs back long enough to smirk and says something like, "Damn, kids, get a room."

I blush because that's probably what we'll see in the headlines tomorrow, but embarrassing news is better than no news at all.

At least *this* embarrassing news will be decadent and true.

I look up at my smoking-hot gambling man and whisper, "Now look what you've done."

He drags me forward a little bit and whispers back, "Wait until I have an hour alone with you then talk to me." He starts to saunter off but then hangs back for another axis-tilting kiss. His mouth is a whisper away when he says, "And Wynn? Don't taunt me . . ."

"Cullen," I groan, flushing.

Exhaling, I meet his gaze. The last thing I want to do is break this moment, but if there's anything as important to me as Cullen, it's my artists. I tug him around. "I promise we can pick this up later and then some, but right now, I have to introduce some incredible art to you, as well as to all my guests."

His eyes gleam with pride.

"Carmichael," Tahoe and Saint call out to him. Cullen pulls his gaze away from me and greets them. "Saint. Roth." They slap each other's shoulders, and Cullen glances at me as I let them have their space and get busy winding around the room.

I can't help but FEEL Cullen looking at me as I greet my guests, and I'm working it extra hard for some reason. Not just for my artists and me. It's as if I need him desperately to see what a bigwig gallerist I am.

I can't believe he came.

He's driving me home after the last customer leaves and Pepper and I are able to close. I'm aching for my gambling man so hard that when we arrive at my building, I tell him where to park and lead him upstairs as if someone's chasing us. Maybe our hormones. Maybe all these days without him. Maybe our hearts. I sigh when I've finally got him inside my apartment. All mine. *All* for me.

Though Silver Eyes looks at me as if it's vice versa. Like I'm all his. All for him.

"This is my place. It's a little messy . . . with the whole gallery opening . . ."

I realize Cullen looks terribly masculine in my feminine space. The space seems too small. The scent of his cologne fills it right up.

I flush.

He notices.

His stare is teasing as he reaches around me, pulling me close to him.

As soon as I gasp, he brushes his mouth over mine, dropping one kiss on my lips. I sizzle as if I've been set on fire. I go up on tiptoes. Cullen leans down for another kiss. This one he finishes with a small, delicious bite on my lower lip. I squeeze deep inside with longing, parting my lips, inviting him to do more damage.

He repeats this kiss—biting me again, pulling back my lower lip from my teeth, sucking gently, causing damage to my whole being. I groan and slip my hands around his neck, then slide them down the front of his chest, aching to touch him.

His hand roams up and down my back while he hungrily nibbles on my mouth and removes my silky gold top. My lace-clad breasts are revealed. He lets my top fall at our feet and his eyes smolder on me. "So gorgeous," he growls, covering my breasts with his bare hands. Sending that same heated look to both my nipples as they salute him.

He tweaks both peaks at the same time. And he watches my expression as he does. I gasp in delight, the pleasure like streaks of white thunder shooting up my veins. His eyes darken as he takes in my reactions. His lips curl, and he does it again, tweaking.

"Oh god. Cullen!"

I nudge him, but when he doesn't budge, I grab his ass, fill my hands with the muscles there, and pull him toward me.

He growls and dives down to bite my lips again, kiss them. *Suck* them.

This kiss becomes more heated, less controlled. We're both breathing hard. I can feel him getting wilder, more possessive, more alpha.

He unfastens his belt buckle, his button and his zipper.

His muscles ripple with his movements and I clutch all over when his belt clatters to the floor. I'm imploding with desire and yearning and something so fierce, I don't even understand the feeling.

I look at Cullen and want to press so close that we're literally one.

I've jumped from guy to guy my whole life, knowing what I need, but never finding it, never feeling like I get it. Now this man is here and he is all I want. I'm so hooked on him that all I want is to give him everything I've got and then some.

I kiss his lips. He kisses mine. He smiles down at me with my favorite smile, masculine, arrogant, elusive—the smile that makes my heart turn in my chest.

There's a question in his eyes as he removes my hairclip. I nod in answer as my hair tumbles to my shoulders. He looks at the red strands with appreciation.

"You don't want him," he murmurs, and then his fingers move under the fall of my hair at the back of my neck.

His eyes are possessive, challenging, as if daring me to keep taunting him with Isaac. With any other man.

My breath catches as his fingers slide under the front of my chest. Fingertips on my skin. The surprising tenderness in the hot, hungry lips on the side of my neck break through all my walls.

I turn my head, parting my lips for him. His palm opens on my cheek. Pinning me in place. And his lips seize mine. I gasp.

He unfastens my bra, and then he yanks it away. I clutch his head at the soft swirl of his tongue over my nipple. "Fuck, oh . . ." I gasp.

His breathing changes, desire clouding his anger.

"You're angry but it isn't me you're angry with," I breathe.

"Trust me. I'm angry at you. I'm fucking pissed at you. You were trying to make me jealous on purpose, Wynn. I don't like it when people play games with me."

"Yes, you *do*," I groan.

I grab his sweater and pull it over his head. His chest beneath my fingertips is smooth and strong. His mouth more voracious over mine. Cullen pulling me closer. Cullen boosting me up in his arms. My mouth on his jaw, neck, fingers on his chest. Muscled, gorgeous chest.

His lips sucking my earlobe. Him whispering, "You gorgeous redhead." Fingers easing under my underwear, stroking my folds. Entering me. I'm gasping in his throat. "You beautiful, sweet redhead, don't you know you've been claimed already? Fucking marked already. You're fucking owned already." He inserts two fingers, then three.

I groan, out of breath, out of my mind.

He presses me up against the door, pushes my skirt up higher and opens my thighs wider, pushes his fingers in deeper, his thumb rolling my clit.

I'm thrashing.

The addictive noises he makes as he licks, bites, and nibbles on my skin undoing me even more.

His warm breath on my cheek. Holding my head and kissing me more, the kiss painfully raw and bruising and slowing down into one that's achingly hungry and slow.

The sound of him dropping his pants. His gaze rises and lashes into me. His erection stretched to its fullest length.

Every touch burns.

The slow surge of his body into mine—his chest as hard as the wall. My hands empty at my sides, I fill them with the hard planes of his muscles as I open my thighs wider.

The increase in his speed. Faster and faster. Pulsing, surging waves crash through me. I smell him, all around me, cologne and soap.

My gasping sobs in his ears.

Holding his jaw and pulling him, closer and closer. The sound of me, crying out. His heavy breaths, as fast as mine.

And the moment I lift my eyes to find him staring straight into mine with a look of wild tenderness in his eyes.

We spend the night all over each other, and late the next morning, I crave to feed my man my best recipe. I cook him my famous cauliflower hash browns, along with Applegate's turkey sausages. Organic and the best. He devours them and I smirk, thinking, *hmmm, he needs the energy to keep his stamina up.* As if he reads my mind, Cullen sets down his utensils. He pushes his chair back with a screech, and crooks his finger.

Just like that. He summons me to his chair.

My heart skips. I can't resist him.

Rising from my seat, I cast my breakfast aside. I settle on his lap. Then I'm kissing him and he's kissing me. Slow but deep. Within seconds, neither of us can breathe.

He makes me weak. I'm trembling with need, but luckily, he's not weakened. He lifts me up and carries me to bed, where we spend the rest of the morning.

"I have lunch with my father," he says when we're done, pecking my lips as he forces me to uncurl my body from his.

"Awww. That's sweet. I'll see you later?"

"It'll have to be night. I've got a packed day. Meeting with an architect to discuss my plans for a hotel in Vegas."

I sit up, wide-eyed. "What? Cullen, that's amazing."

He grins. "I know."

He walks forward, setting his lips on mine. "I'll see you tonight?"

"My friends said there will be a get-together to welcome the honeymooners back."

"How about we meet there?"

"But everyone will notice . . ." I halt when he looks at me as if he doesn't care.

Feeling myself flush as I smile, I devour him with another kiss before he leaves, then I lie back in bed, smiling from ear to ear, never feeling so sexy and delicious in my bed.

FULL HOUSE

'm at Rachel and Saint's with the gang that evening, and I'm annoyed that Isaac is here because it's almost like my friends are pushing something that would be a disaster from the beginning. There isn't any chemistry there and I'm not sure why no one can see this except Isaac and me.

I grab a glass of champagne and head for my girls, ready to address the pending never-gonna-happen arrangement when the elevator dings.

Turning to greet the next guest, I sip from my glass and nearly choke on a bubble when the doors part and out walks Cullen.

He's not a surprise entirely. I mean, we said we'd see each other tonight. But he surprises me every time he keeps his word. And he's been keeping them non-stop.

My heart skips when he walks into the room and looks at me while I look back at him, not even concerned of anyone noticing. His stare is dark and openly admiring, a smile touching his lips.

I feel beautiful under his gaze.

"Do you know he's always happier when you're near?" Gina watches him.

"That can't be true." I shake my head.

"It's totally true. When he walked through these doors, there was this smile on his face. He's into you."

The way he looks at me, that's something I won't ever forget.

I exhale as I hold his gaze, admitting, "Emmett never made me feel like this. Cullen though . . ." I trail off, shaking my head in awe.

He continues approaching, and my mouth goes dry and I nervously gulp down the rest of the champagne, wondering if he'll brush off the others and make his way to me.

I don't wonder long. He nods at Gina and Rachel. Maybe he says hello but I don't hear him.

He's looking at me like I'm his and I can't help but feel an inkling of possession. He looks like he belongs to me as much as I belong to him.

I realize I shouldn't go there, I shouldn't let my mind go to this place, but it's no use. I'm already so drunk on this feeling of belonging to him, of being his girl, his woman.

"Hope I didn't keep you waiting long," he says, wrapping his strong arm around my waist and pulling me against his side. He kisses my forehead and whispers, "You're the most beautiful woman in the room."

And just like that, the anxiety I was feeling slips away. It's gone. Replaced by happiness and warmth and a sense of homecoming.

"You look nice," I say, refusing to leave his embrace for a while.

"Just nice?"

"Fucking amazing. How's that?"

"Better." He grins.

I bite down on my lip and glance down playfully at his crotch, knowing he likes our intimate little games. "I could've said, what do you say we leave this party behind and go fuck until sunup."

He tightens his grip at my back and whispers, "I'd rather stay between your legs, licking you from one orgasm to the next."

I gasp and hope no one hears. My tummy tightens. His words sound too much like a ravenous promise that I wouldn't mind him keeping.

"You wanna play? My turn." I stand on my tiptoes and whisper, "I'd rather have you stroking your length between my lips."

I walk away then, certain his eyes are on my hips as I re-join my friends who are talking about Rachel's mothering skills. Apparently, little Kyle loves reading his mother to sleep and once she closes her eyes, he'll give up the story and close his as well. Their little game has allowed Rachel and Saint more alone time.

"Just what you two need," Gina says. "More time in the bedroom. You'll be pregnant within a month."

"Not happening," Rachel says, turning to me. "And what are you doing over here with us when your man is over there looking like he wants to drag you off to the nearest bedroom?"

"We're mature adults," I tell her. "We can wait until we're alone."

"If you can't, third door on the right is the guestroom," Rachel teases. "Locks and everything."

"Does it have its own bathroom with running water, too?" I tease back.

The double dings announce another arrival and when the door parts, the happy couple enters.

We all cheer as Callan and Livvy gravitate to the center of the room. Everyone wants to hear about the honeymoon. They had a great time and want to share pictures and stories. We're all bewitched by Callan's new storytelling skills. Typically one who doesn't say a lot, he seems eager to share some of their tamer memories.

We're about three minutes into their arrival when Cullen's at my side, locking his hand around mine. Rachel glances down at our union and smiles and mouths, "Running water."

I laugh and Cullen asks, "What's that about?"

"I'll tell you later."

He nods at Saint then and I get the feeling that their insider secrets are similar to mine and Rachel's.

"What's that about?" I tease in a gruff voice similar to the one he just used.

"Why don't I show you?" he easily teases back.

"What do you need to show me?"

"Something you've never seen before."

"Oh, I've seen plenty, Mr. Carmichael."

"Not this." He takes my hand and drags me to the third door on the right. He holds out his arm. "After you, lovely lady."

"This is so inappropriate."

As soon as the door closes behind us, he's all over me. His eyes. His hands. His lips.

Good god, those lips.

"Cullen, we can't."

"We can but we won't," he whispers, his forehead resting against mine as he fumbles for something in his pocket.

"What are you—"

"Turn around." He hits the switch on the wall and the room lights up. We're in front of an oval mirror. He presses his lips to my shoulder and whispers, "I went shopping today."

"Did you?" I'm already so turned on from the kissing and groping that I'm only vaguely aware of his arms sliding around my shoulders.

"And I found a necklace that needed a woman."

"Cullen. You shouldn't—"

"Shh . . ." His lips brush my nape before he latches the necklace and stands back.

I'm touching a gorgeous diamond pendant set in a sea of emeralds. The platinum chain shimmers like it's been brushed in white gold or diamonds. I can't tell and it doesn't matter. What matters is the chain reminds me of Cullen's gorgeous eyes.

"It's beautiful." I touch the pendant and stand enamored, not with the jewelry, but the man. I face him. "I'll wear it everywhere and it'll always remind me of you."

His look turns serious. "You say that like you don't plan to see me after tonight."

"Don't be silly."

"I'm not a silly man."

"Where have I heard that before?"

His smile fades and he turns me to the mirror again, forcing me to watch him as his hand skims up and down my side, slower at the swell of my breast.

Fire settles in my belly.

Fire sizzles at the base of my spine.

Fire is in his kiss.

And his mouth is everywhere.

I curve my arm around his back to hold him closer as I arch against him.

"We can't."

"Oh, but we could," he whispers, nipping my earlobe while holding me against his straining cock.

"This started over a bet," I tell him.

"Fuck the bet," he growls, watching me.

And I see something in his eyes that I've never seen in him or anyone else. I giggle, go up on tiptoes, and give him the hottest kiss of his life. "I love it. I love—" My eyes widen when I realize what I was about to say. I start blushing.

Cullen is staring at me intently.

I can't believe I was about to say the L word!

There's passion and need, seduction and . . . oh god, I'm so in love with him I can barely take it.

I swallow as his mouth holds me captive. His eyes seduce me. I won our bet but I also won something more.

I won the man, a man who chose *me*, a player who should've been back in Vegas by now.

He'll still go back, Wynn.

He has to go back.

Knowledge is a bitch but passion is power and I'm not about to spoil the passion now by thinking about tomorrow. I've never loved a player but I'm falling for Cullen over and over again.

It's like we're new every time we're together.

My inner hussy rears her pretty little head and whispers, "But you're immune to love."

The thought makes me feel awful, because who did I think I was kidding when I thought I could resist him? I couldn't. No matter how much I wanted to stay away.

He picks me up and carries me to the huge cherry dresser where he steps in between my legs, framing my face with those decadent hands. His touch leaves me breathless and now . . . I want to cry.

Why do I want to cry? Because I can't forget the longing in his eyes when he looked at a mother and her son in Vegas.

"What's wrong, baby?"

"You. Me. You don't know what you're doing to me, Cullen."

"I think I do know."

"Then why do you keep doing it?"

"Because I want you." He steps closer. It's sweet, sexy, and intimate but not at all sex-driven. "I need you."

He uses his tender fingers to dry up my tears before he slips his hand down the back of my neck and presses his lips to mine. They're firm but tender and the kiss is sweet and passive, but that tenderness turns relentless and the kiss turns into a claiming.

"I want and need this," he whispers in my ear. "Tell me you need this too." He slips his hand between my legs, sliding it under my skirt as he captures my mouth and kisses the living daylights out of me. The pain out of me. The fear of whatever is happening between us out of me.

Until there is only one giant, tingling feeling—and it's all over my body. A fire shaking through me, under my skin, *in* my skin, in my veins, my tummy, the tips of my breasts, the warm spot between my legs that suddenly feels so swollen, it's uncomfortable.

"Cullen. My friends . . . your brother . . . they're right outside the door."

He shoots me a sexy look that says they can stay there. He doesn't care. He'll fuck me into tomorrow, love me straight through the night. Here or at my place or anywhere.

"We're leaving in an hour. Until then, look at me and know that I'm only thinking of fucking you, pleasing you." He steps between my legs once more and parts my knees, fingering the wet v of my panties. "I'll be right here, Wynn. All I'll see when I look at you tonight is the woman that I'll lay down later and love."

I'm trembling as I grab his hand, and pleadingly strain out, "Let's go meet the newlyweds."

He pulls me back against him, slapping a kiss on my temple as he whispers, "We're not done here yet." And then he lets me go.

Now what do I do? I wonder. I'm in too deep, but just as I know that I'm in dangerous waters, I understand he's treading there, too.

What am I supposed to do?

One of us is certain to drown. I can't let it be me.

I don't know how to love a gambler. I don't know if Cullen's a gambler or a player and if I'm being played. All I know is that I've fallen for my own playboy and while he sweeps me off my feet and makes me feel all these things that I never thought I'd feel, I'm all in and loving the idea of him.

I love the idea of us.

When I rejoin the party, Cullen is talking to Isaac. I pass them, determined not to look at Cullen for fear he'll give me one of those looks that sends me to the floor on buckled knees. I hear him tell Isaac that Lucas is on fire, playing well and winning a lot.

I don't want to think about gambling or Vegas or . . . my eyes meet his and as soon as we connect, the tension is there, the sizzle and the spice and the promises he made.

He's going to lay me down and love me.

I turn around, practically knocking into Livvy and Gina and Rachel.

"Uh-huh," Gina says. "Tell me you don't like that man quite a bit."

"Just a teeny bit," I laugh off with a shrug.

"She's being cautious," Livvy says.

"And were you cautious when you fell under the Carmichael charms?" Rachel teases her.

"Callan's irresistible."

"Cullen's . . ." I can't bring myself to finish what I wanted to say. My eyes meet his again and the heat passing between us is enough for everyone to turn and look at us.

"Damn, Saint. I thought you got those two a room," Tahoe says.

"So much for a private gaze-fuck," I say, hugging my friends. "I need to go."

"You got that right," Rachel says, laughing. "And I think you need to take him with you."

"She does," Cullen says, tucking me at his side when he comes to say farewell. "Ladies, it's always a pleasure." He hugs Livvy. "Glad you made it home, sister-in-law."

"Behave, brother-in-law."

We say our goodbyes and step into the elevator. I immediately glance up at the security cameras and shake my head.

"Why not?" he asks, his tense jaw flexing.

"I want you all to myself."

"And I don't want anyone to see what's only meant for my eyes."

I blush and the heat in my cheeks runs down my neck and chest. His compliment is like foreplay, brushing against me with a whisper of electricity.

The exquisite note of possession in his voice makes me feel alive, but I settle down when we're in the car, driving through the city, heading to my place with our fingers entwined, our hands warm to the touch.

We don't talk. We don't make promises now.

We're already in the moment, thinking about the forthcoming hours. And I'm also dreading the inevitable end that will send my hot gambler back to Vegas again.

ROYAL FLUSH

We arrive at my apartment. Cullen slings his coat over his shoulder as he walks around the front of the car. As soon as he reaches me, he slips the jacket around my shoulders and brings me against him, shielding me from the sprinkling rain.

Everything is so easy with Cullen.

He presses his kiss to my forehead and I feel cherished in some way, like I matter more now than I did the hour before. With Emmett, it was different. With each passing day, we were further apart.

Cullen and I seem to grow closer.

We're in the courtyard when a monsoon strikes, the peppering rain so forceful, it's like a hammering snow.

I squeal as Cullen drags me to the only overhang, a perfect little awning for one but we make it work for two.

"Where's your key and I'll run ahead and open the door!" He calls out to me as the rain slams against the concrete.

"It'll pass," I tell him. "This is typical in Chicago."

He runs his tongue over his lip, eyeing my mouth like he'll never be able to stand here without a heated make-out session.

"Be good," I say. "I have neighbors."

"Who shouldn't be spying on those who are out here weathering the storm."

"Is that what we're doing?"

"Ever fucked in the rain?"

"Um . . . no."

"Me either," he says, smiling as he tilts my lips to his. His kiss is sugary sweet and oh so tender. He smiles into our kiss, taking his time before turning up the heat. "You. Me. All night."

"Promises, promises."

He holds my head as he kisses me deeper, thrusting his tongue between my lips as he cradles me against him, protecting me from the gush of water rolling off the building's roofline.

"I don't care who sees me doing this." He tastes like champagne and sways against me like he might have sipped on the whole bottle.

Instead, he's sipping me. Drinking me in.

I hold him steady and rock with him as he moves us into a slow and easy grind, his cock pressing against me as my back rakes against the brick wall.

"Cullen."

"Not yet," he breathes, dragging his finger down the front of my dress. "I can't have my way with you here but let me just enjoy kissing you."

The knocking sound of the rain against the patio furniture sends a shiver down my body. We're out in the open, making out like no one's watching.

And Oh. My. Lord.

He kisses me crazy.

I'm rocking against him, dying to jump in his arms and enjoy a more primal time together. I want him taking me, plowing into me, ravaging my body, and feeding my dirty mind.

One hand is in his hair.

My lips slide up and down his neck.

One hand gets busy.

And he grins into the kiss.

"What about your neighbors."

"Fuck the neighbors. They should go to bed."

"Then grab it," he says, loosening the button on his slacks. But he doesn't lower his zipper and I know it's a dare. He wants to know how hungry I am, how eager I am to drive him a little bit crazy.

No one can see us. There isn't a camera around. There isn't a window nearby. And Cullen's broad shoulders block the view.

"I want on my knees," I whisper, pulling back to gauge that exotic expression on his face.

"Then we're definitely going upstairs," he whispers, catching my hand before I grab hold of his cock.

I nod once and press my key into his hand.

"I'll hold the door open." He's gone before I can grab another kiss.

And I'm standing there breathless, thinking, *Good Lord, Wynn. Since when have you become an exhibitionist?*

"Wynn!"

I peer around the wall and see Cullen waving me inside. And I run to him, splashing through puddles, and laughing aloud, loving my life even when I almost lose my balance.

But I don't lose my footing because Cullen is there to catch me and it's sweet and thoughtful and loving.

Even better, now that we're home.

We don't wait one bit. I pull him inside and he slams the door behind him.

His mouth crashes against mine and he tastes like temptation. And my body wants to be provoked. The seductress wants to be seduced, trapped by the many pleasures that he uses to tempt me, the kind I'll never be able to resist.

He lures me to a carnal and sinfully delicious feast with many tests and dares and oh . . . my . . . he is such a sexy and careful and diligent player.

My sexy player.

My Cullen Carmichael with the silver eyes and body that makes a woman, this woman, feel like a sinner because of the thoughts and desires and acts . . . good Lord, these acts.

His mouth is working its magic. His fingers thrum and coax and wake me up to joy like I've never known.

I'm free in his arms.

I'm a prisoner in his arms.

His body feels like an invitation to a private party, a tasty offer of sex and sin.

And I want that taste.

My lips and hands are busy as I slide to the floor, dragging every stitch of his clothing with me.

"Damn," he says, his eyes hooded. "What are you trying to do to me, woman?"

"Woo you," I croon, gently pumping him while admiring his wicked smile. "I dreamed of you." I kiss the tip. "This." Drag my fingers up and down the length of his cock.

His hips sway. "I'd like to hear more about this dream."

"I'd like to share it," I tell him, licking his pulsing head around and around. "Show you?"

"Please," he says, dragging his dick across the soft swell of my lips.

He looks like sex dipped in candy and chocolate, sweet as sin and rich and naughty.

I slide down the length of his beautiful and strong cock, riding him with my mouth, sucking him to my throat then rising to the tip again.

My tongue swirls and swirls. The way he hardens at my lips . . . he feels so *damn good.*

His hands are in my hair. He's wrapping my strands tightly in his hand, guiding me. He's taking his time but I want *at him.*

I'm greedy and I'm dying for a better taste, a spicy shot of his pleasure as my mouth stays with him, riding him to the finish. I want to give him what he gives me, that satisfying high that rocks with us in unmatched pleasure.

I'm greedy as I stare up at him, noticing the firmer planes of his handsome and strong face, his tight jaw, the undeniable pleasure in his eyes.

Sweet damn, the way he rocks against my mouth!

I suck him gently as he slides across my tongue. This is pure ecstasy. He is pure pleasure redefined.

I want and need him. I'm dying to feel him thrusting against me, working for that mad gratification, relishing in the seconds, moments, and oh yes . . . every last minute of pure and precious and raw friction.

I bob my head faster when I feel him pull away from me, not wanting it to end. Not wanting to give up. Not yet. Not when I need to feel him, *want to feel him*, giving *me* the control. Letting go of *his* control.

"Come here," he whispers, dragging me to my feet and bracketing his arm around my waist.

"I wasn't finished."

"You're killing me, Red." He kisses me senseless. Touches me until I'm crazy.

I need him inside me, fucking me, loving me . . . reclaiming me as his.

My arms go around his neck as he lifts me higher and cups my ass. "You're so damn beautiful." He buries his face in my tits, his tongue running from one nipple to the next, the suckling and petting driving me mad, leaving me to need and ache and . . . God, I'm about to beg.

I find an easy sway with him, wrapping my legs around his back in an effort to force the impalement. "Don't tease."

"I won't be rushed," he says, eyeing my pussy as he takes his time dragging the tip of his cock to my center, to my clit, and back again. "Maybe I should do this . . ." He releases my hand and thrusts a finger inside me, finger-fucking me until I'm dying, literally dying.

My mouth opens and closes with each swift and firm impalement.

He wears a naughty expression and it goes darker as he replaces his fingers with his cock. "You're mine, Wynn."

The first thrust is hard and virile and all male.

"Say it," he whispers.

I whimper as he pushes my hands above my head, clasping them on either side of the pillow. His hips move side to side as he screws me slowly and meticulously, driving inside me without one hint of speed.

I want to go wild with him, lock my legs around him and drive the passion but he's trying to tame me, trying to keep me grounded underneath him.

"I didn't hear you . . ." His mouth skims mine. His teeth nip at my tits as he pulls out, screws in again.

"Yours," I whisper, refusing to think of what this means. What he wants it to mean.

My breast is in his mouth. His tongue circles the tip as he watches me intently, stirring this frenzy.

"Give me more, Cullen."

"My greedy little angel." His crooked smile is destroying me as he keeps playing and teasing, pumping his cock inside me, withdrawing enough to kill me. He holds me down, eliminating my free will, but I don't want it. Don't need it. I've already conceded. This night he's in control, guiding the actions, plotting each stroke and every single move.

My body is quivering, quaking. I rise up, stretching my neck to his kisses. I want to come. I'm dying to come as he drives inside me and takes me again and again.

But he's not ready.

He leaves my lips and his impassioned kisses speak to me in a feverish manner, in a way that I easily translate into love and longing, acceptance and beauty.

What *is* he doing to me?

He's having his way with me.

He's letting me have my way with him.

The fucking changes in an instant, the sensuality of our bodies smacking together quickens. We're in the throes of it, the heated beats of passion. The pleasure is . . . I'm . . . he's . . . we're . . .

One.

"Fuck," I moan, not even aware that I've spoken until . . .

"Definitely, and you're damn good at it," he rasps, rolling to his back and sliding to my thighs again. Once he's there, his tongue is all over me as his fingers spin around my clit.

He sets me on fire. I'm ready to explode.

Under his touch, this touch, the one before and the one that will soon follow, I lose control.

He's mine. I'm his.

God, this is us.

We're rolling across the bed and fucking like we'll never stop and I can't stop. I'm at the end, rising to the peak, over the edge, DYING as he's loving me.

"Don't ever stop."

"I won't." He takes a serious oath and tone as we settle down and curl up together. "I can't." The silence is sending me into a heavenly and waiting sleep. "I love you, Wynn."

And just like that . . . I'm wide awake.

We're fucking at two o'clock and three, four o'clock and five.

I'm half here and half dreamy at eleven a.m. when he parts my legs and I guide him inside me. We're impossible together, so into one another that I can't help but wonder if my body will go into major withdrawals once he leaves for Vegas again.

It's then when I notice the time with wide eyes. That's why he woke me once again. That's why he's loving me like he'll never let me go.

Because he is . . . going.

And he will . . . leave.

He's leaving and I'm empty inside only I'm not . . .

I cry out in pleasure as he fires me up, rolling me into primal chaos, a carnal world of explicit and extreme satisfaction.

"What time do you go?" I ask breathlessly.

"Now," he whispers, dragging me into his arms and holding me tighter than I've ever been held.

"I'll . . ."

"Come with me."

"I can't. I have the gallery and . . ." I swallow back the realization that his world doesn't run parallel to mine. Nevada isn't over the state line. Las Vegas isn't down the street.

I'm quiet as I remember his last words at midnight.

He loves me.

He said it as if he thought it landed on deaf ears but I heard them. And savored them.

I savor them now.

He props his head on his hand and stares down at me. "I love you."

"No fair," I say, dragging my finger down his chest.

"You love me too."

I tense at that, and sit up in bed, pulling the sheets up to my chest. I can feel his gaze on me, and my eyes sort of feel a sting, but I don't want to cry right now.

"I can't have kids, Cullen! I can't give you a son or a daughter or a family. I can't give you what you need."

"Why? Fucking why?"

"Because I can't. I've seen several doctors, they all agree."

He shifts forward. "I knew this. I went all in with you from the start."

"What?" I'm shocked. "How could you possibly have known?"

"I'm a poker player. I'm good at reading people. I'm an expert at body language. You think I didn't notice it, clear as day, the day you told me about Emmett? You couldn't look me in the eye, you looked away. The way you phrased it, the way you moved was enough for me to know. You don't take a pill, you never once worried about a condom. You wanted me in you, and you didn't have to worry about anything else."

He reaches out and tips my face back, his voice raw.

"You make me happy. You fill that void in my life, Wynn. Just you. Traveling, hell, playing, no longer has any appeal if I'm to do it for no one but myself. Or if I'll share it with random strangers. I want to make you happy. It gets me off."

"I can't do this. We . . . this hurts, Cullen."

"Not as much as being away from each other."

"No, no, no," I deny, shaking my head, my heart crushed in my chest, his love and acceptance so alien I can't even accept that it's real, "This is over, Cullen."

"The fuck it is. You love me, Wynn."

"You couldn't wait for me to tell you on my own terms?"

I'm picking a senseless fight, an argument neither of us can win. It doesn't make sense to him but it means everything to me.

"No. Because you won't. Because you never fucking will. I'm leaving and you're staying here and you're going to overthink us and reconsider my gambling and our distance and . . . the fact that you can't give me children." He kisses me hard on the mouth. "And you won't tell me. And that's all right because you show me in other ways."

I swallow.

He looks at me, clenching his jaw.

My eyes sting and sting, a tear threatening to slip.

"I want you at the tournament, Wynn. Say you'll come." He looks at me, his voice low and thick and emotional. "This Saturday. My plane will be at O'Hare at two o'clock. Please be on it."

My voice is just as raw and emotional. "And if I don't get in?"

He doesn't answer at first, but sets a kiss on my cheek and whispers, "Get in. Take a risk, Wynn. On me."

Before I can stop him, he slides away from the bed and goes to shower. And I feel a little abandoned and hopeless and like the world is tilting and I can't stop the shift.

I'm on the outside, looking in and it . . . well, it sucks. Because I see how much he loves gambling and everything he puts into being a good player. He's dedicated because he's really great at it.

My eyes water as I stare at the red digits on the nearby clock. I'll never survive without him. I don't want him to go.

I'm already pulling away from him even before he goes.

I feel it in my heart.

I feel it in my soul.
Everything is dark and lonely.
This is me.
Without him.

BLUFF

I can't eat, sleep, think, without thinking of him. Being haunted by him.

I mean, this was all a bet. Only it wasn't.

I care about Cullen. Maybe even love him.

Really, Wynn? It's a *maybe*?

Right.

I so fucking love him. I love him from the tips of my toes. I love him when he's with me, love him when he's not.

And I don't know when or how that happened.

I didn't want strings, not because I'm unwilling to let him string me along but because when we're together, we're so connected and that kind of connection can only end in heartbreak. Right?

He's exactly what I need but not at all what I expected. He challenges me and makes me a better person. Cullen—Silver Eyes—Hot Gambler refuses to let me settle for a sliver of the action. He wants me to have the whole damn adventure.

"Cullen," I whimper, rolling around in bed, missing his heat, his warmth, his nearness.

I don't want to leave him behind. It's like I've cut off my only source of oxygen. I can't breathe. I can't survive without air and HE is my air.

I think of not going to his final. And my heart just breaks. I want to go to him, to be there for him, but we had a deal. I kept up my end and saw how he lives. I see the appeal in how he lives.

I LOVED how he lives.

He brought out the wild in me. With him, I have no reservations. I'm free, sexy, and yet pure. How can that be?

He FILLS me.

I'm more of 'me' when I'm with him because he lets me be the kind of woman I have always been, but changed because other men stomped on me.

He gives me freedom.

Makes me feel loved. Wanted. *So damn wanted.*

I can't bear thinking of not being there to give him all the luck he needs, but then what? Will one day he tire of me? I remember the way he told me he loved me. The way he already KNEW my deepest secret, a secret only my friends learned recently. He loved me still.

Why don't I dare seize his love and take it? Accept it?

Emmett. He doesn't make me feel special. Cullen, though. He makes it effortless. I thought breaking up with Emmett was one of the hardest things I'd ever do. But the hardest thing isn't actually learning to love again. But being brave enough to let it in.

A few days later, I'm spring cleaning my apartment, desperate to get him out of my head, when Rachel, Gina, and Livvy storm the place like women with an assignment.

"Before you open your mouths, it's never going to happen."

Rachel sighs and looks at Gina.

"I'm getting tired of coming over here and dragging you out of a rut," Gina says, not meaning it one little bit. "Especially when *you* are your own worst enemy."

"I second that," Rachel says.

"Ditto here," Livvy says.

"How am I self-destructing?"

"Cullen loves you," Livvy says.

I wonder how she knows this. Has he said something to Callan?

Gina narrows her eyes. "She doesn't look surprised."

"This isn't news to her," Rachel agrees.

"He told her." Liv watches me. "Did he, Wynn?"

"Yes, okay, he says he loves me." And a tickle of excitement explodes inside me. This sexy and desirable man, a man who is every dream and illicit fantasy of every red-blooded woman around, told me that he loves ME.

And I didn't say it back?

What the fuck, Wynn? What's wrong with you!

"Oh my god!" Rachel claps. "We'll be planning a wedding again soon."

"Not so fast," I say. "I didn't say it back."

"Well of course you said it back," Rachel says. "I've never seen you happier."

"But I didn't say it."

"He knows," Livvy says. "He told Callan."

"Did he really?"

"No, I made it up," she says. "Of course he told Callan because Callan asked him."

"But wait, back up," Rachel says. "You really didn't say it back?"

"No." And I feel like shit about that now.

"Then you're the single most stubborn woman in Chicago." Gina glares at me like she means it then grins and says, "I don't think the words mean so much to men. So you'll tell him the next time you see him. No sweat, right?"

All eyes are on me.

There's a long silence. Too long.

Finally, I say, "I probably shouldn't see him again."

Rachel rolls her eyes at Gina and Gina says, "Call the guys, Rachel. Let them know we won't be home before dinner."

"What? Why?" Livvy asks, reasonably so since she's still in the honeymoon stage of her marriage.

"Because we're taking our girl to the closest psych ward so she can have her head examined." Gina crosses her arms. "You're so crazy in love that you've lost your good senses."

"Have I? I don't know anymore. I just . . . have this sick sense of abandonment since he left. You know?"

"It's called love," Gina says.

"I can't have separation anxiety whenever my guy leaves me."

"She called him her guy," Rachel points out.

"She did," Gina says.

"Stop!" I laugh.

"Wynn, live a little. Fly to Vegas and enjoy him!" Rachel exclaims.

"Easy for you to say. You don't have a gallery to run."

"Or a friend named Pepper who does an extraordinary job," Gina says.

"Okay, fine." I suck in a breath and they collectively exhale. "I'm scared. All right? I mean, I've landed the hottest ticket in Vegas. Cullen Carmichael is a god out there and he's . . ." A blurred line of good and bad, of hot and sweet, naughty and nice.

The naughty gets me every damn time.

"I'm a coward. That's it. If he ever rejects me, it would truly break me." I shake my head. "This feels so different than anything else I've ever had in my life. This is real love. Real and honest. It's love, the kind that moves mountains."

"Then what are you waiting on?" Liv grins. "He loves you and you love him. I've watched you two together and that kind of love? Girl, it's once in a lifetime."

"And there you go. Unless you have nine lives, you'd better start packing." Gina winks at the other two.

Livvy hugs me. "There's a plane with your name on it. And it's landing in Chicago in just hours."

I shake my head, my stomach in knots. But the truth is . . . I just want to feel his arms around me again, one more time, to be there for him.

Whenever someone mentions him, when his name comes up in a conversation, my stomach wraps up like a burrito. It's not even a feeling of butterflies, it just feels rolled up and tight, almost as if the name triggers some invisible baseball bat to swing right into my stomach. Sounds painful, right? It is! Is this what loving Cullen will feel like?

Shit, what the fuck did I sign up for? It felt softer before, with all the other guys, not this intense, this deep, this life-altering.

My heart feels more broken that it's ever been in my life. I feel weak, and sick, and just dead inside.

"It's just not easy for me, and I don't know why. I don't know why this keeps happening to me. I believe in love being forever, but I'm starting to think that for me, it's only temporary. I mean, nobody marries someone thinking they'll get divorced. It just happens," I tell my friends, aware of their understanding gazes.

But is that reason enough to stay on the shelf?

Is that reason enough to let real love go?

No, every part of me whispers. Every voice in me. The slut and the hussy, the responsible one, even the one that sounds like my grandma.

Every single inch vibrates. I know that I made the wrong choice. That I need to rectify this. That the guy that makes me crackle and shine, tingle and burn, is facing his opponents this weekend in Vegas—and I want to be there with him.

How can I be loved the way I have always wanted to be loved if I don't believe myself deserving of it? How can I love a man with all my heart if I don't love the very heart that I'm giving him, each and every nuance of it, even the body that houses it?

I want to give this man everything that I can give, and even what I can't give him on my own.

VEGAS, BABY

Thongs? Check. Sexy lingerie? Check. All the clothes he loves? Black dress? Boots and sweater? Lucky earrings? Infinite check.

I'm packing like mad when the phone rings.

"Wynn? Pepper. I have a couple of paintings packed and ready to ship. I need to get an address."

I groan. "Can you give me a few minutes and let me jump online? I'll call you once I have the database pulled up."

"Won't be necessary. You probably have this one," she says. "I need one address for Cullen Carmichael."

"What?" I stop packing and stand at the window overlooking the courtyard where we ran from the rain and made out in public like a lust-driven couple who couldn't keep their hands off each other.

That's because we are a lust-driven couple and can't keep our hands off each other.

"He bought a work from the show?"

"Not just any work," she says. "He bought *the* work, the crown jewel."

Oh god. "Oh my gosh, it's perfect!" And my favorite.

"I know. So's the guy."

"Oh, he's *more* than perfect, he's . . . No, I mean . . ." I swallow, not wanting to bore her with details of Cullen's study with its charming art and lavish appointments. The place he calls home, the home that is so overpowering that only a man like Cullen could live there, a sexy alpha who lives his life rather than allowing life to happen to him, the man who takes what he wants and to hell if it makes sense.

My man.

I blink and say, "I'll see if I can get an address for you."

"Okay. Let me know."

"I'll stop by on my way to the airport. I'll see you in a bit."

I hurry out with my suitcase and jump in the waiting Uber. We drive to the gallery. I arrive to find a group of men already unstretching the masterpiece and rolling it in a tube for shipping.

"Careful!" I call. "This is a super-important work!" I cry, hoping Cullen will receive the work in perfect condition.

"We've got it!" Pepper assures me, coming out from around the corner. "Don't worry. Go on—don't you have a plane to catch?"

I blush beet red. "Yes. I just feel bad about leaving again."

"Don't. I'm thrilled for you."

"Thanks, Pepper," I say, hugging her.

After I power off my computer and switch everything off in my office, I grab my keys, ready to head to the airport.

I step out into the hall and spot Emmett standing outside in the gallery room. I slow down my walk as he stares at me in confusion.

"Going somewhere?"

"Emmett, hi." I glance around to see if anyone's with him. "Um . . . yeah. Did you need something?"

He looks rather . . . sad. Did his restaurant get a one-star review somewhere?

He points in the direction of my office. "Can we talk alone?"

"Sure, I guess. I'm in a bit of a rush, so three minutes tops," I say, pushing the door open.

I allow him in. It feels odd having him inside my office. The place doesn't sing with his presence. My body doesn't . . . feel a thing. It's hard to remember a day when I looked at him and imagined him as . . . well, as my forever.

He sits on the edge of a chair. "Wynn, we need to rethink our breakup."

I don't sit because he isn't staying and I'm not missing my plane over this. At the same time, I won't be rude. Emmett and I spent four years of our lives together.

"What do we need to rethink?" I ask.

"You and me."

I frown in confusion, shaking my head. "I don't understand. Emmett, I'm running really late, can we do this another time?" I start for the door, but he stands and approaches quickly and with a hint of a pucker.

"Whoa, and hell no." I put up my hand to stop him.

So much for being polite.

He sniffs and smirks, but it's wicked ugly and doesn't suit him at all. It's then when I realize he's jealous. *Really* jealous.

"It's because of Callan's brother, the gambler?" he says.

"Poker player. Cullen. And yes."

"And yes?" he frowns.

I look at him, stunned that he thinks I'll explain anything to him. We've said what needs to be said and spent the last hours of our wasted time together a long time ago, a lifetime ago, or so it seems.

"Whatever we had, Emmett," I say, glancing at the door in frustration, "it wasn't what it should be. It wasn't love, not really. You'll find love with someone and she'll be great. She'll be everything you wanted me to be and more. I know it. But it'll never be me because now I know who's the one for me. And right now, he's waiting for me. And I need to leave." I wait and he doesn't move for a moment.

He steps aside, and I open the door and step out. Emmett follows.

"Wynn. Can't you see? I made a mistake."

"Then don't make another one," I say, unwilling to give in. "Go and find someone who makes you fall so hard, you won't even have time to wonder what happened." I lean up and kiss his jaw. "I'll see you around, Emmett."

"You were always too good for me," he murmurs, with a small confused smile, turning and walking out of my gallery.

"What was that?" Pepper asks from behind the small reception desk by the entrance.

"Closure. I suppose."

I quickly summon an Uber, checking my watch, dreading the rain that has started, dreading that I won't make it on time.

When the car finally halts before me, the driver hurries out of the car, covering himself from the rain as he packs my suitcases in the trunk.

"Hurry," I tell the driver as soon as I climb into the car. As we head to the FBO to where Cullen's plane lands, I dial Callan's cell phone. "What's up, sister-in-law?"

"Don't joke. It's going to happen."

"You're fucking joking?" He sounds shocked but glad, and I smile.

"Well, not now, anyway. But this is the real deal, Callan, and I need you to help me do something special for your brother. I need to win him back and bring him the best gift in the world after he wins this poker championship."

That's when I hear the screech—and feel the jolt of my Uber skidding on the wet pavement and crashing into the car in front.

My phone falls from my hands, and I glance around, cursing this blasted rain as the driver of the car in front of us gets out and starts yelling at us.

My Uber driver curses in Spanish. "Mierda!" he calls to himself, then glances at me. "You okay?"

"Yes. Just started and jolted and . . . shit, I'm so late, sir."

He exhales and shakes his head. "You're going to have to call another Uber," says my driver.

GAMBLING MAN

Cullen

'm holding her close, refusing to let go, curling up and spooning, just waiting until she wakes. Her hair smells so damn good, like pineapple and coconut. Of course it would. We're parked on a deserted beach with our toes in the sand.

A loud racket in the hallway jars me to an upright stance. I'm on the floor looking around, frantic because I'm still living inside our dream. "Wynn?"

That's when I realize she's not here.

She wasn't here when I dozed off on the couch or when I ambled off to bed at five this morning.

She's not here now that I'm wide awake.

Wynn. Is. Not. Here.

I drag my hand through my hair and look at the black shirts hanging in the open closet. When we arrived last night, Oliver hurriedly unpacked my things then asked for the night off. I'm pretty sure he had a date.

Standing at the window, I wonder where Wynn is now. In a few hours, the tournament starts. In a few hours, it's go big or go home.

And I'm not the guy who leaves the party right after it starts.

I glance at my watch. Wynn should be at the airport. I gave my pilots strict orders to update me when they took off.

I haven't heard from them, but should get the call anytime.

Last night, I had a series of dreams, the recurring beach dream and a new one—a tender, sweet dream that included Wynn and my son. Did I have the dream because she told me she couldn't give me a child? Do I care that she wants children? Do I want more children?

I haven't thought that much about it.

Or right, maybe I have.

Maybe I want to make her mine, in every way. Lady of my house. Mother of my children. Adopted, even.

A casino is a lonely place for serious players. Anyone can get lost in Vegas but I don't want to be lost. And I don't want to be alone tonight.

Am I thinking about this now because of the dream or because I'm waiting for Wynn to take her greatest gamble on me?

With Wynn, maybe it's possible to think about the things I haven't had. Maybe I want some semblance of a family.

Can I open up and talk to Wynn about my son?

I need her to understand and not judge. See that Adam is the sweetest kid, and I am no longer willing to live without him.

Adam's mom is a tough nut to crack. She hates poker and everything about a gambler's life. She berates me every chance she gets. She was a gold digger from the start. We were kids, but she still wanted wealth and status. The country club scene. She wouldn't marry a poker player. Where's the status in that, right?

If only Mom shared her opinion.

She thinks poker players have an endless stream of wealth. Like a few days ago, she called to ask me for "only" thirty grand. I can't help but wonder what she plans to do with my money.

You can't think of it as yours once you give it to her. Callan's words hum in my head. My brother refuses to support her, and maybe that's why I always hand it over without questioning where it goes or who may end up with it.

If I have it and she wants it, it's hers.

I don't have anyone else to share it with. At least not yet.

I'm impatient, checking Wynn's nightstand once more, in case she arrives after I have to take my seat at the table. I've left a note—for good luck. I prop it against the lamp one more time and pace another circle when my phone buzzes, and Tim's name, one of my pilots, flashes on the screen.

Don't wait for me . . .

I clench my jaw as I remember her last words. Like hell I won't. Something about her changed me. And something about me changed her too. We're not the same people that went into this stupid dare.

My lips twitch. Our dare was anything but stupid.

I wanted her. I still do.

I love her like I've never loved a woman. She's in my veins, my damn bones. It didn't make saying goodbye any easier. It made things worse, and as Wynn pushed me away because she fears I will one day tire of her, my chest collapsed onto itself and my damned heart shredded and burned.

Deep down, she knows the truth—the truth that burned into us both as we got deeper and deeper into this dare. That come hell or high water, she's my woman, and I'll never want anyone else.

I pick up the phone, my chest swelling in anticipation. "You're late—I need you to fly that damn bird as fast as you can. I need her here, asap."

"Mr. Carmichael . . ." he says tentatively. "She didn't show. She's not coming."

I take a moment to register his words, my fist clenching on my cell phone.

She's not coming.

Disbelief, frustration, regret, anger, helplessness: it simmers in my veins as I disconnect the call.

I stare at the carpet, unseeingly, unable to believe that she's really done with me. That she won't come. "Fuck me," I growl, swinging out and sending my laptop, the lamp, and everything on top of the hotel room desk crashing to the floor.

Oliver enters the suite right at that exact time. He rushes the bedroom with his hand in strike position, his keys wrapped around his forefinger like he plans to use them as a weapon. "Sir! You all right?"

I exhale, shake my head. "I'm fine. Lucky in play, but not lucky in love, right?" I shoot him a stony smile and try to pretend it doesn't matter, but my jaw is clenched, my heart is burning and crumbling in my chest. I don't like being in Las Vegas without her.

I stalk out of the room as Oliver's phone starts ringing. "Yes, Mr. Carmichael," he answers. "No, he's just left the room," he says as I motion for him that I'm not in the mood to take calls. No more distractions, damn it to *hell*.

I grab my jacket and storm toward the door, struggling to shake off my frustration, and think, *Where are you, Wynn?*

POKER

ours later, and after missing Cullen's plane and catching a last-minute commercial flight, I finally head to baggage claim, anxious to arrive at the tournament.

"Oliver?" I'm surprised to see Cullen's chauffeur.

Dressed in casual blue shorts and a short-sleeve polo, Oliver probably didn't plan on being here.

"Miss Watson." He's smiling like he's sitting on the biggest secret in the world.

"Callan called you."

"Yes. And Mr. Carmichael—Cullen—doesn't know you're here. He was . . . in a bit of a *mood* before I got the call"—his eyes are twinkling, indicating he seems to think his *mood* was because of *me*—"and I thought it better to keep him out of the plan to avoid further distractions before his big game."

"That's perfect. I want to surprise him—I'm not only bringing his usual lucky charm, but I'm bringing him a thirteen-year-old one too!" I clap excitedly, then realize maybe Oliver doesn't know. "Did Callan tell you about Adam?"

He nods once, his smile wide. "He had some trouble wrestling Adam away from his mother, but apparently, a free vacation for her was enough to let us enjoy him this weekend. His plane just landed. He's right over there."

Heart leaping in excitement over meeting Cullen's boy, I follow Oliver's head motion. There's a funny little quiver in my heart as I scan faces in the crowd. It only takes a moment to find the tall and lanky kid, the *silver-eyed* kid. He has disheveled dark hair, probably because he slept on the plane, and is wearing a "Poker Rules the Earth" T-shirt with a tagline: *Approach with Caution. I can read you.*"

I laugh. "He's his dad's son."

"For sure, Miss Watson."

Tentatively, I head over to Cullen's son and wait while he drags bags from the carousel. He has an unreadable expression and I immediately wonder if this was a bad idea. Not all kids like their dad's significant other.

Is that what I am?

Geez, Wynn, this was absolutely a real bad idea.

I'm in the middle of self-doubt when the kid sticks his hand out. "I'm Adam. Uncle Callan told me a lot about you."

I try not to overreact but I'm happy as hell as I shake his hand.

"I'm Wynn. It's nice to meet you. I've heard a lot about you. From your dad."

"Surprised he can talk about me at all." He frowns. "Mom does what she can to keep us apart."

"Well, Miss Watson has brought you together," Oliver says, shooting the kid a kind smile. "And your dad will be pleased to see you."

"How's he doing?" Adam asks.

"No updates yet." Oliver looks at his watch. "He should be arriving at the tournament now. You'll be able to watch the tournament at the hotel. It's broadcasted live."

"Let's go." I exhale happily on Adam's words. He's about as eager to get there as I am.

Forty minutes later, I'm slipping on my lucky black dress and earrings when I spot an envelope on the nightstand, the one that's next to Cullen's bed.

Our bed.

I peek inside and smile at the ten-thousand-dollar chip and the note that says, "Please don't be late. You're my lucky charm."

He's so predictable and it's that predictability that makes me think ahead with my own predictions for my special player.

My man is about to win a title and bracelet.

And . . .

We're on the edge of a winning streak that could last a lifetime.

TEXAS HOLD'EM

Cullen

The new poker commentator is pumping up our credentials when I enter the roped-off area, ready to take my seat. Seven of the final nine players have won numerous bracelets. Only two of us play professional poker and I'm looking at the other one—the man who plans to get a "real" job.

"You haven't retired yet?" I tease.

"After today," he promises.

Lucas comes to the final table with the third highest stack and those chips might as well be mine.

"Where's your luck?" Lucas asks before he sits down.

I glance behind him. His groupies are hard to miss with their bouffant hair, flashy jewelry, and loud voices. "Couldn't you leave the kids in daycare? I hear the casino has a real nice romper room."

He laughs. "Guess your woman isn't coming."

"What's up with the teenagers?" I can keep it real as long as the bantering continues. What I won't do is let Lucas rattle me by talking about Wynn.

Lucas sniffs. "They're all twenty-one or older."

"Never would've guessed, man. I was about to ask who does the fake IDs for you."

"Insult a friend much?"

"Only at the tables," I tease, but I'm done talking so I stick out my hand and we shake. "Good luck, Lucas. Let's get to the final four where the real money is."

Translation: You take fourth. I'll bring it on home.

He frowns at that and it's disconcerting. If Lucas frowns at "luck" then that can only mean somebody's helping him develop his poker skills.

Damn Lucas. I wouldn't care to see you on my heels at the finish, but now?

Can't risk it.

If I don't freeze him out early, he could take the lead and keep it.

Once again, I scan the crowd, looking for *her*, my lucky charm. While I may look like I have it together, I'm miserable here.

I hate being in Las Vegas, at this tournament, *without her*.

The commentator is ready to go. He rises. He says a few final words before turning to the table.

The dealer shuffles.

I have my first hand.

But my girl isn't here.

I peer at the cards.

How the fuck do I slow play this mess when all I want to do is fast forward time and see Wynn again?

Wynn

'm so damn excited to see him that I barely notice the crowd until Mike's beside me saying "Kind of overwhelming, huh?"

"Oh, Mike. I'm sorry. I didn't even see you." I blush as soon as the words tumble from my mouth. I sound like a woman in love. "I zoned."

"It happens." He holds out his arm. "Let me show you to your seat. Someone will be real glad you're here."

Seconds later, I feel his eyes on me. We're walking in front of the press when I notice the familiar warmth on the back of my legs. The pressure at my hips. The tingle across my back.

I tighten my hand on the crook of Mike's arm and almost lose my balance. We're in front of a crowd of women when I hear someone say, "Look. That's her. That's Playboy's girlfriend. Isn't she beautiful?"

Mike pats my arm as if to say, "Go with it."

And I do. I go with it.

I straighten my spine, take a deep breath, and gain every ounce of confidence when I finally turn.

And time stands still.

There's no one there. No one in the crowd. No one at his table. No one next to me.

It's just us.

He tosses in his cards without looking at them.

There's a hint of a smile on his lips as he watches me take my seat next to Mike.

"I'm here," I mouth.

"You never left." He taps his chest near his heart.

"Wow. Did you see that?" someone in the groupie section squeals. "I wish he looked at *me* like that."

I don't even turn around to see who said what.

I don't have competition.

It's just me and Cullen. His love surrounds me as I find my place in the crowd, a seat where I can watch him do his thing.

As soon as I'm settled, I'm gaping at him and feeling his love firing right back at me.

I'm dying to kiss him, dying to hold him, dying to be in his bed.

Dying to be completely his all over again because when I'm dying, that's when I feel most alive.

Stop, Wynn. There will be time for fantasies to play out later.

For now, he's about to win the biggest tournament in the world. I feel it in my veins. I see the shark sharpening his fins as he mentally circles the other players around the table.

He's about to strike.

He'll take the title and the bracelet and the money . . . and then he'll take and devour me.

I finally come to terms with the misery I've felt over the last few days. I may have been in Chicago, surrounded by my belongings, but I wasn't here with the man I love. I wasn't where I'm supposed to be.

Cullen has somehow, in many sweet ways, become my heart and home.

Hours later, there are four players left and the commentators are making predictions as they call for a fifteen-minute break. Lucas Ingram has the lead. Cullen is in second. The short stacks belong to two unknowns, players who probably don't stand a chance now, if the commentators are correct in their predictions.

I wait for Cullen at the ropes and as soon as he clears them, he's in my arms, not caring who watches as he sweeps me against him and delivers a scorching kiss. As our lips meet, part, and gravitate together again, I can't believe we ever spent one night apart.

"Cullen." My face must be as red as summer roses.

"You look great," he says, breathless. "I was beginning to wonder if you'd . . ."

"I missed your plane."

"The pilot called to tell me." He frames my face and looks at me tenderly. "You're a sight for tired eyes."

"Cullen, I'm so sorry. I'm a coward. I . . ."

"Shh . . ." he whispers across my lips. "When I look at you, I see a strong and beautiful woman. These eyes don't see a coward." He waits a second and says, "You're here and don't owe me an explanation . . . for anything."

His words are telling. He must have some inclination, some knowledge of why I'm late.

"There aren't any secrets between us, Cullen."

"Right . . ."

"Emmett was there." I'm ashamed to admit as much because I missed my plane because of my ex. "I'm sorry."

"You don't owe me an explanation." He looks unmoved. "How'd that go?"

"I'm here."

"You are." His eyes twinkle.

"And I told him . . ."

"What did you tell him?"

"Can you give me a minute?" I look up at him and my heart skips a beat. My pulse quickens. My legs go weak. "I want to get this right."

"You. This." He nods at the final table. "We're perfect."

"Then I want to *perfectly* tell you that I wanted to be here from the minute you left me. I need to say . . ."

There's a two-minute warning. The players shuffle by us and Cullen grips my hand. "Later. We'll have all the time in the world." He kisses my temple and leaves me standing there alone.

Mike is at my side. "I had my doubts."

"What's that?" I'm so mesmerized that I don't take my eyes off Cullen.

"I never thought Playboy would settle down, love somebody. And then . . . there you are. You're good for him, you know."

"He's better for me." My words didn't come out like I'd intended.

"You've got that right. He plays better, acts better, wins better—more—and I like you in his life."

I reclaim my seat and think, *I like me in his life too.*

THE FINAL TABLE

The third and fourth place winners are quickly eliminated and it's back and forth, the lead going to Lucas then Cullen then back to Lucas.

"Want to cut a deal?" Lucas asks.

"Best deal I see is for you to go all-in right now." That's a bluff. If Lucas goes in, Cullen will fold.

Given the look on Mike's face, I suspect he knows the same.

Lucas narrows his eyes and folds.

Cullen doesn't show his hand.

The commentators are whispering into the microphone, bantering back and forth as if no one can hear them. Thanks to soundproof glass, the players can't. The crowd seems interested.

I turn to Mike when I catch part of their dialogue. "So Cullen can buy Lucas out?"

"If a deal was brokered, they worked it out on the break. Cullen won't cut a deal when it's down to two." Mike seems sure. "If a deal was cut, you probably heard about it."

During the break, Cullen and I reconnected. I wasn't thinking about poker. Cullen wasn't talking to anyone but me.

I lean forward and focus on Cullen as he makes swift moves, inching his chips forward before tossing in a few extra ones to signal a raise.

On the board, there are three nines.

"Pretty."

"Unless Lucas is holding the fourth one," Mike says. "Don't think he is. He keeps looking at his cards."

Lucas raises.

Cullen folds.

"Not how I saw that one playing out," I say.

Mike shrugs. "You probably read him better than most, but here? He's a different player. His game face at the final table isn't the one you'd see in a cash game." He studies my expression then says, "Cullen has ten million reasons to remain unreadable."

"That's a life-changing sum."

He grins. "Second place isn't too shabby at seven and a half."

I don't respond. I think Mike wants me to react in some way.

"With you here, I'm sort of surprised Cullen's staying in. He could take the money and run. All Lucas really wants is the title."

"Maybe he wants the bigger payday, too," I say. "The difference in first place and second isn't a few pennies on the dollar."

He laughs. "No, it sure isn't."

Cullen pushes his cards back at the dealer and frowns. He folds the next three hands and Lucas seems agitated. The next hand Cullen gets, he plays.

The crowd is antsy. The commentators feed that angst by saying, "Something tells me we may be watching the final hand, Boz."

Boz shakes his head. "This isn't the end."

Only it may be.

Cullen is on his feet. He's all-in.

I stand, waiting and watching, hoping. If I were an emoji, I'd be a couple of praying hands right about now, I'm so nervous.

Cullen lifts his chin and winks at me as if to say, either way, he's got this.

And I've got him.

No one else is in the room. It's just me, Cullen, and everyone else now fading away.

"I love you," I mouth.

His smile is wider when he mouths back, "I know."

Damn him.

Only I like it. His confidence is sexy and pure.

I laugh and wait, hoping Lucas will do this, call him so we can get on with it.

He stands, sits, stands again.

"What do you think he'll do, Boz?" The commentators begin again.

"Based on how the kid has been playing, I think we'll see him call. He's thinking about it . . ."

"We used to be able to see the hole cards," Mike says. "After there was some speculation about how easily that information could be passed to those playing, the rules changed."

"We don't need to see."

"Player has it?"

"Yes. Want to place a side bet?" I say.

"No way." He shakes his head. "Cullen would kill me if I bet against him."

"Yep. You're probably right." I'm worried. "You think Lucas has it?"

"Kid has been on a roll and you're Cullen's biggest distraction." He pauses. "Hard to predict this one." He nods then and whispers, "Here we go . . ."

The adrenaline fires and feeds the waiting crowd when Lucas moves all-in and joins Cullen to watch the cards fall.

"I can't see Lucas's hand," I say quietly, the nerves knotting in my belly.

"You don't want to," Mike says.

The dealer turns the river card in a smooth and theatrical manner. Before it falls, it's so quiet, I'm almost sure we'll hear the card land on the felt. The crowd across the room has better visibility and they're on their feet, cheering like mad.

"Ladies and gentlemen, we have a new world champion! Cullen Carmichael succeeds at drawing Lucas out with his pocket kings, but they weren't enough to keep Carmichael from the bracelet. His queens found a match on the turn and river! Say hello to the new world champion . . . the best poker player in the world . . . Cullen Carmichael!"

"Unbelievable!" Mike says, whooping and hollering, high-fiving the others around him.

Cash is dumped on the table.

Cullen and Lucas embrace, slapping backs. Lucas is photographed with his millions before moving aside so Cullen has the same opportunity.

"Come on," Mike says, dragging me around to the private exit. "We'll meet him on the other side."

I send a text to Oliver.

He did it! He won! Can you bring Adam downstairs?

We're here at the arcade.

Meet me at the tournament entrance?

On our way now.

I pick up my pace. "Hurry, Mike." I can't wait to see Cullen's face. He'll be thrilled to see his son.

A few minutes pass before Cullen approaches from the left. Adam is at my right.

"Everything is perfect."

When Cullen sees us, I realize my word choice doesn't adequately describe *this moment, this* tournament, *his* world . . . Cullen and his son . . . it's pluperfect.

We're better than perfect. We're all here, together.

We take Adam to Casino Kids, a new arcade with a casino-spin to it. We eat pizza and play games, win prizes and have a blast. At the end of a long night, we return to the hotel. I watch Cullen and his son and my heart is near bursting.

"Dad. I want to see you more. I wish it could be like this."

"I know, son." He rumples his hair, pulls him into his arms, and rubs his knuckles on his head. "I'm working on it. Would you like to come to Vegas and live with me . . . and Wynn?"

Sensing the seriousness in his voice, I let my heart soar and devour the moment of belonging. That sense of worth and family and being a member of something bigger than myself, it's like . . . well, it's like all my dreams are falling into place at once.

"Mom won't ever . . ."

"I'm coming to an arrangement with your mother. You can see her for half the year, and the other half, you're ours." He pulls me into his arms, still focusing most of his attention on Adam.

He grins. "You will win," he says.

"He wins a lot," I say, wondering if I should've remained neutral as I slip away from Cullen's arms.

Cullen smiles, his eyes warm as sunlight. "I missed you. Come here, champ." He grabs the back of his neck and steers him into the room. "We'll need to fly you back home tomorrow."

"I don't want you to," he adamantly says, his voice breaking.

Cullen pauses, looking down at him. "I'm sorry it has to be like this for now. I promise you I'll do everything in my power so you can spend more time with me." He pulls his son into his arms and Adam nods. I cry silent tears as I watch them. Cullen's jaw tightens as he guides him to bed and tucks him in.

When Adam finally falls asleep, I watch Cullen stare at his son from the doorway. I'm still crying as quietly as I can. I step out of the room, hurry to our bedroom for tissues, aching to make it better for them both.

I sense a presence in the room and spot Cullen's wide frame in the shadows.

His voice is thick and raspy. "Thank you."

"For what?"

"For being here." He takes a few steps forward. "For bringing him here." He keeps closing the distance. "For being you." He reaches me, tugs me closer and pulls me into his arms, his lips in my hair. "For being mine."

"I'm yours," I whisper into his shirt. "All yours. You don't even know—"

When I tip my face back, he kisses me softly, and I wrap my arms around him. "It's like . . . right here? I could not want for anything more," I admit. "I want you. I want Adam. I want Vegas and Chicago. I want everything."

"I won't have my woman wanting for anything." He pecks my lips, my jaw in his palms. "I'm building a hotel on the Strip soon. I'm fighting Sondra for custody of Adam. I don't want to take my son away from his mother, but I want him to have a father, and I want him to have you."

"I would love to be his stepmom . . . or . . . I mean . . ." I start blushing.

"You know it's happening," he says softly, his eyes twinkling, "Just let me ask you the right way."

I shake my head as if to clear off this wonderful, heady daze I'm in. "When I was very young, I always thought that

I'd do anything possible to find the One for me. Anything. I'd sell my soul. Move to Vegas. And now . . ."

"And now?"

"And now I realize, I was right." I grin up at him, laughing. "I'll have Pepper watch the Fifth Street Gallery and maybe I can open one here—"

"As many as you want." He boosts me up.

My arms fly around his neck. "I won't be easy but—"

"We can handle hard. You and me. Just don't ever quit me."

"Me? I would never fold when I've got a winning hand."

EPILOGUE
TOP PAIR

Cullen

Seven months later

I wake up at my Vegas place with one thing on my mind.

It's not that unusual now that Wynn and I live together. The only thing different about this morning and the previous one is the empty space beside me.

In the next room, I hear Wynn's high-pitched voice and a *tap tap tap* against the floor. Is she dancing?

Amused, I toss a pillow behind me and wait as she parades back and forth, squealing a little louder . . .

"Seriously? Oh, Pepper, that's fabulous! I can't wait to tell Cullen!" The place goes silent and then she says, "Right. That's perfect! We'll do it."

"Come here and share," I growl at her when she hangs up, meaning a whole lot of one thing and a little of the other.

Of course I want to hear her news but I also want that little tigress arching under me, moaning in my arms as I drive into her and show her just how much I can't wait to make her my wife.

She sashays by our double bedroom doors and holds up a finger, shooting me an impish grin. I groan and stretch. When she passes our room again, I hold up the sheet so she can see what she's doing to me.

Close proximity without the first touch is like sipping coffee without caffeine. The need is there but fulfillment is out of reach. I shift my arms and link my hands behind my head.

"Tell you what . . ." Her voice fades as she slips out of sight again and I realize she's still on the phone.

I make a mental note to send Wynn's assistant a token of my appreciation. She keeps the ball rolling at Wynn's gallery so I can keep my lucky charm beside me.

As I contemplate a gift card or basket of wine, Wynn bounds inside our bedroom and tumbles across the bed. I see a blue-white blur as she rolls over, places her phone on the nightstand and peers up at me as if to say, "Come and get it."

I charge at her, pinning her beneath me in one second flat.

"Good morning." I peck her lips and she immediately attempts to pull my button-down shirt down that sexy body of hers to her thighs. "Oh no you don't." I catch her wrists and lift her arms above her head, smothering her lips in a kiss that's meant to lead somewhere.

She sighs into my kiss, taking it like it's all she wants, then she pushes me back. "Cullen! Hang on! I have something to tell you."

"It can wait." I'm already worked up. Hell, this girl works me up without any effort at all. I nibble her earlobe and stare down at the beautiful woman that recently said "yes" when I asked her if she could take me on for a lifetime.

"You're insatiable!" She giggles.

"Then sate me," I say, inching down. "Have I ever told you how hot you look in my shirt?"

"Many times." Her body responds and she bucks underneath my lips, and I get the feeling this little move was meant to throw me aside. "But that's gonna have to wait. THIS is important."

"It sure is," I tease, walking my fingers higher up her thigh.

Her hands land on my shoulders and she yanks me forward. This is Wynn's typical signal when she really wants to fight me off. But it's anything but a turnoff.

"Five minutes?"

Her smile could stop traffic but I don't want it to stop me.

I persist until her hand lands on mine. "Your five minutes spin into two hours, Cullen."

"Some women would find that irresistible."

"*I* find it irresistible." She pecks my lips as I prop up on my shoulders and look down at her. "But you have to hear this first."

"I can do first. That means there's more to follow." I sigh and roll to my back and like it even better after she straddles me. I grip her hips and drag her closer to my cock.

I'm playing but love it when she blushes.

"Stop. Would you?" She giggles again and shakes her head, which sends those flaming red curls straight down her back.

I tuck my hands behind my head. "Talk to me, gorgeous." I'll behave but it won't be easy. Her nipples are beading in plain sight.

She eyes my straining erection. I try one more time but it's a moot effort. She freezes me out by sliding forward.

"Step it up." I snap my fingers to let her know I'm in a hurry here.

"We have things to do, Cullen."

"I know what tops my list," I say.

She drags that succulent tongue across her lips, leans forward, and whispers, "Not a chance."

"Wicked tease." I cup her ass to squeeze it and drag her back in perfect alignment with my cock.

"Okay! Now listen to this!" She tumbles to the side and says excitedly, "Remember the Bensons? They're buying a summer place out on Lake Michigan and guess where they just dumped a shit-ton of money?" She jiggles her shoulders. "MY gallery! Can you believe it?"

"Wynn, that's great!" I don't tell her that we don't need the money. She wants to keep her gallery and open others. It's important for her to maintain independence and I'm supportive. "Wait a minute, you said Bensons?"

"Yes!" She rubs her thumb across her middle and forefinger. "Already paid in cash, baby!"

I pretend to think about it then say, "Maybe Pepper got it wrong. Last I heard, DB Benson had returned to Stonehenge to reclaim his birthright."

"Very funny. They're not as old as they look. In fact, Mr. Benson said they spent so much time in the sun that it eventually caught up with them. He's only sixty-two."

I don't detect a smile so I scoff and say, "Wynn, that man is every bit of eighty."

She shrugs. "*Mrs.* Benson looks sixty-two."

"He's a sugar daddy!"

And it's Wynn's innocence that makes my heart clutch. My pulse pause.

"What?"

"Mr. Benson has a crush on my fiancé."

"That too." Her grin turns wicked and she bends down to kiss my lips. "And you're jealous."

"Damn right. When an old guy throws money at my woman, I pay attention."

We're ready to roll as soon as she slides a little closer to the southern region but right as her brow shoots up in a playful gesture, my phone jingles.

And it's the woman who has better timing than the U.S. Congress when she wants something done.

"Damn it."

"Can't she wait five minutes?" Wynn says playfully, wiggling her hips but then easing off me.

"Don't go very far," I say, taking Mom's call. "Good morning, Mother."

"Cullen?" She sighs dramatically. "I hate to call so early and ask. I know you're out of town with that . . . *girl* . . . but . . ."

"Woman, and she's my fiancé. We've discussed this."

"Right. You've said that. Anyway, can I go by the casino and see Mike?"

"Sure," I say, pissed. Mom hasn't even met Wynn and she's already decided she doesn't like her.

"Don't be crass, son. I need to see him right away."

"Sure you do," I say, wishing Mom would call, instead, to ask about our day. "How much do you need?"

Wynn's working when I hang up. The coffee seems to intrigue her more than I do until I sit across from her. "What are you doing over there?"

"Watching the woman I love while she works." I pick up the second mug on the table and sip. "Want to come over here and work on my lap?"

"Ha! If I come over there, we'll never get anything done."

"You say that like it's a bad thing." Morning sex is probably off the table for now so I prop my ankles up on the footrest and wish for more pleasurable mornings.

Wynn doesn't say so but Mom was on speaker. *Fuck me.*

"Cullen. We need to talk about the wedding."

I sigh. If she's in the mood to plan, passion and pleasure might as well be the forgotten condiments pushed to the back of the shelf.

She grins up at me as if she knows I'll be all the more attentive once I finally get between her legs today. Our eyes meet and hold.

"What?"

"Nothing," I lie, leaning back until her gaze dips down. Satisfied when it does, I say, "Talk to me."

She shakes her head so quickly you could miss it and says, "I think we should get married here. But if we do Vegas, then it can't be a cheesy drive-through wedding, mister."

"Not a chance, *Mrs. Carmichael.*"

She lifts her eyebrows in surprise over the name and blushes. "I love it when you call me that."

"You wear the name well."

She smiles and glances dreamily outside.

"We'll get married wherever you want," I say, eager to make Wynn my wife. "I could get married in the middle of the Mojave Desert or here or even at the underground poker room where we met . . . as long as I have you and you're mine by the end of the ceremony, the day will be perfect."

Her eyelids get heavy and she glances at me as she reaches out to cup my jaw. "I love you. I just can't wait. The wait feels eternal."

"I love you too. And I know what you mean." But she won't have to wait any longer.

I pull her into my arms, finally ready to feast on her, just as Adam pads into the kitchen.

"What's for breakfast?" he asks, voice groggy. I smile and peck my girl, and give her a smile that promises *later*, easing away to whip something from the fridge.

"Take your pick," I tell my champion. "French toast. Omelet. Bel—"

"Waffles!" he says as Wynn rumples his hair.

"Did you sleep well, Adam? How are you finding your room, are you comfortable?"

He blushes, not used to the attention of a gorgeous redhead. "Yeah."

"She's mothering you, let her," I tell Adam warningly.

Adam grins, still looking shy and unused to it. "Of course I let her. I like it. She's my stepmom. Or at least will be by Mon—" Adam's eyes widen when he realizes his near-blunder. He glances at me, and I raise a brow reminding him it's our secret.

"In a few months," he amends with a grin, and Wynn is too distracted whipping out the orange juice to notice the surprise I've got in store.

Adam and I share a smile. Because it's on.

"Think she has a clue about all this?" Callan asks as we head to my new Vegas property a few hours later.

Beyond the wedding tent, multiple crews set up ferns, construct a gazebo, and organize tables and chairs. Everything is coming together as it should. When we say our vows, the sun will set and cast a red glimmer across the sand. We'll move to the reception tent where Wynn's favorite band will sing the songs that have somehow become our songs. It'll be perfect.

"Big brother? I asked if . . ."

"She has no idea we're getting married tomorrow." I smile because I can't wait until she knows. Maybe then she'll understand. I couldn't wait another day to make her my wife.

"Knowing Wynn, she probably thinks he's playing poker tonight," Saint says.

Our friends are supposedly in Vegas for our bachelor and bachelorette parties. When I left her with her friends, Wynn was reluctant to let me go. Maybe I should've reassured her and told her that all I'd be thinking about was making my way back to her bed, straight into her waiting arms.

Damn I'm whipped.

My heart is in her hands and I know it now more than ever before. There's something about this moment, something about making Wynn's dreams come true even when she doesn't know it. I can't explain and can't try. I'm just hoping to deliver so she looks back at our wedding day and believes everything was right. Perfect. Impossibly beautiful.

Just like my bride will be tomorrow night.

"It better be perfect, man," Roth says. "Wynn always dreamt about her wedding day so you'd better not miss a beat."

"Something tells me we won't," I say, watching Wynn's mother, who is standing in the center of the commotion giving orders. While my mom was visiting Callan, I was picking up Wynn's at the airport. Wynn will be pleased once she realizes we spent some time together.

We park in front of the future home of Carmichael Casino. While I'd like to think I can roll out the red carpet for the construction crews entering the scene next month, the fact is, I need Callan on the line in case we run into any unexpected delays. In Vegas, those delays can break a casino quicker than a groundbreaking ribbon-cutting ceremony with A-listers.

"So are you ready for this?" Callan asks, grinning at me to let me know he's not thinking about his investment. He's ready to watch me take the biggest gamble of my life.

Only it's not a gamble because I've never been more certain of anything in my life.

BACHELORETTE PARTY

Wynn

'm positively thrilled our friends are in town, and because we're supposed to take advantage of the weekend and turn it into an early bachelor and bachelorette party, me and the girls gamble like it's the end of an era, and it is.

I'm the last one of my closest friends to get married and while the wedding is still several weeks away, I feel nostalgic now. We're at Cullen's favorite casino. Mike is at our disposal, per Cullen's request. We're partying like there's no tomorrow but when that no tomorrow arrives, we'll be having the royal treatment at the spa—hair, nails, massages, a shopping day, the whole nine yards. Cullen insisted.

I don't think Cullen wanted us back at the house until tomorrow afternoon and since I can't reach Mom and Dad by phone, I take a wild guess and say, "Guess my parents are on their way to Vegas."

Rachel looks at me bewildered. Gina says, "Why would they be coming out here?"

"I . . . well, you're right. I don't know why I thought that. Maybe because Mom wants to be part of my bachelorette party."

My friends laugh uncomfortably and I fear it's because I'm starting to act like Bridezilla and can't seem to think of anything else beside the fact that I'm marrying Cullen in a few weeks.

"Maybe we should check in with the guys," I say, eyeing the dark lounge where I had my first public orgasm, wondering if the guys are around the casino. I feel my face heat as we cross the casino.

"Let's go in here for a drink," Livvy says, dragging me to the door.

I follow them to the bar, then I turn around and stare at the empty dance floor and wish my Silver Eyes would magically appear. To make matters worse, Christina Perri is belting "A Thousand Years" and I think back to the night that we made out to "100 Years" so I sort of summarize Cullen and me, like how it feels when we're together and I'm just mush thinking about it as I listen to the song.

At the sign of tears, I whisper, "I wonder if that's true?"

"What's that?" Gina asks.

I point up at the speaker and cock my head. "I don't know. I feel like I've known him all my life and I wonder if the universe made it impossible for me to marry anyone else. You know?"

"We know!" They chime in together.

Livvy lightens the mood and points to the dance floor. "She almost got fucked right over there." She grins like an elf with a secret package.

"Forgot to mention that?" Rachel asks slyly.

"Seriously?" I order my drink and motion to the others. "A round on me, please."

I place my plastic on the counter and as soon as I do, someone picks it up and thrusts it back at me.

I jolt in surprise then look up at Cullen's go-to host. "Mike, hi! I'm glad you're here."

He eyes my friends. "Aim to please."

The music is loud and I can't make out what Mike's saying. It was something like, "Damn, you weren't joking when you said you have gorgeous friends." And he immediately follows it with, "Cullen said as long as you stick around here tonight, it's on him."

"Controlling men," Rachel says, as if used to staying where she can be seen. Saint likes to know where she is at all times.

"So what do you say we hit the tables?" asks Livvy.

"I'd like to enjoy my drink," Gina says, dipping her cherry in her frozen daiquiri and watching the lights flicker above the dance floor.

I object, but no one cares. Next thing I know, we're three drinks in and the place is still deserted.

"One more round?" Gina asks.

"Why not?" Livvy says, checking her watch.

"Are we waiting on someone?" I ask.

Liv, Rachel, and Gina stare at one another suspiciously like they're sitting on the biggest secret ever. As if those behind the scenes are watching, the lights go down and the glass doors are closed in front of the lounge.

"What's going on?"

Livvy shrugs. "Shall we, ladies?"

I spot three shadowy figures over to the left, signaling I'm about to be abandoned. "Hey, what happened to the gal pal parade?"

"We'll be back!" Rachel promises.

"And you'd better be glad to see us when we return!" Livvy says. "We still owe you an impressive bachelorette party."

I glare at them in confusion and suddenly I sit all alone waiting. And waiting.

And . . . waiting.

And right when I start to feel a little self-conscious and a lot impatient, there HE is . . . waiting.

On the dance floor.

This guy who doesn't dance.

This man who dances only for me.

His hand is out. He looks like a *REAL PLAYBOY* with his white shirt rolled to his elbows and pleated black slacks taut against that evident male package. And girls, I'm telling ya . . . I think I've died and gone to heaven.

"Cullen."

"Are you going to look at me or dance with me?" he teases but he isn't smiling and this look, this "I'm your man and I'll do whatever I can to prove it" look that he owns? WHOA! It makes my knees go weak, my tummy tighten, my bones ache.

I take my time going to him, but it's like he knows that *I* know we both want to savor this moment and take it real slow. We need to make it last for as long as possible because once we touch, it's all over.

He'll dance with me like he's never danced before. He'll set me on fire, make me lose control, not that I want it.

Because I don't. I so don't.

I'm in front of him now and my breath catches at the sight of those silver eyes and the tiny lines in his forehead, his corded muscles showcased by his open shirt. I want to run my tongue up and down his neck, drink him in and indulge so many dirty little fantasies.

As soon as he pulls me to him, his hand cups mine, his hard arm supports my back and I inhale, breathe him in. We're swaying to the music and it's so good to touch him, so damn good.

Too. Damn. Good.

I'm picturing him doing all sorts of things to me, letting me do things to him that I've never done to another.

"What are you thinking?"

"You know," I whisper.

"I do." His lips steal away with mine. And it's a soul-stealing, toe-curling, darkness-claiming kind of kiss that moves the earth and seas and winds and heavens . . . And it's all I can do not to drag him to the corner booth and have my way with him. I. Want. My. Way.

And I want him to have his way.

"What do you say we blow this joint?" He twirls me around, swings me out and back in again. "Go upstairs and play all night?"

"We agreed to have bachelor and bachelorette parties," I remind him. "Besides, I thought you had something to do tonight. Something that couldn't wait. You've been telling me all week about it."

He bends his head down and nibbles my ear. "*Someone,* not something."

"Ah . . . the truth is finally revealed. How long has this been going on? Is it anyone I know?"

"I think you know her pretty well." He spins me, brings me back again, and dips me.

"The man can dance."

"When he's properly inspired."

"Must've been inspired," I say, thinking if I can get him to look at me like this all the time, I'll blow him every day for the rest of my life.

"Say it," he whispers, breaking into a faster dance, spinning and twirling me until I'm dizzy. So dizzy that I don't notice when he's holding me close again, his palm flat against the small of my back. "What were you thinking just then?"

I stand on my tiptoes and whisper it in his ear.

"Promise?"

I bite down on my finger and give him a saucy look.

"Let me taste you," he says huskily.

I lean closer and kiss him. His hand slides down my side and the way he holds me lets me know exactly what's on his mind. The intense gaze lets me guess what he's thinking.

"Not tonight." I rub against him anyway and crane my neck to look around, watching for my best friends, hoping they won't return just yet.

"I didn't ask for permission," he whispers, his mouth devouring mine. And in a matter of seconds, those fingers spin magic.

And he's right. He didn't ask for permission. And he sure as hell won't seek forgiveness.

After dancing with my guy and then having another drink while I try to wheedle out what he and the boys will be doing later, I'm standing all dazed and confused watching as Cullen, Callan, Saint, and Tahoe walk away from us like they're high-strung badasses (because they are).

We watch them go and have a boys' night and watch as every woman there seems to notice them.

"Watch those men work their swagger," Gina says, not at all worried. Tahoe is so in love with her that we all believe the man plans his day around when he'll be able to drag her off so he can have her to himself.

"Watch and weep, girls," Livvy says, narrowing her eyes on Callan.

"Yep, if all heads turned before, now they'll snap out of their sockets." I laugh and sure enough, every single woman this side of Texas suddenly seems interested in our men.

"Come on, girlfriend. The night is young," Livvy says, steering me away.

I follow my girls to the roulette table. And as soon as I buy in, I stick all my chips on two. After an hour with my man, it's a VERY lucky number.

Go figure.

Later that night, Livvy and I stumble into my suite sometime after midnight. Rachel and Gina are staying across the hall because their guys apparently can't sleep alone.

"What wimps," Livvy says, slamming the door behind us, but I get the feeling she's missing Callan and feels like she ended up babysitting the bride-to-be.

"Hon, you can call him. Have him come and get you. I'll be fine." I'm better than fine. I'm one Mai Tai away from being drunk enough to perform an opening number for a Vegas headliner. And that would be pretty damn interesting this time of night.

She thumbs the adjoining bedroom beside ours. "I think I'll take you up on tha—" The door slams and I jerk, realizing that Livvy just sort of fell behind that closed door. Startled, I creep closer to the door but immediately relax when I hear laughter.

I hear Callan say, "Strip."

Her response is somewhere between provocative and silly. Since I'm not sure if I heard her right or if I wanted to, I amble away and close myself up in my big and empty room, a space that's quite humongous, dark, and lonely without Cullen's larger-than-life presence.

It's three a.m. when I wake up with all my clothes on. Cullen's not here. I wish I'd called him.

I roll over at four. Bed is empty. Kick off my shoes and now it's five, five o'clock and I'm vaguely aware of large and gentle hands undressing me.

And no one undresses me better.

No one has the right to undress me. Or hold me. Or kiss me.

"Cullen."

It's six. I'm spooning him. Six-thirty, he curls around me like a blanket.

Seven. He's playing with my hair, whispering how much he loves me.

At eight, the spooning is over and the fucking is unbelievable and sexy and fulfilling and . . . OH MY GOD . . . I LOVE THIS MAN.

So much. Too much.

By nine, he's crawling all over me, telling me he can't get enough, will never have enough, can never be enough or do enough or surprise me enough . . .

But he's wrong.

Because at ten, I find out he's just pulled off the surprise of a lifetime.

It's my fucking wedding day.

I pound on Livvy's door then shoot across the hall and do the same. "Rachel! Oh my god, Gina! Somebody!" I fly back across the hall, pad across the floor, knock on the door again.

"Dude, what is it?" Tahoe stumbles into our suite, looks at Cullen and smirks, and then hops over the sofa, making himself at home. Gina darts across the room and does the same.

Those two are perfect for each other but right now? I'm kind of pissed at their perfection because they kept the perfect secret.

Livvy. Callan. Rachel. Saint. They arrive in that order. Cullen leans against our bedroom door with his arms crossed, looking too cool, too sure of himself.

And I'm a mess.

"It's my wedding day. Would someone please tell me what I'm supposed to do first?" They watch without speaking. "I mean . . . this is terrific." I'll be married tonight. I'll be MRS. Cullen Carmichael this time tomorrow.

I look at Cullen and I'm so damn in love but then . . . I'm so frantic.

"I've got to call my mom. And Alessandra. I promised her . . . we planned for this. She's supposed to do my hair!" I throw my clasped hands against my forehead. "And Pepper!" I spin around because, let's face it, I'm already spinning so fast in my head anyway. "Cullen! We can't do it today. We can't possibly get it together by tonight."

"Actually . . ." Cullen looks at our friends. "We've got it under control."

"What? There's no way. I mean . . . I had this down to a science. I had the caterers lined up. I wanted Bonnie B to do my cake. Flo's on the Corner was doing the flowers. One Direction would handle the wedding announcement. Adele. I wanted Adele to sing. I had people. You know that. I had MY people . . ."

Rachel laughs. "And you'll still have your people."

"Yeah," Gina says. "What do we look like?"

"We handled it," Livvy says. "So you can have a stress-free wedding day."

"But there's just an itsy bitsy problem with that, girls."

"WHAT?" they say together.

"I don't have a wedding dress!"

"Yet . . ." Cullen winks, tucks his phone away, and opens the door. "Bring them in, ladies."

An hour later, I stand in front of the full-length mirror, punching in Mom's cell phone number. When she finally picks up, I breathe a sigh of relief. "Mom! SOS! I need you to help me pick my wedding dress."

"I've already seen them," she chokes out.

"Wait. Are you . . . tell me you aren't crying. Mom!"

"I'm not." She sniffs. "Okay, so maybe I am. A little."

"So you met Cullen?" I hold my phone to my ear while using my hand to swish the skirts of the belle-of-the-ball gown, a throwback from the Victorian era and definitely not a gown that will make my top three. "What'd you think?"

Rachel thumbs the rack of dresses while Gina holds out her choice, a fitted white gown with rolling lace around the short train. "Um. No. It looks like a mermaid gown."

"Don't do the mermaid gown," Mom says. "It's big in Chicago right now and the girls are having such a hard time walking down the aisle in those."

"No mermaids, Mom." I remember she hasn't answered me and I say, "Back to Cullen. What do you think?"

"He's charming."

"Yes."

"Handsome."

"For sure."

"And so in love with my daughter. How could we not love him?"

I breathe a sigh of relief. "I wish you were here. You should be here."

"Darling, I've seen the gowns and my favorite is the Monique Luhillier. Try it on and see what you think."

"But where are you?"

"You'll find out soon enough. We love you, Wynn. And we love Cullen. We're so excited for you!"

We say goodbye for now and I turn to my girls. "So let's see the Monique."

They swoon before my eyes as they unzip the plastic garment bag. The floating silk and lace gown has a matching veil adorned with tiny flowers and cultured pearls. It's perfect and my friends and I know it before I even slip it on.

Minutes later, I'm zipped and staring into the mirror, thinking how quickly everything has progressed. I'm shivering, maybe from nerves and all the excitement or maybe because I can't believe that the lovely bride staring back at me IS ME!

BOYS

Cullen

Saint treated us to lunch and a round of golf. I don't know how anyone can play golf on their wedding day but apparently that's what Chicago dudes like to do.

I bear it, but barely. Three more hours and I'll be a happily married man. I'm content, not one bit nervous. When a man knows he has the right woman at his side, everything else just comes together.

My phone rings as we're returning from the greens. I hold it up and see an unknown number, and I wonder if it's the Children First in Nevada, a local adoption agency we've been applying to.

"Cullen Carmichael."

"Mr. Carmichael, this is Dana Vanzant. I'm Jack Cavanaugh's lawyer. Do you know him?"

"Jack Cavanaugh. Three-time world champion in Hold'em. Yes, I know him."

"He's passed away."

I look at my brother and he flinches, solely by the expression on my face.

"I'm sorry to hear this," I say, knowing he had two precious little boys. Hell, it was only recently that I wondered what he was up to. Jesus Christ. Now he's gone.

"He named you his sons' guardian, Mr. Carmichael."

The words are somehow there, but it takes my brain a moment to register them.

I glance at my watch and imagine Wynn's face when she finds out she can be a mother, a mother of two more boys, and decide I have time to pick Adam up from school along with Wynn. Maybe then we can go meet Jack's boys.

I turn to my brother, suddenly too fucking confused here. He knows more about these things than I do. His best friends are dads, and some of the best hands-on dads at that, but what if I can't be a better father than Jack was and what if I one day find myself in a similar situation and what if . . .

I won't.

Because I'll be a better man and better dad.

She says, "Mr. Carmichael, the boys are asking for you. They have a letter for you. We'll talk when you get here. I'll look forward to seeing you, Mr. Carmichael."

I hear myself say "likewise" but it's becoming increasingly obvious that I have no idea what's going on here.

I hang up the phone and meet my brother's stern expression. "Jack Cavanaugh died. He left a letter for me. And . . ." I pause. "Two boys."

"Tell her before you go."

"Would you tell Livvy?" I pace, shoving my hands into my pockets.

"Yes. Wedding day or not, you have to tell her."

"I can't get her hopes up only to let her down, especially today."

"Then get her hopes up by building up her trust in you. Tell her what you're doing, man. She'll understand."

So I walk outside and place the call. "Hey, beautiful. What are you doing?"

She squeals. "I just picked out my wedding gown and . . ." A pause. "It's perfect, Cullen!" Her friends cheer in the background.

"I have something to tell you."

"Is everything all right?" Her voice changes.

I nearly wince, dreading the news, and at the same time, hopeful this will be a good one in the end.

"No. Yes. I don't know." I exhale. "I need you to come with me, Red."

I pick her up at the hotel, explaining the phone call, aware of her wide eyes as she listens to every word I say. When we walk into the lawyer's office, all I can think about is how she feels about this.

"Mr. Carmichael?"

The older boy can't be more than eight years old but he looks older, more mature, when he sticks out his hand and says, "I'm Stevie Cavanaugh. You knew my dad."

"I did," I say, admiring his firm handshake and wondering how much these kids know. Jack's youngest son is over in a corner working a puzzle and I nod to Adam and he takes off to strike up a conversation with him. "I'm sorry to hear about Jack."

"Thanks."

This boy has an odd maturity about him, like he's wise and worldly way beyond his years. I'm guessing this kid has been through hell. His mom left after her second son was born and she was never much of a mother anyway, from what I remember. Jack spent ten to twelve hours a day in the casino, seven days a week.

I never asked who watched the boys for him.

I assumed they had someone.

I'm guessing they had no one.

Now, I'm at an odd disadvantage but don't quite understand how true that is until the kid thrusts an envelope in my direction. "He never had a chance to ask you. You know, if you'd take care of us, you know. If something happened to him."

"I . . ." Quickly, I turn to Wynn, who smiles at both boys.

Stevie waits for her to speak.

"This is Wynn, my future wife," I introduce.

"Hello, Stevie. That's a pretty name," she says sweetly, her voice raw with emotion, and I squat in front of Stevie and see sorrow and pain on his face. He's looking at me as if he thinks I hold all the answers.

"Aren't you going to read it?" he asks me.

"Sure," I say. "Do you want me to read it now?"

"That would be really great, Mr. Carmichael. If you *both* read it." He looks at Wynn lovingly, and she smiles and nods as she follows me.

I glance at Adam as I draw Wynn to a nearby table and pull out the letter. I can tell he isn't getting very far with the younger boy. He meets my gaze and shrugs in answer. I nod, hoping he'll keep trying.

As soon as I start to read, I can hear Jack Cavanaugh's voice in every word, listening to Wynn's soft gasp beside me. I clench her hand in mine, as we read it together.

If you're reading this damn letter now, I've fucked the hell up. And I'm sure you'd like to drag me out of the grave so you can tell me so but don't bother. These boys are better off without me. I've provided for them so they won't be a lot of trouble with a nice trust set aside for them but they need a dad, a real present, hands-on dad. Take care of them better than I did. You and that nice woman settle down, maybe someplace away from Vegas. Don't fuck this up, Carmichael. You always said if you could do things over again, you'd be an attentive dad. So here's your chance. Be good to my boys because they're now yours. And thanks, Playboy. I'll owe you one when I meet you at the gates assuming we end up at the same place.

This letter hits its mark. Jack was always that kind of guy. He said what needed to be said in a way that made people pay attention. But when it came to taking his own advice? The man couldn't do it. He was a fuck-up.

Then again, maybe not. Maybe he finally did something right.

I slowly turn to see the youngest one watching us as if he thinks we'll leave him here, leave him the way his momma did when she left town and never came back. Or maybe leave him like his daddy did when he owed the casinos more than he could pay. If there's a trust somewhere, I doubt the casinos know about it. If they'd known, maybe Jack would be alive today.

Be good to my boys because they're now yours.

"Cullen." Wynn slips her fingers deeper through mine and whispers to everyone in the room, "Will you give us a very brief moment? I promise we're not going anywhere."

She pulls me outside, her eyes wide and bright with tears, her cheeks flushed.

"Those little boys . . . the letter's saying that . . ." Tears are streaming down her face now, and I can tell she can't even try to hold them back. "Are they yours now?" she asks.

Adam steps out, overhearing. He leans closer to Wynn and whispers, "They're kind of yours, too." He shrugs. "I mean, they are if you still marry my dad."

"Adam." I want him to hush until I pull my thoughts together.

"Dad."

"Wynn." I want her to say something, anything.

The two boys peer out the door and timidly approach.

Wynn quickly wipes her tears and looks from one to the other, smiling that warm smile I'm fucking addicted to. Decimating them just like that smile decimates me.

"I'm Shawn," the little one says, looking at Wynn as if he wants her to notice him.

"I'm . . ." Wynn looks at me, then drops to her knees in front of the little boy, holding out her arms. "I'm Wynn, Shawn. I'm sorry about your dad." She looks up at me and the tears gush, then back at the little boy. "And if you'll let me . . . if you and your brother and Adam and Cullen will let *me* . . . I'd really love to be part of *your* family."

When the boys start to cry from what's closing and what's opening, Wynn pulls them into her arms, and I pull Adam into mine, waiting for the two boys and Wynn to collect themselves. They do, and Wynn helps them to their feet and presses them up against Adam and I.

My arms go out to encompass all of them. I've felt lucky in games, felt at those times like I'm turned <u>on</u> for some reason, like everything is going in my favor.

But I've never felt as lucky as I do now.

Wynn and I exchange glances. There'll be paperwork to fill out and a shit ton of stuff to do to welcome them into our new home. But I don't want to leave them now, and so I leave the boys—all three of them—in Wynn's embrace as I step into the room and ask permission to have them at our wedding tonight.

When I step out, Adam looks comfortable. Eager, almost. As if he's just realized he's finally got two brothers he never knew he wanted until now.

"Well?" Stevie expects an answer. What I say next will be important. Maybe the only way to set the right tone for the rest of our lives.

So I say the first thing that comes to mind. "Well, boys, looks like we need to go find you a couple suits."

FOREVER

Cullen

"What were the odds?" My brother asks the question and I'm so busy watching Wynn with the boys that I can't focus on what he's saying. Something about odds and taking the leap of a lifetime.

He's right. What are the odds?

What are the chances that any gambler would think of me when making decisions about a child's future?

My eyes water as I contemplate Jack and how much trust he must've had in me. I never knew. Never had a clue.

I zone out, watching Adam. He has such a kind spirit. I'm proud of him. So proud he's my son. We've had a chance to spend more time together in recent months. I credit Wynn and my brother for making that happen. They brought him to Vegas and Callan somehow broke the ice with Sondra, made her see that Adam needs both parents in his life.

Tahoe and Saint watch me as if they expect me to crack under pressure. Maybe that's what some gamblers would do but I'm not just a gambler or even a player anymore. I'm a dad with responsibilities. A husband already in my damn heart. Sondra agreed to joint custody and I wonder now if maybe everything in the universe lined up so evenly because of Wynn, because the woman I love made it all possible.

Adam hovers over Jack's boys and his actions throw me back to another time as well. It's like he understands that I need him to help make Shawn and Stevie feel at home.

Callan points and nods at the three.

He gets it.

He understands.

My son is a mini-version of me and how did that happen? He wasn't around me. We spent very little time together and yet there he is, showing Shawn how to clip on his bowtie and giving Stevie the once-over to see if he's perfect.

He is. Those three are . . . well, I can't even think it or I'll get all choked up.

"We could've gotten Adam a real tie, Carmichael," Roth says.

"Loan him yours," Saint suggests.

"Yeah, swap," Callan teases.

Tahoe laughs. "I'm happy to go without one."

"But you won't," Gina says, wrapping her arm around his waist when she joins us.

"How's my bride?" I glance at Gina, then check the time on my gold watch, a wedding present from one of the online poker rooms.

"She's about to put on her dress," Gina says.

"Then I'll be right back." I motion for Adam to keep an eye on the boys and he nods and smiles. He really likes having Jack's sons around.

"Whoa there, young man," Livvy says, stepping in front of me. "Your bride isn't quite ready for you."

"Let me just kiss her and tell her good luck."

Livvy turns her cheek up and points to it. "Put it there and I'll deliver it for you."

"Livvy. Come on. Give him a free pass." Callan's voice sounds like a dropped grenade over the commotion. "They've already seen one another so the traditional superstitions are squashed."

She shrugs. "Can't blame the gatekeeper for trying." She moves aside. "But five minutes."

I breeze past her and to the stairs. I picture my gorgeous bride darting from one side of the bedroom to the next and call over my shoulder, "Make it fifteen. I need to talk to her about something important."

Behind me, there's an explosion of laughter and I'm fine with that. They can place bets on what will transpire, but today's our wedding day and it started out in a nontraditional way. I have a little something on my mind to keep with that tradition.

Inching inside our bedroom, I close and lock the door behind me. "Wynn?"

"I'm in here." The bathroom door is shut. "I'll be out in a minute."

I knock because I'm impatient, but also because I hear her sniffles. "Honey, open the door."

"I can't."

"Why not?"

"Because everything is just so perfect and I have to leave it this way. I'm afraid if I open the door and . . . well, I'm afraid if I change anything now it won't be so perfect and it won't be real and maybe it won't even happen!"

"Open the door or I'm picking the lock." I jiggle the doorknob. "I want to see my beautiful bride. Please?"

A few seconds pass before she emerges and as soon as she does, my eyes fill with tears and I'm not a dude who cries, but I've never seen a more beautiful woman.

Never.

Not in magazines.

Not in movies.

Not even in my fantasies.

"You take my breath away."

"I'm in my robe!" Her hand trembles as she brushes back a tendril of hair. "My makeup isn't even finished."

"You're perfect." I mean it. She is stark raving beautiful. "Want me to call the minister and ask him to come upstairs and marry us here?"

"I thought we were getting married at the casino property."

"We are." I tilt her chin to mine and slant my lips over hers. "But we can say our vows anywhere."

"Cullen, we have people waiting for us."

So what. "I, Cullen Carmichael, take you, Wynn Watson."

"To have and to hold?" It doesn't take her long to play along. "In sickness and in health?"

"In sickness and health," I agree, admiring her as she stands a little taller.

"And?"

"For richer and richer and richer *and* richer." I rock against her.

She frowns. "Very funny."

"I'm counting my riches by those who'll be seated around our family's table."

"Oh, Cullen," she breathes. She latches her arms around my neck and her forehead rests against mine. "You're everything I ever wanted."

"But?"

"But we have a lot of wedding guests waiting."

"Yes, we do," I say, pulling away but not unaware of how her fingers tighten on the back of my hand. "I'll behave, but only because I can't wait to call you my wife."

"I do," she says.

I look at her and read her perfectly. "I do, too."

Smiling recklessly, she pulls me to her in a kiss that's meant to lead into a quickie. "I need you, Cullen. I can't do this if I don't know . . ."

"You know," I whisper, dragging my fingers up and down her arms. "You know how much I want you, need you, and love ONLY you."

"Then don't wait until the vows have been said in front of our friends. We've said them here. We're not good at waiting."

"If I start . . ."

"I know," she says, rolling her eyes. "You'll go all night."

I smirk. "You're fucked for that little comment."

"Cullen, I'm so happy right now I don't want to wake up from this ever."

I seize her chin between my thumb and forefinger. "Ditto to that, Red," I rasp, leaning over and kissing her on the lips.

She parts her mouth, kissing me like only she can.

"We'll work it out. With the boys. Don't worry for a second—"

"I'm not worried. I'm so happy."

She wraps her arms around my neck, and I hold her, squeezing her tight.

I need in her. The emotions too raw, too on the surface. I start to kiss her for real, faster and harder, my girl trembling from all the excitement of the day and what's to come.

There's love and lust and passion and forever.

I back her to the bathroom counter and boost her up, exposing her nakedness beneath the robe. I unzip and thrust inside her as hard and wild as I can, watching as my dick sinks between her thighs and that age-old look of satisfaction washes over my young bride's face.

"Faster," she whispers, scooting forward.

"I'm not getting in a rush," I tell her, pulling out and going to my knees. I quickly put her legs on my shoulders and rub my jaw against her thigh. My words are softly spoken as I coax her, making her settle down before I settle down too, but in a different way altogether.

My lips lower. Her back arches.

My tongue is *there*. Right. Fucking. There.

She throws her arms behind her hips to brace herself and thrusts forward, my mouth capturing her most intimate lips in a lust-filled claiming that I'll never forget. She's wet for me as I tongue my way to her sweet center, my cock painfully hard the second I taste her.

"Cullen," she breathes, her hands in my hair as she pushes down on my head.

I eye her full breasts and just about lose it. This woman—my woman—is the whole damn package.

"Cullen," she whispers, her legs tightening against my head.

I lick her long and lovingly, enjoying the way she bucks and writhes. Sure, the honeymoon is tonight, but I can't wait. Won't wait. *Don't* wait.

I jerk my head up and watch as her eyelids flutter and her lips pucker and so help me, I can't help myself. I can't stop.

Giving her more, I tip her clit with my thumb and bend down to have some more, taste her pleasure as her orgasm rolls over her. I drive her closer and closer, fucking her with my tongue and right when her body tightens, I rise up and drive inside her.

"Cullen!"

"Say it again and again," I whisper, eating at her lips, fucking her like crazy as her pussy shatters around my cock.

We come together, rocking out a sweet and crazy-passionate climax.

When we finish, we're kissing and laughing and still physically joined together. And it's not even a surprise when the explosive end leads to another round of mind-blowing, toe-curling, body-rocking, and obsessive-as-hell fuck-fest.

Wynn

We're late to our own wedding. Okay, so we're not that late, but we're late.

My mom and dad are waiting. Oliver is here. Some of our Vegas friends and neighbors. I squeeze Rachel's hand while shooting Livvy and Gina a big smile.

"Oh, girls, I didn't even mention your dresses. They're beautiful!" And familiar. I frown at first and then as if they read my mind and I read theirs, we all burst into laughter.

They're the dresses from Livvy's wedding; Livvy's probably wearing mine.

"Okay now, stop," Livvy says, holding up her hand before we say it. "We can't laugh or cry because we'll mess up our makeup."

"It must be said," Gina says.

"For real," I concur, waiting for it.

Rachel rolls her eyes and in an exaggerated voice says, "These dresses are so pretty. Your bridesmaids will wear them to countless events, long after the wedding is over."

It's the sales pitch from every bridal shop in America.

Rachel says, "We did good though, right?"

"They're the best," I agree, growing nervous.

"We didn't have time to get anything altered," Rachel admits.

I twist my hands and Gina says, "Oh, I almost forgot." She opens the limo fridge and pulls out a bouquet full of lilies. "Now you're ready to walk like a bride."

"You thought of everything."

"Cullen did," Rachel says, pointing behind us. "Looks like they're ready for us."

"This is it, girls." I breathe out a dreamy sigh, knowing the guys are in the limo behind us and wondering what Cullen is thinking. "He won't back out, will he?"

"Why would he back out?" Gina asks, rolling her eyes. "I mean, it's not like he rode the horse before he had the saddle strapped to its back."

"Ha!" We all burst out laughing.

"That was pretty good," Rachel says.

We laugh again.

The casino's chauffeur rolls down the privacy glass. "Oliver gave me strict instructions to wait here."

"We'll cue everyone from here," Livvy says, pointing to Gina. "You're up first, girl."

Minutes later, the door swings open and Tahoe is there, looking like her dashing prince as he offers his arm. They walk down a beautiful white carpet with potted plants on either side before making their way to the gazebo.

"There's an orchestra?" I can't believe it. They're playing a beautiful ensemble but I can't quite make out the tune.

Rachel is next. "I'm up."

"You're beautiful," Sin tells her when he helps her from the car. He plants a sultry kiss on her lips before guiding her to the carpet.

Livvy and Callan stroll about a hundred feet behind Rachel and Sin while I struggle to catch my breath, but it's impossible to breathe.

I don't know if I can do this or not.

My nerves are getting the best of me.

In and out and in again.

Breathe, Wynn. Breathe. Breathe.

And then I see HIM.

He's so polished and pulled together and looks like the man I wanted to marry in my dreams. He IS the man from my dreams. He's so perfect and handsome that it's almost as if I dreamt him straight into my life.

I'm about to open the car door when I see the boys take their places beside him. Adam, Cullen's sweet and handsome son, is to his dad's left, standing between Cullen and Callan. I focus on the way he stands there proudly and I feel a deep-rooted sense of pride when I see him take little Shawn's hand and motion for Stevie to join them, too.

I press my lips together and pray. *Don't let me cry. Please don't let me cry.*

My dad is there, opening the car door for me now, and as he reaches for me, he whispers, "Only one other bride was this beautiful and I married her forty-one years ago today."

"Oh Dad," I say and as we embrace, I look down the aisle at Cullen and the rushed wedding ceremony on this particular day makes perfect sense.

He did this for me.

He did this for them.

He thought of absolutely everything.

"He's a great guy, sweetheart." He pats my hand and tucks my arm under his, leading me away from the car to stand near the ceremonial gardens, the gardens that weren't there until my sweet Silver Eyes and best friends and parents made it possible.

"Ready, sweetheart?"

"Ready, Dad."

He nods and the bridal march begins to play.

I walk toward my handsome groom and just can't take my eyes off him. He's so perfect that I can't believe he's mine and I'm his.

"I'm lucky," I say, mouthing the words to Cullen but saying them to my dad.

"I think so," Dad says.

"Yes, you are," Cullen mouths, meaning something else altogether.

We reach the gazebo and Cullen accepts my hand from my father. I turn and hug him and he seems to be okay with letting me go.

"Hi," I whisper, suddenly timid.

"What took you so long?" he says.

"Don't rush me today, Playboy. I've been waiting for this day for most of my adult life."

I was a little louder than intended and the audience erupts in laughter. I peer over my shoulder and spot more of our Chicago friends—Pepper, the Bensons, Valentine, and Isaac—and a few recognizable faces from Las Vegas—the lady from the adoption agency, Jack's lawyer, a couple of gamblers, and Mike.

Then, I also spot two expected guests sitting unexpectedly together—Cullen and Callan's parents. I smile at my in-laws before turning to my own parents and mouthing, "I love you."

I refocus on my husband-to-be, my sexy Silver Eyes. Next to my handsome groom are the boys who will soon think of me as their mother. And Adam, already mine, my boy in every way that counts.

"How'd I do?" he asks, holding my hand.

"Everything is perfect, just like you," I say, standing before the minister and ready to do this.

The vows and wedding music, everything is just as it should be. Honest. Pure. Lovely. While we may not have had a traditional wedding day, the customary ceremony is beautiful and I wouldn't change a thing.

As I'm reveling in my happiness, thinking it can't get much better than this, it does. I mean, it really, really does.

Adam holds out his arm to us and turns to the crowd and says, "Ladies and gentlemen, I'm proud to present to you . . . Mr. and Mrs. Cullen Carmichael, my dad and stepmom."

He then nudges Shawn who shyly says, "You're supposed to kiss her now."

Cullen grins. "Then turn your heads, boys, because I'm doing this right." Our kiss lasts and lasts and I've never been happier.

I wanted a love that lasts.

I longed for my happy ending.

Cullen gave me everything in one beautiful wedding day. I couldn't ask for anything more . . . except maybe a little girl.

DEAR READERS,

Thanks so much for reading *Playboy*. I hope you enjoyed Cullen and Wynn's story as much as I enjoyed writing it. They were so addictive that I couldn't leave them, not for a minute or a second. Hope your reading experience was just as immersive and exciting!

XOXO,

ACKNOWLEDGMENTS

Although writing is a personal thing and sometimes quite a lonely profession, publishing is a whole other beast, and I couldn't do it without the help and support of my amazing team. I'm grateful to you all.

To my family, I love you!

Thank you Amy and everyone at Jane Rotrosen Agency!

Thank you to my editors, copy editors, proofer, and betas: Kelli, CeCe, Anita, Mara, Monica, Nina, and Kim.

Thank you Nina, Jenn, Shannon, and everyone at Social Butterfly PR.

Thank you Melissa,

Gel,

my fabulous audio publisher,

and my fabulous foreign publishers.

Special thanks to Sara at Okay Creations for the beautiful cover.

Thank you Julie for formatting,

to all of my bloggers for sharing and supporting my work—I value you more than words can say!

And readers—I'm truly blessed to have such an enthusiastic, cool crowd of people to share my books with. Thank you for the support.

Xo,

Katy

ABOUT

New York Times, *USA Today*, and *Wall Street Journal* bestselling author Katy Evans is the author of the Manwhore, Real, and White House series. She lives with her husband, two kids, and their beloved dogs. To find out more about her and her books, visit her pages. She'd love to hear from you.

Website: www.katyevans.net

Facebook: https://www.facebook.com/AuthorKatyEvans

Twitter: @authorkatyevans

Book Bub: https://www.bookbub.com/authors/katy-evans

Sign up for Katy's newsletter:
http://www.katyevans.net/newsletter/

OTHER TITLES BY KATY EVANS

Made in the USA
Lexington, KY
23 October 2019